I0739421

Books by Christopher Woods
<u>Soulguard Series</u>
Soulguard
Soullord
Bloodlord
Rash'Tor'Ri (forthcoming)

<u>This Fallen World Novellas</u>
This Fallen World
Broken City
Power Play (forthcoming)

Soullord | Christopher Woods

All rights reserved
Copyright ©2015 by Christopher Woods

Cover art by Derrick Gallagher

Acknowledgements:

I'd like to express my thanks to several people who have helped me along the way. My aunt, Janice, who told me I could do it is one. My brother, Brisco Woods, I thank for being there at any time to talk out scenes. I thank Derrick Gallagher for the awesome cover images. I thank my family for loving my work before anyone else had ever seen it. And I thank my wife, Wendy Woods, who encouraged me to put my work out in front of the public. I'm sure there are others I should list here, but I'll just say I thank all of you who have liked my work enough to buy it and give me the opportunity to do what I love to do for a living.

Soullord
By Christopher Woods

Prologue

I stood on a dark plain surrounded by my dead, and I knew that it was over. This was death? I heard a voice that seemed to come from all around me.

"It's time to leave," it whispered, "time to let go. Come with me."

I almost accepted it, but I couldn't do it. If I quit, if I die, everything falls squarely on the shoulders of the only other Soullord left. It falls on a sixteen year old girl to protect the world from the Demon hordes that will surely be coming, and I couldn't accept that.

So I stood my ground and refused to go.

"I can't go. I'm not finished yet," I answered the voice that came from everywhere.

"You will come, one way or another," the voice returned.

I saw darkness from across the plain surge forward toward me, and black tendrils began to spring from that roiling mass.

I settled into the beginning stance of the Dance of Blades with two red-fired Soulblades that sprang to life in my hands.

To my horror, all of the dead around me stood and came for me. These were my own dead. How could I strike down the very people who had already died for me? I saw Janicek and I saw Wilson. I saw men, women, and children from Morndel Academy. To my dismay, two forms strode to the front of the group, and I was looking into the eyes of my mother. Not Kyra, my real mother. I have her face seared into my memories from the many times I've seen her from Kharl and Kyra's memories. I would know her face anywhere.

How could I strike down the very person who gave her life protecting me? Then I think of a sixteen year old girl who would have to take my place, and I can't give up. I can't leave it all on her shoulders. I just can't do that to her or the rest of them either. They need the Soullord now, more than ever. Not Colin Rourke, but the Soullord. The man who can do the amazing things needed to fight this war.

In time, Lyrica could take my place, if I fall. But she is not ready for all of this. Not yet. And I have an Archmage to kill. I will not go until that is settled. No way in hell will I go down without a fight.

As my sword blurred, and time seemed to slow to a crawl, I saw something in my mother's eyes. Something that gave me the strength to do what I must. There was pride. She was proud of the decision I had made and before my sword could strike, she and my father both faded away, as did all of the dead from my past.

But the tentacles neared me, and I could see creatures from nightmares at the tips of each of them. They closed on me, and I Danced. I Danced like I had never Danced before. They fell to my blades, but more surged forward from the darkness. I felt the rage explode within me, so I embraced it.

With a roar, I met the horde of creatures, and began the toughest fight of my life. The fight to keep my life.

I jerked awake in a sweat, and Soulfire was burning all around me. I shut down the Soulfire that was covering me as the dream faded. It was the same dream I had from the day I awoke from the Source coma, and it scared the shit out of me. It scared me, because it felt more like a memory than a dream, and the last thing I want to think about is the Afterlife, and what will happen when I finally die.

If the dream is true, I might have pissed something very important off with my refusal to go.

More than likely, I'm just going crazy after the things I've done.

A pounding at my door interrupted my thoughts.

"Come in, Ric," I could see his Soul with my Inner eye. He was furious and worried as well.

He opened the door and entered quickly, "They got the Kid, Boss."

"Oh hell."

Chapter 1

"I can't believe the bastard actually blocked his own son from the Source," Rictor muttered, "his own freakin' son."

The private jet owned by the Soulguard was much quieter than the C-130 we'd been in before. The seats were much more comfortable, too. But it was hard not to fidget with my impatience.

"If he wasn't already dead, I'd kill that bastard every Tuesday for a month," I returned, rage burning inside of me like a furnace. "Then to leave him inside a shield, that's just evil. I hope he's alright, I really like that kid."

"He's been four days without food or water," Rictor said. "That's gonna be rough as hell, but he's a tough kid. He'll be ok, Boss."

"God, I hope so," I said with a shake of my head. "I knew something was wrong when he wasn't there at the Last Rites. I should have done something right then."

"There's no way you could have known about this, Boss. Don't beat yourself up over it. Not everything is your fault, even if you always blame yourself anyway."

"It is my fault, Ric," I said. "I knew, two years ago that they had to be faced, and I didn't do it. I knew it, Ric. Instead, my Guards died, my friends died, and Lyrica has to live with what she had to do. It's what I should have done. So don't tell me not to blame myself. But I swear this, it'll *never* happen again."

Rictor was actually taken aback at the vehemence in my voice, but he didn't try to argue with me.

"When it *needs* done, it will *be* done," I said, "damn the consequences."

I hated the fact that Lyrica had to kill the Council. She's a Soullord, but she's not like me. Thank

God. She has a kind heart, and she shouldn't have had to do something that was so completely against her nature. She has always been a sweet girl with a smile always on her face. I can see the torment in her Soul as she faces the consequences of her intervention on the behalf of Gregor and Guilefort.

She's every bit as powerful as I am, probably a great deal stronger, but she isn't like me. I'm almost as bad as the foes we fight. If I didn't have the Kresh to fight, would I be some monstrous person? A psychotic killer? Would the rage rule me if I didn't get to use it on the Demons?

Lyrica, thank God, doesn't have that monster inside of her. She will fight, like any other Guard, but she will only fight when she needs to. I fight because it is the one place I feel completely at home with myself. What does that make me? I guess the future will tell.

"You tell 'em to have some food ready when we land? The Kid'll be starving when I unblock him."

"Yep."

***

The black SUV's tore into the driveway of the mansion in Texas where Kevin Graves had spent his childhood under the harsh rule of Roman Graves. There were several people waiting for us as we exited the vehicles.

An elderly grey haired man in a suit met us.

"This way, Sirs," he ushered us into the front doors. "The young Master is through here."

I could see the genuine concern and outrage flowing through the old man's aura. He cared a great deal for Kevin, this was obvious.

I rounded the corner ahead of us and my mouth dropped open. The room in front of us was contained inside a shield bubble that was tied directly to the Source. The expected sight of a nearly dead man wasn't what we found, though.

Kevin Graves sat calmly on the bed in the room. Off to the side of the bed, a tendril stood straight up from the floor.

"Never ceases to amaze me," I mumbled and sat down in the chair in the hallway where I assume the elderly gentleman had spent many hours. He'd actually untied the block, himself.

Seeing that the Kid wasn't in any danger, an idea sprang into my head and I reached into the sack I carried with me. I slowly unwrapped the double bacon cheeseburger and with a sigh, I took a huge bite out of it.

"Really?" he said as he licked his lips, "Really?"

I laughed aloud and tossed the sack toward him. As it neared the shield, I tried something new. If it didn't work it would look a bit awkward, though. I reached out with my mind and literally ripped a hole in it. The sack soared across the room to be caught quickly by eager hands.

He eyed the shimmering shield and the hole ripped in it. Then he shook his head slowly.

"Is there anything you can't do, Boss?" he asked as he unwrapped another cheeseburger.

"Underwater basket weaving," I answered.

He almost choked on his cheeseburger and laughed loudly.

"So," I said, "You unblocked yourself. I'm beginning to think that the question you asked would pertain to you, too."

"I can't weave baskets under water either," he answered between bites.

He moved toward the edge of the bed, pointing toward the tendril of power jutting from the floor, "It's right there, isn't it? When I untied it, it wasn't touching me anymore. I can't feel the flows very well when they aren't touching me."

"That's why you haven't dealt with the shield yet then," I said with a nod. "I was wondering why you didn't just take it down too."

I reached out with a tendril, and built the jumper like I had done years ago at the Academy. As I clamped down on the two feeders for the shield, I cut my connection to the tendril and the shield dropped.

He walked forward and grasped my outstretched hand, "Really is good to see ya, Boss."

I handed him the super-sized coke in my other hand, and he smiled as he drank deeply.

"The Source can keep you alive for a great deal of time, but it does nothing for hunger or thirst," he said, "Poor Gerald sat out here for the last day worried to death."

"He tries to blame himself because he wasn't here when that bastard did this. My father had given him a week off. There was no way he could have known what the Mages were up to."

"The strange part is," he said, "my father wasn't in charge of the group that came after me. It was that woman with the burns, Regina Worthington. She ordered everyone as if she was the friggin' Archmage or something. It was so unlike my father to take orders from someone so much weaker than himself."

I have replayed all of the memories in my head from everyone involved, and I was beginning to have a disturbing idea of what had occurred at the Academy. And what may have been occurring for many years before that too.

"Now I have to face the bastard," he said with determination, and fear. There was probably not another person that the Kid fears more than his father. His fear is rooted in the past from the torment dealt him by the person who should have been his one safe place in the world.

Once again, I wished for Roman Graves to be alive again just so I could kill him.

"That might be a problem, Kevin" I said. "I don't really know how to say this, but Roman Graves died with the entire Council when they attacked Gregor Kherkov and Simon Guilefort a few days ago."

"The Truthseer and Gregor?"

I nodded. He was silent for a moment, and I watched the emotions playing across his aura. Relief, anger, and ultimately ending with sadness.

"Who can I thank for this? You?"

He would find out soon enough, there was no point in hiding it, "Lyrica Jayne intervened before they could kill Gregor and Simon."

"Lyrica? The crazy girl from the Academy? She's only, what, sixteen?"

"Yes,"

"Unbelievable," he muttered.

I took a deep breath, "Get cleaned up, and pack your stuff Kid. We're heading back to Montana. There's been a great deal of changes, and you can see them firsthand."

I squeezed his right shoulder and turned away. I never know what to say to people who have lost family. It was even harder in this situation. The Kid didn't know whether to be happy or sad at the loss of his abusive father either.

I looked at the tendril jutting from the floor, "Any particular tree ya want to enhance, Kid?"

Chapter 2

"What the hell do I know about running a war, Greg?" I asked.

I sat in Gregor Kherkov's office at the Academy. He had requested my company a little while before, and I had come to see him immediately.

He looked at me, and shook his head a little with a strange look on his face.

"Colin, you're what we would call a natural leader. People follow you almost automatically. That is a very dangerous attribute for anyone to have. It would be easy to abuse, but one of the reasons you have it is that you wouldn't abuse it."

"What do you mean? People follow me because I'm the one who's there. I'm not something special, I just do the job."

"Horse shit!" Rictor's voice came from behind me. All of the new Mages who were with me in Kansas had gone to their new training locations.

Two of them refused to go and I actually seem to have become their Mage instructor. Rictor and Andrea refused when they were instructed to leave. Rictor had just stated, "Someone's got to keep an eye on him."

"This is complete and utter horse shit. We follow because of who and what you are, Boss. You're the Soullord. And you're the man who put himself into a Source Coma before letting another of his men die."

"He's right, Colin," Greg said, "By all rights, when you reached Kansas, command should have gone straight to the most powerful Mage present. But even the most powerful are ready to follow you. I don't think we would have survived under anyone else's command, mine included."

"You have a gift, Boss," Andrea Prada said, "and you see things none of us can. We need that skill in charge considering what's coming. We all know that this ain't over. There is a great big hammer about to slam down on this planet, and we need you to use everything you have to prepare for it."

I just shook my head in wonder. I still don't quite understand how the people around me can show me so much loyalty. A hundred and five deaths in Kansas alone. Because I'm not learning how to use what I can do fast enough. But I know I can't get bogged down with the guilt. No matter how hard it is, I just do the best I can. Time to get down to business.

I pointed at the map stretched across Gregor's desk, "I think we need shields here and here. They can be support for the main shield here. I would like to put the installation here, underground. With the numbers they'll bring, I want as much protection for the Guards as I can get."

"I would suggest multiple facilities, if we get the time to build," Prada said.

Rictor nodded, as did Gregor. "Boss, we need to evacuate Newton for sure, and if we can manage it, all of the surrounding area. Probably Wichita as well."

"Paige is working on getting the support we need from the Senate and Congress," I said, "The President is ready to support us but the others are a little harder to convince. I've got a meeting with her in an hour to see what we have."

"I don't want this one to be like the last battle there, and we know the Demons aren't stupid. They'll make allowances for what happened last time. I'm thinkin' the one big gate will be accompanied by other gates so they won't be stopped if we shut down the one gate. It's what I would do."

"True," Gregor nodded, "if they have the capability to open the big one with others in the area, and we'll have to go under the assumption that they do."

"The thing that worries me is what the Wraith said. It said there are seven of these Gates didn't it?" Rictor asked.

"Yeah," I answered, "But this is the only one we know the location of. All we can do is try to make this one so costly they won't use it again. But we can't pull all of the Guards here, either. If they pop out somewhere else, we have to be prepared."

"We'll do our best, Boss," Ric said, "it's all we can do."

"We need to actively recruit for the Guard, too," I said. "There just isn't enough of us, and we need the recruits to begin training as soon as possible."

"True," Greg returned, "but it takes time to train Soulguards. The focus lessons alone take months. Not to mention, the actual tying of the Soulstreams."

"That's why it's so important to get the backing we need as soon as possible," I said, "I'll let you know where we stand after the meeting with Paige. She's been doin' all of the work in that area. I understand we have backing in several countries already."

"Yes," Gregor said, "We've got complete backing in Scotland, England, Germany, France, Argentina, and Russia is looking to be pretty solid as a backer soon. Some of the groundwork had already been in place in some of these countries before last month."

I stood up and turned toward the door. "I'm heading to the meeting with Paige after I get something from the mess hall to eat. I'll get back with you after the meeting."

"By all means, don't miss a meal or anything," Gregor said with a sarcastic look on his face. "I keep hearing rumors of that bottomless pit you call a stomach."

"I have no idea what you're talkin' about," I returned as I opened the door. Rictor chuckled and Andrea snorted. Both followed me out the door.

As I left Gregor's office, and rounded the corner with my two shadows following, I found Lyrica standing in front of the receptionist who ran the office. Georgia DuMorne worked for the Soulguard from the day she and Lyrica came to Montana. She was pretty much a fixture around the Academy.

"Thanks, Nana."

That was the only name I'd ever heard Lyrica call her since the day I found her in Tennessee. She'd made herself at home amongst the Guard, and she always had a smile on her face for me.

"You're welcome, young lady." She turned her head as I entered, 'And you, young man need to be a bit more careful. You gave us all a scare last month, and we would truly hate to lose you. Now come give me a hug."

This was actually the first time I had seen her since the Source coma, and I was happy to give her a hug. She really is a nice woman.

As she hugged me she whispered, "Watch her, please, Colin. She is hurting inside, and needs all the love from us we can give."

"Yes Ma'am," I whispered and stepped back. She smiled, but I could see the worry still in her aura. I knew Lyrica could see everything I could, but she didn't say anything that might embarrass the woman who had cared for her as a child.

I turned to Lyrica and her two shadows, Trent and Mattie, "You wanna join me for lunch?"

"Sure," Lyrica said with a smile. She was smiling again, maybe not as much as before, but any was better than none.

I turned to start out of the room and stopped, "Georgia," I said, "Can you get Terrence Pickney out here for me? I have somethin' in which I need his expertise. Rictor can give you his information."

"I'll send for him, immediately, Colin."

"Thanks," I turned and headed toward the elevator.

If what I feared was true, there was a very uncomfortable explanation for the actions of the Archmage and his Council. And even for the actions of Gavin Price, all those years ago. There is one common link between every action that was taken. She lay in the infirmary in a coma.

I'd gone to see her a while back, and the remnant of Soul that clung to her body looked very familiar. What was left of Regina Worthington's Soul looked like the purple and black Soul of a Demon.

Chapter 4

"It's so damn infuriating," Paige said as she sat down behind the huge desk of the Archmage. "They don't listen to me at all. I'm just a child in their eyes, and I can't stand the sanctimonious pricks."

Unfortunately, now that we are dealing with the public, people don't realize that the man or woman in front of them is actually not a teenager. I never had even thought about the problem until recently. Tying the Soulstream in the Guard knot sends so much life force into a person, they heal incredibly fast. A side effect is that age is something that the Source heals as well.

I'm thirty years old but I look like I'm eighteen, as does Paige. She is thirty one yet the Senators see an eighteen year old standing in front of them. They have a hard time taking her seriously. The ones who have a history with the Guard try, but the others are a bit more difficult.

"I don't know how to get it across to them that we are a force to be reckoned with," she said.

"I've got an idea," I said, "They haven't accepted what has happened yet, but I think a demonstration on the plains of Kansas would be beneficial."

"What sort of demonstration do you have in mind?"

"I would expect a show of power needs to be made," I said, "They think their military can protect them. I think I'll show them it can't."

"That," she gave me a wary look, "makes me very nervous."

"That gate is there. I don't know how long until it opens again. We don't have time for this bullshit," I said, "I need their support for the defense of our whole damn planet. And I'll have it if I have to set the whole damn Capitol on fire!"

"I'm thinking something a little less drastic, but you're right. They won't take us serious until we show them what they are really facing instead of the teenagers they think they are facing. Go ahead and set up the demonstration. I think you should include something you would like for me, personally, to do. All of this power scares the shit out of me, but if it will hammer the idiots into listening, I'll use it."

I smiled, "I think I can come up with something that needs a great big hammer to take care of it."

"Sometimes," she said with a shake of her head, "that smile makes me very nervous."

I stood and chuckled. Then I turned to start for the door.

"I'm sorry, Colin," she said.

I turned back to see her tiny figure sitting behind that huge desk. I could see regret and sadness in her aura.

"For what?"

"I never understood how hard it must have been for you, knowing that everyone was afraid of you. I'm sorry I became one of those people instead of the kind of person you deserved."

"It's ok, Paige," I said softly. "I've accepted what everyone thinks of me. I'm ok with it, now. There's a lot about me that inspires fear in others, but there's much more that would terrify them if they knew. They need not fear what I'll do to them. The Kresh, on the other hand will learn to fear me with good reason."

"But it's a lonely way to go through life, and I apologize for adding my fear to it. I actually see the other side of it now. There aren't many people who don't cringe when I drop my screen. Almost everyone is now just as scared of me as they are you."

"It's a hard thing, the wielding of Power," I said, "But you have the iron in you to stand. I know this, I can see it in your Soul. Never forget it, never doubt it."

She sighed, "Thanks for the vote of confidence. I know you are one of the few who doesn't fear me, but of course, you don't have enough sense to be afraid of anything. Only a fearless idiot would tie himself to the Source while two hundred and thirty-seven new Mages stood within a hundred feet of him, any of which could have served as support in our place."

"Hindsight," I said with a grin, "is twenty-twenty."

"That it is," she said with a smile.

***

"Hello Doctor," I said with an outstretched hand, "Thank you for coming to Montana."

"I go where I am needed," he answered in his precise voice. "I saw what happened in Kansas on the News. That certainly is not staying away from stressful environments."

"Yeah... I had to take option two."

"Use the Rage as much as you can as a release," he nodded, "Not the best way for you, but apparently it is the best way for everyone else. If no one else has done so, I must thank you. There is no way to even imagine the destruction they would have caused if you had not stopped them."

"Wasn't just me," I said, "Close to four hundred men and women were there with me."

"As you say," he returned with a nod, "and what would you like me to look into for you? You already know I have not found anything for you to use against the Demon DNA. Is there something else?"

"As a matter of fact, there is. In our Infirmary there is a woman in a coma. I need you to do a DNA test for me. I think it will confirm my suspicions and clear much of the confusion surrounding the Archmage and all that occurred over the last fifteen years."

"You think this woman has the same sort of problem as you?"

"I'm not sure but I need to know, and if you don't mind, keep this between you and I for the time being. Most people don't know about my... situation."

"You know I can be discreet," he said with a solemn look, "I've kept your secret for the last six years without revealing anything."

"True enough," I nodded. "That's why I sent for you and not any other physician. Your discretion is much appreciated."

"I will begin immediately then, and we will see what we will see," he said and stood up. "I am familiar with the Infirmary and the compound. I will make my way there now, if you have no objections."

"No problem, and thanks again."

He gave a short nod and turned away. As he left my office, I wondered if my suspicions were true.

If they were, there had been a Demon spy in our midst with possible skills unlike any that we have been trained to defend against. It was actually possible that she had gained mental skills that a regular human doesn't have. I'm almost certain the Demons have some form of telepathic connection with one another. Could she have some way to force people to do things with her mind?

My ability to project to the Guards around me could also be based on a telepathic sort of communication gained from my Demon DNA. Lyrica doesn't seem to have any ability in that area. She can't push a memory into someone else like I had done back when we'd found that child molesting bastard in Knoxville.

It would explain why the Archmage had done something that would endanger the whole human race for his own ends. Not even a bastard like Price should have been able to do what he had done. And the eerie way the whole Council seemed to have the single goal of destroying Gregor and Simon without thought of defending themselves at all? It just didn't make sense to me, unless someone else was in control.

But I would find out soon enough if my suspicions were true. I had a demonstration to set up, and I was thinking seriously about tanks.

Chapter 5

The Hooters in Missoula didn't have a large crowd, except for us. There were twenty-two of us from the Academy seated around five tables that the staff had pushed together. Now that we didn't have to keep our Soulguard ties secret, we scheduled these get-togethers once a week.

"How many wings have you already eaten?" Kyra asked me in amazement as I ordered another plate from our waitress. It was all you can eat wings day and I was taking advantage of it.

"I'm not sure but there are a lot of flightless birds out there somewhere," I answered.

"They don't fly to well anyway, son," Kharl said with a chuckle. "At least you didn't eat their legs. They can still run."

"That's mean," Lyrica punched Kharl's arm, "Those poor chickens."

"And the chicken breast you just devoured?" Mattie asked.

"At least I'm not leaving a bunch of crippled chickens running around. It's much more humane," She answered easily.

Mattie snorted and laughed aloud.

The very well-endowed waitress returned with another plate of wings for me and I saw Kharl's eyes drawn to the same place as most of the other men at the table. She smiled and headed back to the kitchen.

"Really?!" Kyra asked. "She's a biscuit older than Lyrica you lecherous old man."

"But... damn it, woman." He answered shamelessly.

"She'd end up cutting those things off the first time she drew a blade. Her arms aren't long enough to swing the blade around them."

"I beg to differ, Mom," Lyrica said, "the first thing she remembered after seeing the Soulguard uniforms was when she won the Championship at her school in fencing. She's really pretty good at it."

"Now why would you say something like that?" Kyra asked, "Now every one of these apes wants to try and convince her to go home with them. And you better not even think about it, Old Man."

"I'd never," Kharl said. "I've got everything I could ever want right here."

He wrapped his arm around her shoulders and she smiled. With his other hand he acted like he was wiping his forehead, and he mouthed a silent "Whew" out of sight of Kyra.

"So," Lyrica said, "let's hear a good story from the vast store of BS seated around this table. Anyone have something to share?"

"What about the Chattanooga thing?" Andrea asked.

I cringed. Of course it would be something about me. It always ended up going there before the night was over so maybe it was good to go ahead and get it out of the way.

"You want this one?" Prada asked Ric.

"Sure," He answered with a grin, "Why not?"

"We were just finished with a patrol just north of Chattanooga, and our illustrious potentate over there needed something to eat," he began.

"Big surprise there," Mattie said from over beside Trent.

"Yeah, isn't it?" Ric returned with a shrug. "Anyway, the boss was just steppin' up to the counter with the biggest cup of coke I think I've ever seen. What was it? Sixty-four ounces?"

I nodded and he continued. "So he's standin' there, and this guy runs in the door and sticks what looked like a 44 magnum right into his face..."

"Oh my God!" Kharl interrupted and looked at me, "Did ya put yer finger in the gun?"

"Have you already heard the damn story?" Rictor looked disappointed.

Kharl laughed loudly, and shook his head. "I always wanted 'ta do that."

Prada looked at Kharl with a sad shake of her head and said, "Just knowin' that you raised the man explains so much."

Kyra snorted and said, "There was no way I could even stop it. I tried so hard to prevent the insanity from passing to the child, but I had to sleep sometimes, and I just couldn't stop it."

There was laughter all around the table.

"So there we were with this kid standin' there with his finger in the barrel of a 44." Rictor continued after a moment, "It was just so ridiculous, the cashier was shakin' with her mouth hangin' open, and I racked my brain to find a way to stop the madness..."

"Bullshit!" Prada exclaimed, "You're just as bad as he is! I didn't see any trying to stop anything!"

"What?" Rictor returned.

"I remember that the only thing you did was ask the guy with his finger in a 44 whether he wanted his twinkies with icing or the plain ones."

"That was a ruse..."

"For what?" she asked, "When he said the iced ones you just picked them up, and walked toward the cashier like no one was there."

"I was strategically placin' myself where I could intercede if it was necessary."

"Really? You were behind our fearless leader where you couldn't even see what was happening anymore."

"Well, you know how important it is to get the Boss his twinkies. If he didn't get 'em he might do something crazy. I was just doin' my job."

Lyrica laughed merrily. She was watching memories in both of their auras.

"That's just not fair," Kharl said. "She gets to watch stuff happen while we gotta wait for these slow asses to get on with it."

"Any way," Prada said, "so the Boss stands there with his finger in this guy's gun, and the guy starts cursing, and trying to pull back on the gun, but the finger follows as fast as he can move the gun. Then the guy actually looks at Colin's face where he gets a shot of the Crazy Eye. He just screams, and lets go of the gun, and sprints back out the door."

"Crazy Eye?" Mattie asked, "What's the Crazy Eye?"

"Ahh, it's that look when you can see the Soulfire burning inside of them, and you start to think he might just rip your spine out or something equally unsavory."

"Yeah I saw that one," Kharl said, "He was still carrying the spine when he got back into the shield."

"Yeah," Prada said, "Right, that's the look I'm talking about. The Crazy Eye."

To be totally honest, I don't know what possessed me to do it but it was so hilarious I couldn't stop myself. I'd pushed a shield out to stop the hammer if he pulled the trigger. There was no danger of him actually doing anyone harm. I had almost forgotten the whole incident, but I'm not allowed to forget anything for long before someone always brings it back up. Usually at one of these grand get-togethers that I tend to be a party to.

"That's awesome," Kharl said with a grin. "God I hope I get the chance to do that someday."

I pointed at his huge hand, "He better bring a twelve gauge shotgun so your finger will fit in the barrel."

"True enough," He laughed and reached for another hot wing from the platter in front of him.

Everyone had their round of laughter at the antics of a Soullord who has seen too many cartoons. When they settled down I looked at Lyrica.

"So I know we've all seen the extremely smelly dog that's taken up residence at the Academy. It seems that it came to the Academy after our esteemed colleagues returned. You know, the ones who were on vacation in Scotland, while we were all workin' so hard here at home. Anyone care to explain the presence of the ugliest, stinkingest creature I have ever laid eyes on?"

"I'm not sure if 'stinkingest' is really a word," Jacobs said, "Smelliest, might be right, or most smelly, odiferous even."

"Yeah," Rictor said. "I've never seen any animals that would get anywhere near a Soulguard, much less follow a group of 'em around."

"And what the Hell is that damn thing?" I agreed. "I mean, I can tell it's a dog but, damn. Its whole body is all wrinkled up. Its wrinkles have wrinkles."

"I think it's adorable," Prada argued.

"Once again," Kharl said in triumph, "Proof positive that all women are crazy. That's probably the ugliest animal I've ever seen."

Trent was snickering and looking at Lyrica, who was trying her best not to pay any attention to the rest of us.

"It happened the other day," he burst out. I think Trent would probably explode if he really had to keep a secret. The man is hopeless.

"We were down on the highway below the Academy giving Lyrica a chance to work on her driving skills. Skills that she doesn't possess at all," He began.

"Humph," Lyrica looked around the room.

"Anyway, we topped a rise, and this dog is a couple of hundred feet from us. It turns around and like most other animals, runs like hell when Soulguards approach. Unfortunately, the car in the other lane hit him, and he flew back out of the road."

"Here's part of the girl's lack of driving skills," Trent said, "She was out the door and running before the dog had even hit the ground. She didn't stop the car; she didn't even touch the brakes. She just stepped out and ran for the dog. Of course, now, we're in a car flying down the road with no driver, and Mattie is screaming in terror..."

"Now wait a damn minute! I recall the screams coming from the back seat, not the front," Mattie interrupted.

"Nope, definitely from the front," He answered quickly, "But regardless, by the time we stopped the car and got out, Lyrica is holding this ugly thing's head in her lap, and we're feeling her Pull through the dog's stream."

"Then it followed us home," Lyrica said, "And now I finally get to have a puppy. A sixty pound, smelly puppy, but a puppy, nonetheless."

"It's a Shar-Pei, by the way," Kevin Graves offered. "They're actually a very expensive breed."

"People really buy dogs that ugly?" Jacobs asked. "They pay money, real money for 'em?"

"Lots of folks do," The Kid answered.

"Well I'll be damned," Jacobs mumbled, "Who would've thunk it?"

The waitress returned with the check and before she could ask, twenty-one fingers pointed straight at me. I sighed, she laughed and handed me the bill.

"Jesus, you people are gonna put me in the poor house," I mumbled and handed her my debit card.

It would take quite a bit more than that to hurt the money I had squirreled away in the bank. Warren was still doing wonders with my finances. I really needed to take a trip back to Knoxville and see him, and see the Twins, too. I had only seen them once since the whole fiasco in Kansas. They'd really come through with finding more Guards to back us up there.

Maybe I could go in the next few weeks, maybe after the demonstration in Kansas.

Chapter 6

I awoke the next morning early and decided to go for a run. As I left my quarters I saw a figure exit the room that had been given to Jacobs. With his leg and arm gone, he wasn't made to stay out in the regular barracks. The elevators were closer to one of the rooms in the underground facility.

I recognized the woman as she turned and waved at me with a smile. It was the waitress from Hooters. I smiled and waved back.

"Good morning," I said.

"It's a very good morning," She answered and her aura told me that she didn't lie.

Jacobs rolled out the door with his chair, "Hey Boss."

"Ivan," I nodded in greeting. Out of all the men who had been hitting on the beautiful woman at Hooters, she'd went home with Jacobs.

"Boss, can I talk to ya a couple a minutes?"

"Sure," I stopped beside him, "What can I do for you?"

He turned to the woman, "I gotta talk a bit here, Darlin'. I'll see ya later though?"

She bent down and kissed him quite thoroughly.

"Count on it, Hero," she said with a smile. She turned and headed for the elevators.

"You tellin' your war stories to that girl, Ivan?"

"To be honest, Boss, she knows as much about us as any regular person I know. She recognized me from the news reports on the battle. She says I'm a hero."

"Well, she's right, Ivan," I said, "But if you repeat what I just said, I'll deny it."

He chuckled, "Maybe I should start recordin' conversations so people can't deny the fact that your's truly here is a hero."

"Speaking of hero's," I said, "I have a small project I would like for you to work on for me."

One thing I know about Ivan Jacobs is that he feels useless now that his arm and leg were ripped off. He's always been a fighter, and now he can't do what he's been doing for forty years. It tends to make a person feel lost when their life has such a drastic change.

"As long as it's not typing, I'm up for it.'

"If you type like I do, I doubt the Soulguard can afford the time it would take you to type anything out," I returned, "No, what I want is someone to really put some time in to figure out how to imbue a bullet."

"That's not something that'll be easy to do, Boss. Powder is tricky around Soulfire, but I got a couple of ideas I've kicked around over the years. I'll definitely see if I can get some results for ya."

He looked at me for a moment, and I could see the emotions rolling in his aura. He wanted to ask me something very serious, and was almost afraid to do it.

"Just ask," I said softly. "What is it?"

It came out in a flood, "Dammit, Boss, I'm friggin' useless. I can't fight anymore! It's all I know how 'ta do. It's the only skill I have that's worth anything!"

"I know it's hard, Ivan. You'll learn new skills." I placed my hand on his shoulder. "You just have to give it some time."

He was silent for a few seconds before he asked, "Will you make me a Mage?"

This was the question. Somehow I knew it was what he was going to ask, and I knew, also, that this was what he needed. But it was dangerous, very dangerous. Three Guards died when I did that Pull in Kansas, including Patrick Shoffner.

"It's a very dangerous process, Ivan, but I do understand why you want this," I said. "We lost Guards when I did that last time, including Pat. Think another week on it, and if you still wanna try it, then come see me. If your focus slips for an instant Ivan, it's the end. Think about it, and think about your focus skills. Make damn sure this is what ya want. The Source is one unforgiving bitch, and she will burn you down in seconds."

"I've thought for a good bit, Sir," He said. "But I'll wait another week to tell ya the same thing. I'm useless as a Guard, but as a Mage, I can still fight."

"There's no guarantee, Ivan, how strong you can be," I said. "You may be no stronger than a support Mage."

"Boss, a support Mage can still be used in the war, a one armed, one legged Guard can't."

I nodded and gripped his shoulder, "Just come see me in a week if ya still plan on this. I'll have to clear something like this with the Archmage. I could do it and ask for forgiveness instead of permission, but it really sets a bad precedent if I do that. If she supports it, I will try my best."

"Boss, that's all I can ask for. Thank you," he said. "I'll get right on the other thing as well. You know anyone with a gun that is willin' to risk it getting blown up?"

I handed him a credit card, "Buy whatcha need. This is high priority, Ivan. We need it for some surprises I have in mind for the next Kresh visitors."

"A very nasty surprise, I hope?" he asked.

I smiled, "Very nasty."

***

"That's not surprising," Paige said, "I wondered who would be the first to come forward and request this. I'm a bit surprised it was Ivan Jacobs, though."

"Why?"

"I mean, he's already been through the mill. He's received injuries that would have killed him under normal circumstances. Yet he wants to run right back toward the fight. I would have thought he would be ready to say he's done enough."

I chuckled, "If you spend as much time with the Guard as I do, you'll understand. There is one thing above all else I learned about them. Soulguards never quit. You take his leg, he'll hobble to the fight. Take his arms, he'll hold the blade in his teeth. They fight because it's who they are. There will be a new breed of Guard after this, though. Our Guards are warriors. The new Guards will be soldiers."

"What is the distinction between them?"

"Warriors fight because it is who they are," I said. "A warrior lives to fight and fights to live. He fights for the fight itself."

"And a soldier?"

"A soldier goes to war when there is no other recourse left," I said. "A soldier fights for a cause or for his home or his people."

"Don't get me wrong," I said. "There are soldiers in the Guard. But the majority of the Guard were enlisted after the Demons destroyed families and friends. Vengeance and retribution-these things breed warriors. You'll see that the threat of the world's end will breed a new Guard of Soldiers, and we will bring those bastards to their knees with this army."

"But as for Jacobs?"

"Jacobs is a warrior born and he won't quit, whether this works or not," I said. "I want to do this because he needs it. But, even more, because I think we need him and every one like him for this war."

"I agree," she nodded. "You can do it then. Thank you for asking me before you just went and did it though. That's not very characteristic of you."

I laughed. "Probably true but it's the way things need to be done, and that's the bottom line. You are our Archmage, not a figurehead. If I won't follow the rules, how can we expect anyone else to do so?"

"True enough," she said with a grin. "How is the demonstration plan coming?"

"I have to meet with a General tomorrow to hash out the details. I'm trying to get automated drones to put against our men. Don't want to hurt any soldiers."

"Good luck dealing with Generals," she laughed bitterly. "Maybe they'll listen to you better than they listen to me."

"They'll listen," I said with a little of my rage trying to surface.

She was taken aback for a split second, then laughed again, "I bet they do."

Chapter 7

"How is this going to be a real test without any of our men in the field?" General Reginald P. Gasper almost yelled. He was standing behind his desk with both fists planted firmly on the desk top. His whole head was turning red.

I had flown into Washington D.C. specifically to meet with this man about the demonstration. It was our job to hash out what we needed for the event.

"As I said before you interrupted," I returned with a bit of rage surfacing, "I don't want to hurt any American soldiers in a simple demonstration."

The General was taken aback by the tone of my voice, or maybe I was projecting my rage a bit. Maybe my eyes were burning again, I don't know. Either way, he stepped back half a step.

"What I want is for you to provide automated tanks or drones of some sort if it is possible. The more actual soldiers that are in the field, the more my Guards have to hold back. You need to see what the Soulguard is capable of, and I need to know that innocent men and women aren't going to get hurt as I show you."

"You honestly believe your men with, humph...swords, can stand up to my main battle tanks?" he scoffed.

"I think your tanks will be utterly outclassed, but you just get them there and we will see."

I stood and turned toward the door, "I suggest you bring some you are prepared to lose, and bring plenty."

I knew this was like a slap in the face to the man, but it seemed to be the only way to get the arrogant bastard to listen. God I'll be glad when we can get past all the bullshit, and get to work on the defense of our world, I thought.

I heard him as I left the room, mumbling, "...why that cocky little bast..."

I chuckled as I rounded the corner. You could bet he'd bring out his best for this now. It's the best way to show them exactly what they face, both in the Soulguard and in the foe that we must face together, if we are going to survive as a species.

As for the capabilities of their tanks, I was working on several ways of dealing with them, although I was sorely tempted to just let Paige blow them all to hell by herself.

***

Waiting for the government to do anything was torture. I know that the U.S. government is a large institution, and it's going to be slow getting results. But that doesn't help the rage burning inside of me. Hell, if the Kresh want to get rid of me, they may only have to stay away for a few years. I might spontaneously combust.

It was time to return to Jacobs, and see if he was still set on being turned into a Mage. Rumors had gotten out about it. Lyrica had seemed to be trailing me for the last day. I think she was afraid I would hurt myself again with the Pull.

"Is my shadow still close by?" I asked Ric.

"No doubt, Boss," he chuckled. "Everybody knows what you're plannin'. You can't really blame the girl. You almost died last time you did somethin' like this."

"It was a much larger scale," I said, "but I'm more worried about Ivan. If his focus fails, I'll kill one of my closest friends."

"He's a big boy, Boss," Prada said. "He knows the risks. Besides, he won't slip. He's got a good bit of skill at focusing. I know we lost a few of our men last time, and you feel it's your fault, but it's not. We all took the chance. We all accepted the risk for the opportunity to end the battle without losing more lives."

"She's right," Ric said. "We lost three lives. If we had just continued to fight them, we would have eventually lost hundreds. They died no less heroes than any of the others who fell in Kansas."

I pointed at my head, "I know this up here." I tapped my chest, "but I still feel here that it was my doing. I know it's not really logical, but it is what it is."

I do know that what they say is true, and we are in a war, although some people don't truly understand that yet. But I just feel that I should have learned what I could do faster. I should have been pushing the boundaries much harder than I had been. That is part of why I chose to do this for Jacobs. If I succeed without incident, there will be more who request the change. In all honesty, we will need as many Mages as we can get.

My actual thought is that every veteran Guard will be Mages, and the new recruits will be the Guards before all of this is done. I don't think I will try to increase any Guards who haven't been there for quite some time. Focus is essential, and the ones who had died in Kansas were relatively new recruits. But these are just my own thoughts on the matter. It will be subject to the Archmage, and her Council to decide if I can proceed with this.

I entered the Dome with my swords in the harness on my back. Before I go get Jacobs, I needed to work off some of the rage that has been building for weeks inside of me. Rictor and Prada both followed with their weapons as well. In moments, Lyrica and her two shadows followed us in.

As I took my place in the center of the Dome, Lyrica stepped up beside me. She held two swords as well. Behind us I heard swords unsheathe as Rictor, Prada, Mattie, and Trent all drew weapons.

I drew my blades and settled into the first stance of the Dance. I let my mind relax as I flowed from that stance to another, then another. That is what the Dance of Blades is. It is the seamless flow from stance to stance with the least amount of wasted movement. I heard the others doing the same, wordlessly.

I began to speed up and I began to release the rage I held pent up inside myself. Faster and faster I Danced. It seemed that the more rage I released, the more I wanted to let it all out. It would be a relief to just let it go. The older I get, the stronger the rage seems to become. The Demon DNA inside me is still altering me at a genetic level, and I don't know where it will take me. It scares me to think what I could become in the years to come.

I've seen what that DNA can do to an evil person. Regina Worthington had indeed had the same sort of DNA. Pickney had confirmed it for me the day before. She had been consumed by hate when she walked these halls. I had seen the ugliness inside her, and not really understood where it came from. I do understand where it came from now, and I have the same thing inside me.

I just fight it where she relished it. I don't want to be a monster. But if it is my fate to become one, I will use that monster to fight the Kresh. I will fight with everything I have.

My thoughts returned to where I was. I had no idea how long I was off in my own little world but I was soaked in sweat, and my rage was noticeably less than it had been.

I brought the Dance to an end, and I heard the harsh breathing of the others around me.

"That was a little eerie," I heard Paige say from behind us.

I turned with a smile, "How was it eerie?"

"When you started, all of you started in different stances," she said, "In moments, you're all synchronized."

I looked over at Lyrica who shrugged, "I just started going with the stance that felt right."

"Me too," Prada said. The others nodded as well.

"You were doin' that thing again," Ric said, "projectin' your moves to us."

"Interesting," Paige said. "Were you trying to project?"

I shook my head. "I was a million miles away. I was running on autopilot."

"I wonder how far you can project what you want done," Paige mused.

"It worked with a hundred Guards in Kansas," Rictor said. "There's really no tellin' how far it will work."

"I don't really try to do it," I said, "it just happens. It will take some experiments to really find out the limits of it."

She nodded. "So, when are you going to get Jacobs and do this thing? Everyone is waiting with bated breath. I think some of them will explode if you don't get on with it."

Rictor laughed, "At last, someone has the guts to bring it up. She's right, Boss. Just get it done, and we'll see what happens."

"I just wanted to get myself centered for it. The Dance helps me get myself together."

"Bleeds off some of the rage, too," said Lyrica. "It's noticeably less after that workout."

"True enough," I answered. "All right, let's get to it."

Chapter 8

"What do ya need me 'ta do, Boss?" Jacobs asked.

We stood out near the giant oak tree behind the Guard Barracks. It had a trunk nearly thirty feet in diameter, and it towered above the Guard barracks like some huge sentinel. The enhanced Stream that fed it had even grown with the time that had passed since I had unblocked Paige so many years ago.

When I had gone to get him, Jacobs had been waiting. Gina Peters, the girl who had come home with him from Missoula, had been there as well. Apparently the two of them had struck it off quite well. She seemed to be a nice person, and I can say that after seeing her Soul. A person is the sum of the things accrued in their Soul, and Gina's was vibrant with color.

A Soul that is ugly with browns and greys is typically that of a person who has done evil things. Demon Souls are black and purplish, but they are more than just a color. They have a sense of evil or repugnance that emanates from them that I sense.

I'd only seen one Soul that had been pure black but hadn't been the black of evil. It was complicated with this man. He had done some very bad things, but he'd done them to very bad people. Much of what your Soul displays is the way you perceive what you have done. If you do evil and know it is evil, your Soul will reflect that with a repugnance that I can see and feel. His Soul was black, yes, but it held a beauty of its own as well. His acts, that would have been considered evil, were tempered with the righteousness of his cause. He killed monsters that walked in human form. He was known as The Whisper in the Night by all that knew of him, and that was a small list of people.

My thoughts returned to the task at hand. "When I Pull, you focus on steering that power straight up into the sky. Before, I used the power I Pulled, so I had them steer to a particular point. Since this is not for a purpose past the Pull itself, focus straight up into the sky."

I lit up my Soulstream, formed a tendril that went to the side, and turned it straight up.

"This is what I want you to form," I said. "Then concentrate all your focus to send everything I Pull out that tendril."

I watched as a tendril formed on the side of his stream, and began to form into the exact shape I had shown him.

"Don't lose focus, Ivan," I said with a warning tone. "The Source is an unforgiving bitch, and she will burn you down in a heartbeat."

"I know the stakes, Boss," he said. "I'm ok, so do your thing."

I nodded and stepped forward. As I started to Pull, I felt three hands land on my shoulders. I turned my head to find Lyrica on my right. She raised her eyebrows as if to dare me to say something. I chose not to say a word. I looked left to find Rictor standing with his hand on my left shoulder. He shrugged and I knew it was hopeless to even think he wasn't going to be Support if it was needed. I didn't even need to see who was behind me. Andrea Prada was undoubtedly standing there.

"On three," I said, "one...two...three."

At three, I Pulled through Jacobs stream. Power poured into the sky, but I wasn't Pulling hard. I just wanted to be sure it was going where it was supposed to. I watched for a second as the several people who had come out to watch looked on. I could see various stages of nervousness around us in auras.

Then I Pulled a great deal harder. I could feel power flowing through my Supports. Nothing like what had ripped through Gregor, Darrel, and Paige while in Kansas. But the power flowed through them easily. Jacobs stream, on the other hand had become a huge gout of Soulfire spewing into the sky.

I watched his Soulstream closely as it stretched wider. His focus was staying steady, so I Pulled harder. People began to step back from us, and there was a bit of fear now flowing with the nervousness in them. I knew it would come, it always comes out. But, as I had told Paige, I've accepted the fact that everyone fears me.

Somewhere along the way I felt that I shouldn't go any wider than I had it, and I eased off. I'm not sure where the feeling came from, but I seemed to sense how much his stream could take before stressing it too far. Perhaps part of it was the squeeze of my right shoulder that Lyrica had given almost at the same instant I had sensed the limit.

Regardless, I stopped Pulling and the fire spewing into the sky ceased. I looked at Jacobs to find his Soulstream had gone from about three and a half inches to close to fifteen inches. It was as large as my stream without a doubt.

I placed my hand on his shoulder, "Welcome to the ranks of the Mageguard. Don't play with it till you get some classes in or you'll go blind."

There was amazement rolling through his aura as he felt the massive increase in pure Lifeforce entering his body from the larger stream.

"This is amazing, Boss," he said. "This is what you feel all the time?"

"You get used to it after a bit, and I'm serious, don't play around with it till you get some classes in."

"Yes Sir, and thank you for this," he said with a huge amount of gratitude rolling through his aura, "you have no idea what this means to me."

"As a matter of fact, I do, Ivan," I said and smiled.

I turned away to find Lennox Flynn standing there in what seemed to be shock, "Ye did that wit two hundred Guards at one time?"

His thick Scottish brogue couldn't disguise the awe that filled his voice or his aura. "I had read the reports, but the bloody scale of it had na really registered on me brain till now."

"It scares the shit outta me," I said quietly so that no one but Lennox could hear me. "I'm not sure how much I can handle with enough Supports. The Supports gave out long before I could even tell a strain on me physically. Perhaps, with enough Supports, there is no limit. I have no idea and that scares the hell outta me. Cause I have to find out."

He looked at me with confusion rolling through him, "Why?"

"Because if I don't use everything I have, and more of my Guards die because I didn't, I can't live with that."

"I see."

I nodded, 'So as soon as we get the problem with our government support taken care of, I have to begin the tests of my power."

"'Tis anythin' I can do?"

"Actually, there is," I said as we started walking toward the Academy, "I'm gonna need a sort of squad of Mages and Guards to work directly with me. I'm thinkin' multiple Nationalities cause we're gonna be workin' all over the world before this is over, if I don't miss my guess. And sadly, English is the only language I can understand."

He was nodding and there was great interest in his aura, "Would tere be any problem if I was part of tis force?"

"Absolutely not, that's why I'm bringing it to you. I want you as one of the members. I also want Rictor and Andrea, here to be part of this group. But I don't know anyone from the other Academies except Len Yueh, who I would also like to have on this, if he's willing."

"I'm sure 'e will be," Flynn said.

"I only want volunteers, as well," I said. "One thing I can guarantee is that we will be in the thickest of the fighting, because that's where I'll be. And I can also guarantee that there will be a lot of unorthodox ways of doing things going on so I need open minds, too. The more I learn about my skills, the more it flies in the face of tradition."

Flynn looked back at a still dazed Jacobs, "Tis a fact, that."

He turned back toward me, "And do ye intend to do this wit more of the Guards?"

"Absolutely," I answered, "Think of it. Every veteran Guard ascended to a Mage, and all the new recruits brought in as a Guard."

"Recruits?" he asked.

"Oh yes," I said. "Soon there'll be many recruits. They'll flood in, and I want them trained as quickly as we can train them. The Academies in Scotland and China will be flooded soon too, I think, and Russia as well. Once people really understand what is happening, our ranks will swell like you wouldn't believe."

He was looking at me with a great deal of respect rolling through his aura. "We old timers just are'na used to de tings ye expect. I suspect we will all have some changes in our expectations, Lad."

"If I could manage it, I would have the whole human race with Soulguard knots. Let the bastards try to make victims of humans after that."

After hearing the fierceness of that statement he looked at me strangely, "Ye actually mean that, don't ye?"

"Damn straight, I do."

Chapter 9

"I kept goin' at it wrong, Boss," Jacobs said, "But I didn't really get the right results till after you juiced me up to Mage status."

"So what do you have on it now?" I asked. I could see the excitement rolling through his stream.

"Well at first I kept havin' to push the Soulfire from my hand into the gun. It always seemed to get the bullets when I did that. That's the reason we always assumed that bullets couldn't be imbued. But after I got the new abilities, I could look at it from another perspective."

He began to concentrate, and a tendril formed that ran from his stream to the end of the barrel. He kept his focus quite well. The tendril enveloped just the end of the barrel and Jacobs stopped. I could see the tiny anchors in the tendril latched on to the gun. He then opened the portal at the base of the tendril just a little, and the end of the barrel glowed with Soulfire.

I smiled as he aimed the .45 toward a target with a thick wood surface behind it. Behind that was a concrete wall and an earth bank behind that. The pistol boomed and the bullet slammed into the target with an explosive reaction. The concrete wall cracked as the imbued bullet slammed through it, and a gout of earth exploded into the air behind the wall.

Jacobs turned to me with a huge smile on his face, "And we have Soul rounds!"

"That's great, Ivan." I reached into my back pocket and pulled out a folded piece of paper.

"But a Mage for each gun probably isn't feasible.." He stopped as he saw the picture on the folded piece of paper. A smile spread across his face, and I saw even more excitement roll through his aura, "That is freakin' awesome Boss."

What we were looking at was the picture of an AC-130. An assault version of the C-130 we had ridden in to Kansas. This plane had two 20mm cannons, one 40mm auto cannon, and a 105mm howitzer jutting from the side of the plane.

"See, if we can have the Mages imbue these guns, we will have a real crowd pleaser," I said.

"No shit," he said. "You don't think small Boss."

"As soon as we get our government backing, I intend to put you inside one of these to see what ideas you can come up with. You can work out details when we get authority to work with the National Guard on this. Until then, work on your Mage training. I hear you're doing quite well with the training."

It had been close to a month since Jacobs had made his ascension.

"I'm doin' alright," he said. "I have a good imagination and that helps."

"I have something else that might interest you, too," I said.

"What's that?" Ivan asked.

"I was watching one of the techs play a video game the other day. It was one of the Star Wars games, and one of the characters intrigued me. He had a force field about right here," I pointed to my forearm, "connecting his arm to his hand. The first thing I thought of was a shield prosthesis tied directly to your stream that would give you at least some more movement in..."

"Son of a Gun!" he exclaimed as what I said registered. "That never even occurred to me!"

"I can help with that whenever you're ready," I said, "I can light up your stream for long enough for you to build the shield you need. That way you can put as much detail as you want into it."

"Really?!"

"Just let me know when you want to get started, Ivan."

He was silent for a moment, "I don't even know how to respond Boss. You can really light up someone else's Stream?"

"Yeah, I discovered that when I was in the Academy," I said. "Just let me know when you're ready."

He nodded, "Let me work on a design, and I'll get back with you. Thank you Boss."

"Any time Ivan," I said. "Now figure out how many barrels you can imbue at the same time. I wanna know how many Mages we gotta put in one of those planes."

"You got it Boss."

***

"That's the ticket!" I yelled as I watched disks of Soulfire slam across the Dome into the targets. I had strengthened the shields around the targets so that the new weapons didn't destroy them as easily.

Rictor grinned from ear to ear as his disks spewed forth, "Hot damn! Now that's a fire!"

This was his first time using the disks. We'd spent a great deal of time just practicing the Pulls themselves. He and Prada were both doing quite well with channeling enough power to run the disk launcher.

"Always remember to let enough power through to keep your shields strong," I said. "Your shield is what keeps you alive."

I saw several of the Mages who were watching our session. They seemed a little confused to me about the necessity of keeping the shield at full power. It seemed that every time I ran a training session with Ric and Prada, we ended up with an audience.

"That's how we lost one of the most powerful Mages who went to Kansas," I explained. "Nora Kestril was a great one for focus. She was too good at it. When she was firing her disks at multiple targets, she kept the overflow from herself. But she kept too much from reaching the shield, and the Wraith that hit her from behind got through it. It's a fine line to have to walk, and experience will be the best teacher."

"Oh crap," Rictor said as he saw the smile on my face.

"Mattie," I said turning around where Lyrica and her two shadows stood at the back of the crowd.

"Oh no," Ric muttered.

"How 'bout you come, and make sure Ric focuses like he should."

There were chuckles from the crowd of Mages and Guards nearby.

As Mattie stepped close to Ric I said, "Start on the left side, Ric. Work your way to the right. I want every target hit ten times, then reverse and work back to the left side. Every time she gets into your shield, stop, and start again at the beginning."

"This should be interesting," Prada said and chuckled.

"Don't get too happy about it Andrea, you're next," I said.

She winced as Ric started, and didn't even get ten shots into the first target before he grunted as Mattie's fist landed in his left Kidney. He stopped and turned to see Mattie smiling.

"You're enjoying this way too much," He mumbled.

She shrugged, "What can I say? I love my job."

Experience is truly the best teacher, and by the time he completed his run, I know he was bruised all over. But the last run across the targets was flawless.

Prada fared a little worse, but I think they both did quite well. I doubt I could do anywhere near as close with the focus. My shield stays strong because I don't stop enough power. My body just has a huge tolerance for power overload, and I can bleed it off with healing, or throw some of it back out through my attacks. If my body didn't have this high tolerance, I'd have been dead long ago, back when I Pulled for the first time at Morndel.

Chapter 10

It was so hot in Kansas. Nearly a hundred degrees. The pavilion kept the Senators and Generals shaded, but it really didn't do much for the heat itself.

Senator Samuel Deacons was seated near the front, and smiled as he saw me approaching. He knew what the Soulguard could do, and he was actually enjoying himself immensely. The last few months he had been hammering at the committee to back us. Naturally, he would be here for this.

I also saw General Gasper sitting next to Senator Losner, the most vocal of the Senators speaking against giving support to us.

"Thank you for coming out here, ladies and gentlemen," I said. "Some of you have met Soulguards before, and some of you don't really know what to expect here today."

I saw nods at my statement. "General Gasper has been generous enough to provide a number of remote operated vehicles for this demonstration, and I hope to show you what the Guard is capable of accomplishing. I asked for remotes so that my men won't have to hold back."

I saw snickers from some of the military personnel around General Gasper. There were quite a few uniforms scattered through the crowd, and most of them were taking this quite serious. All I could do was show them, and see where it took us. One way or another, I would stop the Demons here in Kansas with or without the U.S. government's help. But it would be so much more difficult without their assistance. We really needed this to work.

"The first thing I would like to show you is what a single Soulguard can do." I turned to the young man who was directing the vehicles. "Send one of the tanks out to meet my Guard. Use every weapon you can, and try to stop him."

He looked skeptical, but he nodded.

I turned to the assorted Guards and Mages standing in ranks and pointed toward the plain.

"Trent, take it!" I barked.

Trent was in full Soulguard body armor, and his shield was hot. I had worked with him on a shield that utilized the full strength of his stream. The feeder tendril was his whole stream. It was passive so it was always the same strength. It was as strong a shield as a Guard could raise, but the real weapon for him was his speed.

"Yes Sir!" his voice boomed, and he shot forward. He left his starting position hard, and earth flew skyward as his feet pushed him forward. Dirt and dust burst out behind him.

"Jesus Christ!" I heard from behind me and smiled. The operator of the remote tank gasped, and began running his hands across his controls frantically. The tank began firing, but Trent was on one side, then the other.

As the bullets neared him, he would surge to the other side, and throw it off. The main gun fired, and Trent launched himself up and then forward. The ground behind him exploded as the shell impacted where he had been.

Then he was next to the tank, and his weapons surged to life with Soulfire as he pushed Lifeforce from within himself into the blades. His swords impacted the treads on the left side of the tank and ripped through the hardened steel. The vehicle ground to a stop, and he proceeded to go from weapon to weapon, destroying its capability of firing the guns.

In a few moments, the tank was silent and still.

"Now, when we compare our Guards to our foes, I can say we are superior in power one to one. The Kresh, as they call themselves, have different levels of classes, you might call them. The lower level are called Kresh. For a thousand years we have called them Demons. Recently we found out what they call themselves, and I will use both terms as I describe them. The Kresh are not as powerful as a Guard. But they wreak havoc with normal humans. The next class is the Soldier Demon, or Kresh'Far. They are much closer to par with a Guard. Still not as powerful as a Guard but much closer. Three or four of them could do much the same as Trent did to that tank."

"Unbelievable," muttered someone. There was awe rolling through the crowd of observers after what Trent had just done. If they thought that was impressive, they'll really enjoy the next one, I thought.

I saw disbelief roll through the crowd, and it struck me a bit strangely. It seemed to start at one point and spread. Then I felt something that felt like a nudge at my own mind.

What the hell?

"The next class," I continued, "is the Wraith or the Kresh'Sor'An. A Wraith can kill Guards with ease, and has to be taken by Mages. My next demonstration is what a Mage strength Guard can do to a tank."

I turned to the man in charge of the tanks again, "If you would be so kind, send another out."

He nodded and once again I turned to the ranks of Guards and Mages.

"Kharl," I said, "Take it."

Kharl Jaegher is a big man, nearly six and a half feet tall, and four feet wide at the shoulders. Now his Soulstream is twenty inches in diameter, and his training as a Mage was still in progress, but for the purpose of this demonstration, he was perfect.

His shield flared to life, and it was similar to Trent's. But it was so much stronger then Trent's, there was no comparison.

He charged forward straight toward the tank. He didn't waver or dodge, he went right down its throat. That's Kharl's fighting style all the way to the bone. Bullets slammed into his shield, but he didn't slow down. He'd even added a sloped front to his shield to turn the projectiles as they impacted. The main gun fired, and the shell slammed into the front of Kharl's shield, and turned skyward as it exploded. He still didn't slow down.

"My God!" I heard from behind me. I swear it was General Gasper's voice.

Then Kharl was at the tank, and his shield dropped. He didn't draw blades, his whole body seemed to burst into fire as he used himself as a weapon. Another of Kharl's preferred methods of fighting.

I saw a movie a few years ago where they adapted the comic book "The Incredible Hulk" into a movie. The Hulk had went head to head with a tank, and I swear this was almost a reenactment. Kharl planted his feet, and began ripping the whole machine apart. At one point, he held the whole turret by the barrel, and swung it in a complete circle to send it flying away from him. I could actually see the complete joy he was feeling as it rolled through his aura.

He was going to be unbearable after this because he got to stick his whole fist in the gun barrel.

I turned back to the observers to see another wave of disbelief. This time I saw where it started, and I almost gasped as I saw the Senator in the back row-his Soul was disgusting.

But I recognized it immediately now that I knew what to look for. It looked a great deal like Regina Worthington's Soul had looked, and I realized why we had so much difficulty with getting support.

As I now understood the feeling that tried to insinuate itself into my mind, I latched onto it with my mind. Then I reached down into the massive well of rage, and hate I knew lived inside of me, and I Pushed back.

I was looking into his eyes when it hit him. His face went completely white, and terror burst out and flooded his Soul. The Senator was looking right into my eyes, and he knew. Yes, he knew, without a doubt, what I was, and he knew I was much more powerful than him.

"Kharl is relatively new as a Mage, so he fights like a Guard would fight. He is just way more powerful."

"Jesus," one of the Senators muttered.

"A well trained Mage would have destroyed the tank before it could even fire. Kharl is working on his weapons at the moment, so he did it the way he knows best."

The interference from the Senator in the rear had stopped completely.

"What would a trained Mage have used?" a woman who sat near Deacons asked.

"We have an assortment of offensive weapons, if you would like to see them. But the important thing I need you to understand is that even with all of this power, it will be nearly impossible to stop them all without the aid of the U.S. military. We need to clear out the general vicinity of the gate, and evacuate any civilians for miles around. But we can get to that later. Let's see what a Mage can do from a distance."

"Gregor," I said as I turned, "you're up."

I nodded toward the tank operators, "Send three please."

I turned back toward the observers as I knew Gregor was stepping forward.

"Recently we have learned that the Demons have Mages as well," Gregor Pulled, and I saw eyes widen in awe, and some of them winced as they felt the power he Pulled. "That sensation that you are feeling is what it's like when you are near someone who is Pulling from the Source."

I heard explosions behind me as Gregor ripped through the three tanks with disks and a huge Soullance. I know I had hedged my bets with my choices of participants in this demonstration. Gregor is as powerful now as the former Archmage, probably more, since he can use the majority of the power at his call.

"The Kresh call their Mages Kresh'Ma'Nar, and there aren't near as many of them as the Wraiths and Soldiers. We have come into contact with two so far, both killed."

"Did one of those Mages kill them?" Gasper asked, pointing at Gregor and Kharl.

"As a matter of fact," I heard Paige as she walked up behind me, "Colin here killed both of them."

One of the Generals I hadn't met looked at me. "Young man, I've spoken with a great many of your people, and I've heard several terms of rank you use. I've heard of Soulguards and Soulmages, but I also hear the term Soullord. I would love to have someone explain what that is. Every time I ask, mouths stop moving."

"A Soullord can do a great number of things, General," I said, "They can see all of the power flows around them and can tap into a much greater source of power due to this."

"And is it true that you are, indeed, a Soullord?" he asked.

Someone had been blabbing. Of course, it's not really a secret.

"Yes," I nodded, "it is true."

He stated, "I understand that you were planning one more demonstration with your Archmage, here. But what I would like to see is what a Soullord can do."

I turned to Paige who was smiling at me and she shrugged. I could see the mischief rolling through her aura, and I didn't need to look far to know who was blabbing.

"I can bring a great deal of power down on them, but once they're into the ranks with our own, I am as limited as anyone else. This scale of destruction would be indiscriminate. But I will show you what you want."

I turned and walked toward our ranks, "Mages to the front! Five supports, link up! The rest send it straight into the sky when I say Pull!"

Then I looked toward the operators. "Send all the rest of them except one."

The commander's eyes widened, "That's forty three tanks Sir."

I nodded and turned back to the field. I felt hands land on my back and shoulders as I looked out to see tanks start tearing across the plain.

"Pull!"

It felt like the world was being Pulled inside out. I reached up with my mind and raised my hands, more for the theatrics than need. As my mind touched that power, the Source began to surge from my Supports into me. My body sucked it up. My stream pulsed as well. My stream may have been enough, but there were a lot of Mages here so why try something that may be dangerous.

I began steering that huge maelstrom of power into a spinning vortex, and as I dropped my hands, huge gouts of Soulfire began to slam into the tanks. In moments there was nothing but the wreckage of forty three tanks. The metal glowed with the heat that had been applied.

"Cease!" I ordered and let the rest of the Soulfire in the sky dissipate.

I turned back to see awe in the auras of most of the observers. The Senator in the rear showed terror rolling through his. I was definitely going to have to do something about this man, and soon. If he was working for the Kresh, I would end him.

"G-Good God man," I heard a voice stammer.

There was one more thing I wanted to show them. I wanted to show them the imbued barrel of one of their tanks.

"So, do you have any solid rounds for the main gun on the last tank? I have something I think we should get together on..."

Chapter 11

I approached the walled property from the north in the dead of night. I would say the wall surrounded close to five acres right in the center of Chicago. This was one of three such properties the man I stalked owned, and I was certain this would be the one he was located at currently.

I leaped over the wall easily, and stopped there leaning up against it. I opened my inner eye, and looked at the power flows of the world around me. There were several Souls I could see patrolling the inside of the wall. None were near me, so I moved forward silently.

I could also see several dogs that had been wandering inside the fence. They, wisely, had all relocated as far from me as they could get, and huddled together in the darkness. I really didn't want to hurt them, or the guards around the house.

After a few moments, I found a window that was open. It was on the third floor, so it was assumed it would be safe from intruders. I think not. I jumped up easily, and landed on the balcony outside the window. I slipped inside, and proceeded to search for the room I needed.

Inside the room, a man lay asleep in a large, canopied bed. I sat down in a very comfortable looking chair, and looked at the ugly Soul that slept there. It would be the simplest thing to snatch the life right out of him along with his Soul.

But I needed information badly. I needed to know who he served, and why he was here, and if my suspicions were true about human traitors working, and living among us. Perhaps he was a fluke like I was, or maybe something much more sinister. The only way I would know was to question him, and I had to be prepared to do whatever would be necessary if I took that road.

My decision would have to be a quick one though, because Senator Calvin Heltor opened his eyes, and looked straight into mine.

"One sound, Senator," I said softly, "and it will be your last."

Fear rolled through his aura, "Are you here to kill me?"

"To be honest, I haven't decided," I said. "The answers I have to the next few questions will decide your fate."

"I've heard of your oath not to harm humans.."

I was suddenly standing directly beside him, looking down at the man, "We both know you aren't exactly human though, don't we?"

He was silent, and I could see his fear and several memories flowing through his aura. I saw him actually speaking to the Kresh, and my first question didn't even have to be asked.

It would have been to ask if he was some sort of fluke like me, or was he some sort of spy for them?

"How much do you know about your masters?" I asked. "Is there enough to convince me not to rip your heart out right here?"

"I-I will tell you everything I know," he stammered.

"How did they recruit you, and why were you willing to betray the whole human race?"

"They took thousands of us and injected their DNA into us," he answered, "There were very few survivors. Some refused to serve them, and were killed and eaten. A few of us accepted their offer. We live as long as we serve them."

I stared at him for a few moments, "Where were you taken from for these experiments?"

"They rounded us up on the Homeworld, Kresh," he said, "most of us, anyway. Some they dragged back through the Portals to the other Colonies."

"Colonies?"

"Fifteen worlds where they harvest humans to be slaves and food for their larders."

"Enough," I interrupted. "There are two ways you can survive this night, Senator."

I actually saw a bit of hope flow across his aura. He was sure that I would kill him, and there was no doubt that I really wanted to.

"One, you flee back to your masters, and trust that they won't have you destroyed for failure. I don't think they reward failure, but that's just my thought. Perhaps you know them well enough to make your own judgment."

I saw the terror run through him at the thought.

"I thought as much. They would kill you and eat you, I would think. Am I right?"

He nodded.

"Option two. Tomorrow, you turn in your resignation and leave. You report to the Academy in Montana, and turn yourself in to the Soulguard. There you will confess everything, but you will live. You will give us everything you know about them and their plans. Everything you know."

I leaned closer to him. "And if you ever Push another human being with your mind, you'll wish that you'd gone back to your masters."

I reached out with mental talons, and raked them through his Soul. His body seized and shook, losing his control over his bowels, and every other part of his body.

"I am a Soullord. I can rip your Soul to shreds with a thought. And you know as well as I do what the monsters inside of us feed on. It would be so easy for you to become a feast for mine."

"I-I see," he said after the spasms ended, "why they want you dead so badly. You're one of us gone rogue."

I laughed then said, "They don't even have a clue about that. They want me dead because I'm a Soullord. I'm strong enough to fight them, and they can't have that. They don't have a clue what they created when they tried to slaughter my mother before she could give birth to me. They created their end when they failed."

My rage was almost pouring from me as I spoke, and the Senator cringed away from me. "My resignation will be tendered in the morning."

"Good choice," I said. "If I have to come back for you, you will surely regret it."

I stood straight and turned away. I walked calmly out of his bedroom, and back to the window I had entered. There were no alarms, and I made my way back outside the property.

I sat down on a park bench some distance away from the Senator's home, and held my head in my hands. I was feeling a bit nauseous. Not because I had tortured the Senator, but because when I did it I enjoyed it. Something inside me actually enjoyed it, and it sickened me.

But no matter what the monster wants, I have to fight to be the man I was raised to be. It was just so hard sometimes.

I stood back up, and headed east toward the airport where the jet awaited me. I was on a trip to meet a couple of Generals in Washington when I had received the call from the man known as the Whisper in the Night. He'd located the Senator for me and I'd been sorely tempted to let him take care of it. But it was my job, I felt, to deal with people with the Demon blood. And I'd needed to know if he was truly working with the Kresh.

Several of the things he had said led me to the conclusion that we needed this man alive. We needed to know what he knows, and if we had to deal with the Devil to learn it, it would be my responsibility to do so.

Fifteen total colonies? There were fourteen more planets of humans being slaughtered and eaten by those bastards. I know my responsibility is to my world, but does it end there? I don't think it does, and I think there is a much longer war in our future than we had ever thought. And do I have any right to ask my Guard to do what I feel might need to be done?

I don't know the answer to that one. But first, we must win a war on our own planet. That will be hard enough without thinking of a war of liberation afterward.

***

"General Gasper," I greeted the man who met me at the door, "it's good to see you again."

He looked at me a moment, searching for the mockery he half expected. He didn't find any, to his surprise. I truly meant what I said to the man.

"I must say, Mr. Rourke," he said with a nod and a budding respect rolling through his aura, "I believe I do owe you an apology for my previous attitude."

"No apology necessary, Sir," I shook his hand, "we only know what has been shown us. And it really seems ridiculous that men with swords can do so much. We've found that weapons that are connected to us can gain a lot of the same benefit as the body after the Soulguard training. Until recently, we haven't had much success with guns."

"Your demonstration with the last tank would say you've had some breakthroughs in this area?"

"Yes, Sir we have," I said as we seated ourselves across the desk from each other. "Back when guns were fairly new, it just wasn't feasible to put a Mage to imbue the single weapon with his essence. But guns are so much better now. I've got a few ideas I'd like to cover at a later date if you don't mind."

"Certainly, Mr. Rourke."

"Colin, Sir," I said. "No need for formality."

He was a bit hesitant. The military is steeped in formality. It's part of the whole discipline of military service.

"Not asking to be on an informal basis with you General. I do understand a little bit of the situation here. My former Guard Captain is an Ex-Marine Master Sergeant. I do understand military discipline. I just don't have a clue what title to address the Warmaster of the Soulguard," I laughed and continued, "So just call me Colin if you don't mind."

He chuckled, "Colin it is then."

He stood up, "Now that I've gotten my apologies out of the way, what say we head to the meeting room, and meet some of the folks you'll be working with when the approval goes through. And after what I saw in Kansas, I'm relatively certain there will be some sort of agreement."

Chapter 12

"You want us to turn over an AC-130 to you and your people?" Colonel Travis Wayston asked.

I could see the almost outrage rolling through his aura.

"No, Sir," I answered, "What I want is several AC-130's placed at the airport in Wichita where we can work with your men to use them in a battle to defend our world."

He sputtered, "We just don't let anybody have access to..."

"Read your orders, Colonel," I said with rage nearing the surface, "Read them now. I'll wait."

He took a step back. I think I was probably doing that whole Crazy Eye thing Prada had been talking about at the Hooters. But there were so many of the officers we had to deal with that hadn't been at the demonstration, and they keep seeing an eighteen year old talking about using multi-million dollar pieces of military hardware for experimentation.

"If I'm not mistaken," I said after a moment, "they say you are to give us any military hardware we request. I stress, any hardware. This includes aircraft, assault vehicles, cargo vehicles, and cargo aircraft. I can even get a staff vehicle if I want to request it. All I need at this moment is three AC-130's at Wichita to use in our defense. Count on the fact that there will be much more needed before this is done. Get used to it, because I've waited as long as I'm willing to for government support."

"It's been approved by the President, himself." I stepped closer to him-- "I will not wait any longer to get started down there. The Kresh could return at any moment, and we *will* be prepared for them when they come back."

The things that Calvin Heltor had revealed so far to the interrogators at the Academy had sent chills up my spine. They would come back. Not an *if*, but a *when*. We hadn't even scratched the surface of their numbers. The figures I'd come up with from the interrogation of the Wraith were not even close to the true numbers of Kresh. And I know that Heltor spoke true, or at least what he thought was the truth. I'd watched several of the interrogations just to test him for truth, and for his skill at Pushing people.

I was never where he knew I was there. And terror would spike through his aura every time my name was mentioned. The Kresh even had a name for me. Rash'Tor'Ri. In their language it meant ender of all life, or life-ender. I liked it.

"I will be relocating my forces to Kansas over the next few weeks, Colonel," I said with finality. "I expect to see my planes there when we arrive. Soon after, I expect to see cargo craft there to take us, and our forces where we are needed if they choose to show up somewhere else. These are things that have already been discussed, and approved at the highest levels."

I turned around, and walked away from Colonel Wayston before he could say something else that would spark my rage even more. It seemed that I had to fight the rage almost constantly. The only time I seemed to be able to escape it was when I could get away from everyone and just sit alone for a time.

It wasn't easy to get the time to do so, but it was necessary for me to function. So I would take the time. As soon as I got back to Montana, I would hit the Guard trail and run through the mountain tops. That always seemed to calm me. Sometimes, Lyrica would join me and she was one of the few people who I could be around at those times. She never seemed to awaken the rage in me.

***

I love to run in the woods above the Academy. There are rock bluffs and sheer drops all across the mountain range in Montana. The air was cool and I spent nearly as much time airborne, leaping from one outcrop to another, as I did on the ground.

I had run for nearly two hours and sweat was pouring from me. Two hours at extremely high speed. I stopped in a quiet spot and sat down, leaning against the trunk of a large oak.

I opened my Inner eye to see the power flows of the world as I relaxed and something immediately caught my eye. There was a large tree a little ways from me. And it was absolutely teeming with life. Squirrels, to be accurate. There had to be thirty or so of the critters leaping amongst the branches.

I'd never seen so many squirrels at one time in a single tree. Of course, the hawk that circled above probably thought the same thing. It was probably thinking, like I was, about lunch. Although I wasn't thinking about eating squirrels, and the hawk most definitely was.

It dove toward the tree, and as it passed the peak of the tree, I saw a brown blur slam into it from the tree. Feathers exploded in all directions, and the hawk plummeted toward the ground. As it slammed into the ground, I watched in astonishment as the largest squirrel I have ever seen leapt back toward the tree and turned to face the hawk. The hawk launched himself back into the air and fled.

I began laughing harder than I had laughed in a long time. Not because of the hawk's circumstance, but because the squirrel that was gripping the side of the tree trunk, glaring at me, had a Soulguard knot.

"Lyrica Jayne," I muttered as my laughter had run its course.

I stood and nodded toward the squirrel, "Go protect your people Squirrel King. I'll go protect mine."

I turned away from the Squirrel King and started running back the way I had come. I had to stop several times along the way to let a bout of laughter run its course.

I guess, when you have a Soullord raised from age six to fourteen running through the hills of Montana, there's no telling what you'll find lurking in the forests.

I'm sure that a good laugh was something I would need since my next act was to face a reporter who had come to the Academy to interview several of us. Paige had done her interview and Jacobs had done an interview as well. But they wanted me there, too, and I would rather face a ravenous horde of Demons than talk to the damn Press. But I also know that we need the publicity to draw more volunteers to the Soulguard.

Mine might be a little easier, as well, because I planned to do it with some of the Guards training behind us, where people could see some of the amazing things a Soulguard can actually do. Perhaps that would keep some of the attention from yours truly.

Chapter 13

"Is it true Mr. Rourke," Jennifer Alstead asked, "That anyone can become one of these Soulguards?"

"I wouldn't say, anyone," I answered. "There's a vetting process, of course, and a person has to be able to pass the tests for certain attributes that are a necessity in becoming a Soulguard."

"And what might these attributes be?"

"First and foremost," I said, "is the ability to focus. It is the paramount skill needed to do the things necessary to become a Guard."

"What things?"

"You know I won't answer that, Ms. Alstead," I answered. "I understand everyone else evaded this subject in their interviews. So let me be blunt. There is an oath involved in the joining of the Soulguard. It is an oath that defines us as Guards and as people. We use these skills we have gained to protect Humanity from the Kresh. Up until recently, we only knew them as Demons, a name given to them centuries ago when we became aware of their existence."

I looked straight into her eyes, "If a person is not willing to swear this oath, they will not learn what it takes to become a Soulguard. We do not use our skills against other Humans. We fight the Kresh. We will not be used against other countries, we are a worldwide organization. Therefore I would appreciate if you quit asking my people about it. They won't answer so don't bother."

She was taken aback for just a moment at the severity of my statement, but she wasn't silent for long. "Ok, then, we'll change the subject a little bit. Is it true that some of the people around us are actually over one hundred years old?"

I knew it was coming. They couldn't go without asking that question, and Paige had been very good at evading questions earlier. I'm not so good at it.

"Yes, that is certainly true. One of the men who fell at the Battle of Kansas was actually two hundred and forty years old. It takes a great dedication to become a Soulguard and fight our enemy. The service is long but there are benefits as well. As you can see, we don't age nearly as fast. The downside of it is that we spend many more years fighting the Kresh than a normal hitch in a military branch would have."

I hid a smile as the camera began to stray. I knew what the man was watching behind us, and Soulguards training would definitely draw the eye of someone unfamiliar to it.

"Interview is over here, Keith," Alstead said and chuckled.

"Sorry Boss," the cameraman returned, "but you gotta see this."

She turned around as Kharl threw Trent half way across the Dome to hit the "Mat".

Trent got back up, quickly and looked around to see if anyone had been watching. As it turned out, Keith, the cameraman had caught it all on tape.

"Aw man," Trent whined, "did you tape that?"

"Keep yer mind in the fight boy, or you can ask him," Kharl said as he pointed at me, "where you end up."

"I wouldn't try anything stupid, Trent," I said. "It always results with your face in a wall."

Alstead was watching the two as they began their match again. She didn't even say a word for several minutes.

Kharl tends to wipe the floor with whoever he spars with, and this was a demonstration for the new recruits who stood off to the side. And with the new stream, he was faster than lightning. There was no beating him in unarmed combat now.

She turned back to the camera, "That is truly amazing. But let's finish the interview, and then we'll watch the training."

Keith looked sheepish and brought the camera back to us.

"I think we were on the subject of age," she said, "How long does a Soulguard live, Mr. Rourke? Will you die of old age?"

"Probably not, Ms. Alstead," I answered. "We're fighting a war, and I expect I'll die in battle."

"But what if you were to stop fighting right now, and go become some sort of monk or something? Would you live forever?"

"In all honesty, I really don't know."

The camera started to stray again, and Jennifer coughed to get his attention. "Well, it seems that my cameraman can't retain his focus very well, so I'm going to go out on a limb and say he's probably not Soulguard material."

I laughed as he jerked back to focus on us.

"I have a sneaky suspicion that someone doesn't like interviews, and may have just set it up to have his where there would be a great deal of distraction."

"I have no idea what you're talking about," I said and smiled.

She shook her head and laughed. "Ok Keith, watch the match. I think we're done with our victim now."

As Keith turned the camera back to watch the Guards practice, Kyra was entering the ring with several new trainees to work on their sword skills. She saw the camera, and looked my way with narrowed eyes.

I sighed as she pointed to me, and crooked her finger for me to come over to her.

"That," she pointed at the camera, "seems to be your fault, so now you have to be the one who works out in front of it. And since I'm not as fast as you anymore, I think you should practice with someone who is."

She pointed behind me to someone, and crooked her finger just as she had done with me. Somehow I knew who was there. I smiled as Lyrica walked past me.

Kyra's right, Lyrica is as fast as I am. In fact, she's much faster. Her stream is twenty two inches in diameter, and she can channel power just as I can. The only thing in my favor is the fact that I have more experience.

I love to spar with her. We both open our Inner Eye, and it seems like we can read each other's actions before we even make them. It's one of my favorite activities, and I know she feels much the same about it.

"I'll go easy on you old man," she said and laughed as she was handed her practice swords. It was a musical laugh, and another reason I loved to be around her. There had been a lack of those laughs for some time after the fight with the Council, but it seemed that they were back.

"He's over there," I said motioning to where Kharl was standing, "I'm just a pup."

A young Guard trainee approached me with something akin to awe rolling through his aura to hand me a set of practice swords. I really wish they wouldn't do that. It makes me a bit uncomfortable.

Lyrica gave me a knowing smile as she saw the same thing in the man's aura as I did. I could see a bit of the pity she felt for me over it.

As the Trainee left the ring, Lyrica settled into the first stance of the Dance of Blades. With a slight salute with her right hand weapon she said, "Defend yourself!"

I settled into the beginning stance and laughed.

She lunged forward, incredibly fast. But I wasn't there. I had already dropped and rolled to the right while flowing into a new stance.

"Not gonna be that easy," I said and launched an attack of my own.

She parried, and we began the Dance in earnest. Our blades blurred with speed to the eyes of the people who watched. But to us they still moved at a normal pace. The world just seemed to have slowed down around us.

That's the key to all of our skills as Soulguards. We have to have the focus necessary to let our minds move as fast as our bodies. It wasn't the amount of power you could use, but how fast your brain could move that gave us our limits on speed.

Except in a case like Kevin Graves. His body couldn't move as fast as his mind, giving him the awesome control he had over his power when using it. His focus was so great that he never even slowed down his Pull after he started it. He stopped when the job was done.

I had reached closer to that focus than ever before back at the Battle of Kansas. I can't just turn it on like him. I need a trigger. But it's good to know I have limitations, to keep me from buying into this reputation that seemed to be building around me. If for no other reason than that.

I felt the crack against my ribs as I had let my mind wander. The rage surfaced just a bit, and the world slowed even more. In a split second, my left blade slipped inside her guard and connected with her side, just below the ribs.

She grunted and kept coming.

We continued for some time when I heard someone say "Halt" in an incredibly slow voice.

We both spun to a halt, halfway through the moves we were in the process of. I could see the joy in her aura, and it gave me a warm feeling. She enjoys the sparring as much as I do, and surprisingly she likes to be around me as much as I do her. The kinship of being Soullords is a part of it but the nicest part was the total lack of fear and awe that seems to be what everyone else feels while we are present.

As we started to walk from the ring I turned to her. "So I was running through the mountains, earlier, and you won't believe what I saw. There was this great big squirrel..."

The look on her face was priceless.

Chapter 14

"I can be a great help to you and your cause," Jennifer Alstead said.

We were sitting in the cafeteria for Mages in the Academy complex. There weren't many of us left here now that the move to Kansas had begun. Newton was suffering from a different kind of invasion than the last.

Soulguard forces were arriving each day from all over the globe. We couldn't pull too many from any one place, but we knew that there was a Gateway there, and had to build up a defense for when they came back.

"What exactly, do you want from me?" I asked.

"The world needs to know the Soulguard, Colin," she answered, "and that means it needs to know you."

"Why me?"

"You are already the most famous person connected to the battle in Kansas, except for Jacobs, maybe."

She turned her phone toward me where I saw the footage of the Battle of Kansas. It showed where I had gone berserk when Kyra was struck down by a Wraith. I thought I was about to lose my Mom, and I had left a path of destruction that was hard to believe.

"It's gone viral, and you wouldn't even believe how many views this file has received."

"I don't know what else I can do for you," I said. "I won't reveal what it takes to create Soulguards. All I can give you are my own personal views. I don't understand what good that'll do you."

She shook her head as she looked at me in disbelief.

"You really don't get it," she said. "I see how everyone looks at you. They treat you like the second coming of Jesus Christ. You walk on water as far as they are concerned. Your personal views mean a great deal."

"But that's not exactly what I mean," she continued, "I would love to record a documentary on you, personally. It would make my career, but what I'm talking about is to show the Soulguard in their everyday endeavors."

"You want to follow the Guard around and record it?" I asked.

"Exactly," she answered, "I want to show the world that you are human, and I want them to know you. If we do this right, the people of the world will want to *be* you."

I snorted as she said that.

"What?" she asked.

"No one with half a brain would want to be me. I don't even want to be me. If people saw me as I am, they would run away screaming. But this is what I am, for better or worse."

"This is part of what I'm talking about. You're a friggin hero. What would you want to be that could rival that?"

I looked at her for a moment, "A carpenter. Maybe build something instead of blow something up. I don't know."

She didn't have an answer for that.

"You go sell your pitch to the Archmage," I said. "If you convince her to let you follow us around, then that's what we'll do."

"And a documentary on you, personally?" she asked as she showed me the scene on the phone again. "Let the world know what makes a man do this."

"I'll have to think about that." I said, "I'll let you know."

***

"Where the hell is that girl?" I muttered as I crossed the Academy grounds. Today was the last day before we head to Kansas, and I wanted to see if she wanted to go for one last run through the mountains. But Lyrica was nowhere to be found.

I opened my inner eye and searched for her Soul. No luck, although I did see someone's Soul who may know where she was.

I headed toward the Dome where I could see Trent's Soul as he was working out inside the mountain. It never ceases to freak folks out that I can see through solid rock when it came to Souls.

I entered through the main entrance, and stopped right inside the door. I stood there for a few minutes while no one knew I was there. Most of the Guard tend to get all formal now when I'm around. I missed the ease I used to have with them. Some still acted as they did before, like Jacobs, Rictor, and the majority of the Knoxville guys that had gone to Kansas with me. But most of the others didn't have the same sense of ease that they did.

"...Soullord."

"...think that's him..."

"Thought he would be bigger..."

I almost laughed when I heard that one whispered. Most people don't realize how far I can hear them. The whispers made the rounds, and I could see the sense of tension rising in most of the Souls scattered through the Dome. Most of them were trainees, and over the last few years the Academy had been rife with rumors about me.

I made my way over to where Trent had just sheathed his swords. He, just as I do, uses his fighting weapon for his workouts unless he is sparring with other Guards. I feel it keeps one familiar with his weapons much more than a training blade.

"Hey, Boss," he said with a wide smile, "What's up?"

"I was looking for Lyrica," I returned. "She seems to have disappeared."

He shook his head sadly, "Teenagers, what can ya do?"

I chuckled and said, "I know she's not nearby. That stupid dog is laying out beside the Tree. If she was anywhere near, he'd be following her around."

"True enough," he said. "She and Mattie are in Missoula. It's kind of a secret, though."

"And they told you?"

"I am the soul of discretion. I'm like a fortress that holds all secrets in sacred trust..."

"Really?"

"Oh ok," He said, "she's been volunteering at the Hospital there for the last month. She's healing people."

I stood there with my mouth hanging open. It really hadn't even occurred to me. Just one more glaring example of the difference between the two of us. She takes her skills and goes where she can help others. I spend my time devising new ways to use my power to destroy.

"You ok, Boss?" he asked, "You're not mad at her are you?"

"Lord, no," I said, "I was just thinking how much difference there is in our approach to power. I wouldn't interfere with that for anything. As a matter of fact, I think I'll go to Paige and see if we can't help her out with her endeavor."

"I told 'em you wouldn't be upset about it."

"Not upset at all," I said. "Well, perhaps a little upset I didn't think of doing something similar. But that has nothing to do with it."

"You already have plenty on your plate, Col," he said, "No need to feel guilty because you're not her. You're doing what we need you to be doing. And honestly, I think she's doing what we need her to do too. The scope of this war that's coming is so much bigger than what the Guard is familiar with. It would be a great benefit to have a Healer out there with us."

"True enough," I said, "And it's something she would be well suited for."

Chapter 15

I stood quietly in the shadows, out of sight of the two people standing in the Dome. Kharl and Kyra stood near the center of the open space, and Kyra was slowly working through the forms of the Dance.

I felt a stab of pity as the muscles in her right side seemed to lock up.

"It's just no good," she said, "I can't do it anymore."

"Honey," Kharl said as he placed his hands on her shoulders, "It's alright."

"I'm just not much use in a fight anymore," she said holding her right side. "Something just isn't right inside there anymore."

"You have to tell him," Kharl said. "He needs to know so he doesn't send you out in the middle of a mob of Demons."

"I know," she said, "But you know him. He'll think it was his fault and blame himself for it."

"True, but he still needs to know."

"Ok," she said and hugged him, "I'll tell him."

She was partially on target. It is my fault that she hadn't healed right. I didn't have a clue what I was doing at the time. It doesn't matter how fast a person can heal, or be healed, if the parts weren't in the right place beforehand. I know that if I hadn't done what I did, she would have died. But, if I had known more, I would have understood what else needed to be done.

I hoped that Lyrica would learn more than I had about where things were supposed to be before she heals much.

I eased back out to the door, and opened it loudly. When I walked around the corner I saw them both sitting a ways from the ring. They looked up and saw me. Both were happy to see me, but I could see the chaos of the deception in their auras as well.

"Hey guys," I said cheerfully, "I was just looking for you."

"What's up, Son?"

"I've figured out where I want you guys, and I know I'll be asking a lot of both of you," I began, seeing Kyra start to interrupt, "I need the new recruits trained by the best, and that means you."

She stopped herself. I hated to play them like this. She needed a place off of the front lines, and I know she didn't want to cause me pain with the knowledge that I hadn't healed her right. This would solve both of those issues.

"I need you, Mom," I said, "to take command of the training programs, here and in Kansas, when we get set up there. There's gonna be a great deal of recruiting going on now that we're free to proceed. You know the Guard well, and know who we need to place where to get the best out of our new troops. Will you do this for me? It would be a huge relief to know someone I trust, completely, is in that position."

She looked at me for a moment with a little suspicion rolling through her aura. She's not a bit slow. She knew what they had just been talking about, and coincidence is truly a rare thing.

"Yes," she said, "I'll do this. But there's something I need to tell you first."

I stepped forward, and hugged her with extra care not to put pressure on her right side, "I know, Mom. You can't hide something like that from a Soullord. I know things could have been better. I'm learning as fast as..."

"Son, you saved my life," she said and placed her hand on my cheek, "and that's enough."

"Thanks, Mom."

We were quiet for a moment and I turned back to Kharl. He had a small smile on his face, and I saw relief roll through his aura.

"I have an idea," I said with a grin. "After the demonstration for the Senators, I thought about something that would suit your fighting style."

"Experimenting again?" he asked with one eyebrow arched.

"Oh yeah," I said. "Take a look at this."

I backed a good distance away from him, and opened a portal on my stream. Then I lit up what I was doing so they could see what it was in detail. I had formed a shield that was fed by a tendril that was almost as big as my stream. Just enough was left to carry into myself the strength needed to push the shield.

"Holy shit," Kharl muttered. "That's gonna be awesome."

"That's what I was thinking," I returned. "What do you think a group of say, twenty or so powerful Mages with this sort of shield could do to a pile of Demons? Now that we're not in the caves, it seems to make sense."

What I had created was a shield of blades. They started at a point about fifteen feet in front of me. They spread out to the sides, and above me like some sort of multi-edged arrow head. The front was an edge that went from inches above the ground to ten feet over my head. The blades ran back at an angle. This would destroy a group of closely packed Demons.

"A strong Mage pushing that would be unstoppable" he said, "A literal juggernaut."

"That was my thought," I said. "I want you to get that group of Mages together and work on it. If you guys come up with a better design than the one I have, by all means, we'll use it. This one is just a prototype, of sorts."

He rubbed his huge hands together, "This is gonna be great."

"He's got a new toy," she looked at me in disgust. "I'll not see him for a damn week now."

"That's a bad thing?"

She chuckled and answered, "Now that you mention it..."

***

"Isn't your plane about to leave?" Paige asked as I walked into her office, "It will set a terrible example if the Warmaster is late for the war."

I laughed and said, "They won't start without me will they?"

"Never can tell with those crazy Guards," she answered. "What can I do for you, Colin?"

"It's something involving Lyrica," I said. "She seems determined to be a healer. She's spent a lot of time in Missoula at the hospital, and I want to do something to help her out. There's a doctor we've used several times named Pickney. I want to put him on the payroll permanently, and have him work with her. I want her to know how to put people back together, and he can help her a great deal."

"I think that's a wonderful idea," she said. "I'll send for him immediately. But I need to know where to send him. Here or Kansas. Where will our little healer be?"

"Here until the defenses are in place, just like the trainees and trainers. Once we get set up they can all be brought down there. By then, we'll need the space if things go right. I'm really hoping the recruit levels keep growing. We need as many Soulguards as we can get."

"This is true," she said. "The story Alstead did was a great boost. I was surprised that she did what she said she would do and didn't try to hurt us."

"I looked into her Soul, Paige," I said. "She has a good deal of integrity, something sorely lacking in the majority of journalists these days."

"So what do you think about her request to work with us on a semi-permanent basis?" she asked.

"I think she can help us a great deal," I answered. "If she keeps the integrity she has shown so far."

"Good, I was about to approve the request, and I wanted to hear your views on it first," she said. "Have you thought about the story she wants to do on you?"

"I'm not sure that it will do anyone any good," I said. "If I see a benefit for the Guard in that, then I'll let her. But I'm not sure it would be in our best interests for the world to see me too closely. You know what lurks inside of me."

She looked at me for a moment, "There's more than that inside of you, Colin. If that was all there was, you wouldn't be where you are at this moment."

"Maybe so, but if they get too close, they may see much more than they want to."

"It is your choice," she said. "I, for one, think there is much more good that would be seen than the darkness. But that's just my opinion. On another subject, what do you want done with the ex-Senator?"

"I need him sent to Kansas," I said, "Where I can keep an eye on him. But I need a few weeks to get some facilities built, first. If you see anyone acting funny around him, you call me. And you stay the hell away from that bastard. You know what chaos Worthington caused with much the same type of skills as this man."

"The same type of thing you can do, as well. Be very careful with that particular set of skills, Colin. It would be so easy to use it badly."

"Very true, I spend a great deal of time worrying about what I'm fated to become. So far, everyone who we've found with the Blood is evil as hell."

"If what Heltor has said is true, they had evil beginnings," she said. "You started with the opposite. You'll never become like them. It is an impossibility."

"I hope I can live up to that," I said as I stood to exit the room. She was right, I did have a plane waiting for me, and I needed to go.

"Georgia has Pickney's contact information. I'll see you in a few weeks, when you get down there."

"Bye Colin," she returned. "If you need me to push any buttons with the Government, just give me a call. I'm having dinner with the President on Wednesday. And I think the English Prime Minister is going to be there for an introduction, as well as the Russian head of state. I'm not positive yet what he is called. Premier or President, I'm not really sure. I guess I should look that up before I stick my foot in my mouth."

"Probably a good idea," I said. "Let me know what it is when you find out, I don't have a clue either."

"Hard to believe we are the ones in control of this whole thing, and completely politically ignorant, the both of us."

"You're the one who gets to deal with the politics," I said with a laugh. "I just blow stuff up."

She was actually giggling as I left her office for the   waiting   plane.

Chapter 16

I could see something was up as the plane touched down. There were way too many Souls outside of the plane. It seemed that I had a reception committee waiting with well over a thousand people out there. Many were Mages, and a good many Guards too, mixed with the souls of quite a few normals also. Their Souls looked so dim beside the others that it was easy to pick them out of the crowd.

I steeled myself as the plane taxied in toward the crowd, because I hate all of this, pomp and circumstance, you might say. I would rather just get down there and start building shields.

"Just doesn't work that way, now, does it," I muttered.

"What's that, Sir?" one of the newest recruits asked. There were five of them that had just graduated to Rookies. They had been sitting quietly throughout the whole flight.

I had seen the tension in all of them at being in the same plane as a Soullord, and I was quite frustrated. But it wouldn't do to let them know that.

"It seems that they have prepared a reception for us outside the plane, so put your best face on and let's go see the show."

I stood and strode to the door.

"How does he know that?"

"Shutters down on the windows..."

"...didn't get call..."

I heard the whispers behind me. I straightened my Soulguard uniform, and stepped out the door of the plane.

They had formed a sort of corridor of Guards from the plane to the terminal, all of which stood at attention as I stepped down the stairs. I made my way toward the terminal, and nodded at a few of the Guards I recognized. I realized that I was familiar with a great deal more of them than I had thought.

There had been several Guards cycle through Knoxville while I was there. I hadn't realized exactly how many until this moment. I couldn't put names to all of the faces, but I could name quite a few.

There were a lot of flashes as the Press started with the pictures. Over the years, I had watched what the press reported, and I had very little use for them. There were exceptions to that observation however, as Alstead had kept her word, and made it a point not to trash us. There was so much a reporter could have turned against us with the detailed report she had done, the least of which was the knowledge of the Demons being kept secret for a thousand years.

At some point there would be the accusations from that choice. I still think we should have come forward long ago, but it may have precipitated what was happening right now much earlier. It's a touchy subject, and I'd rather stay away from the topic, if possible.

We made our way through the corridor of Guards to enter the terminal. Inside waited another group of people. These weren't quite so dreaded as the reporters would be. Several men in uniform waited surrounded by a group of military guards. There were three Guards and three Mages waiting as well.

Lennox Flynn, Gregor Kherkov, and Daphne Cavanaugh were the three Mages. Each had a Guard standing beside them. I recognized two of the Guards from the battle of Kansas. They had been two of the Denver guys that worked with the Kid. The other was unknown to me but his stream was large enough to classify him as Elite.

Gregor stepped forward and greeted me, "Welcome back to Kansas, Colin."

"Perhaps we can have a better outcome than the first time," I said and shook his hand. "Lord knows we need one."

"With preparation," he said, "I think we can do a great deal better."

I could see the memory of Nora Kestril exploding in a massive fireball when she Magebombed during the battle.

I'd heard the term a few days after the Last Rites, and it is as accurate as any other way to describe it. She'd Pulled everything she could as hard as she could until the explosion destroyed all of the Demons around her. And Nora was a very powerful Mage, indeed.

Gregor turned to the Guard beside him, but before he could introduce him, I nodded to the man and said, "Adam, good to see you made it through that last mess."

"Yes Sir," I could see that the man was impressed because I remembered his name. I'd only met him once, and it was in the middle of one hell of a battle.

I remembered him from the fight because, I'd spent hour after hour memorizing as many of the names as I could. I want to know my men. I don't want them to be numbers that I spend like currency. There are a lot of them, and I want them all to survive what's coming.

I know this is an impossibility, but I have to try my best to keep them all alive. We are about to be in a war, and I know I will lose men. I've already lost many, but I feel it's my duty to know who they all are. And I will try my best to make each life cost the Kresh so much that they will, eventually see that Earth would be better off left alone.

I turned toward Daphne and the Guard with her, "Through with training, Daph?"

"Just got in, was over in Scotland and hopped a flight with Flynn."

"Good to see you," I nodded to the Guard with her, "Rex, how are you doing?"

"Fine Sir," he said with much the same reaction as Adam had.

"Len," I said as I turned to Flynn, "How are things coming on our group?"

"We've got ten Mages on their way with ten Guards apiece," he said. "This should make a pretty decent crew fer you. We can test with it, ta see if we need more. I included yer two shadows in this group, and I leave it ta them ta form their Guard squads."

I nodded, "Good man, and who might this fellow be? I don't think I've ever met him."

"Colin Rourke, meet Colin MacGregor."

"Colin," I said in greeting.

"Colin," He returned in a Scottish accent.

"Nice to meet you," I said, "But I'll get better acquainted with you in a bit. Gotta go meet with the Officers over there."

I approached the group of officers and saw General Gasper standing in the front of the group.

I nodded to him, "General."

"Welcome to Hillsboro, Mr. Rourke," he said with a smile.

He turned to his left toward, if I was reading the rank insignias right, a one star general, "This is General Seran Polomo of the Army National Guard."

"General," I said and shook his hand.

Gasper turned to the right, "And this is General Marcus Stratton of the Air National Guard."

I shook his hand as well.

"You've thrown the whole Military situation in a turmoil with this Demon invasion of yours," Gasper said. "They are squabbling about who takes charge of the situation back in Washington. So while they try to figure out what they should do, the National Guard has stepped up and taken charge of the situation. Their Mandate is to protect our country from within, in short, while our Military branches work outside the country. It's not a rule so much as a long standing tradition."

"I see," I said.

"These men are ready to support you in any way they can. National Guard forces are being called up all over the country. I understand you requested several planes before you came down, and they will be here tomorrow."

"Great," I said with a bit of excitement running through me. I really wanted to see how the Soul rounds worked with the big guns. "If you guys can give me a few hours to get settled, I'd love to meet with you to discuss an overall strategy. I really need some experienced advice on this. I know our enemy but the Guard has spent the last thousand years fighting the bastards down in caves more than any other way. And it looks like that has changed, completely. I would love to talk about some surface strategies that we can use to mesh our forces."

Polomo spoke first, "I think we can help with that. Both Stratton and I are vets. We may have some useful advice. And I've been briefed about the age thing with your Soulguard, but can you tell me how old you are, just for my sanity's sake. I swear you look younger than my sixteen year old son."

I laughed aloud and said, "Thirty one, next month. I'm not one of these insanely old codgers masquerading as a youngster."

As I said that I pointed toward the group of Mages, "Like Gregor, over there. I've heard rumors he's close to two hundred years old. Can't seem to get him to confess to it, though."

"Two hundred years," Polomo muttered in amazement, "Jesus Christ."

"He looks like he may be thirty," Stratton said. "He's really two hundred?"

"According to the rumors," I answered.

He shook his head in silence for a moment and then continued, "I guess we have some things to learn from you as much as things we may be able to help you accomplish. Shall we set up a meeting at, say, fourteen hundred hours."

"No problem," I said, "That actually gives me five hours to get situated, and find out where I stand with my forces. We've got Guards coming in from all over, and I need the time to see what numbers we can bring to the table at the moment. One thing I know, the Kresh will come. I just hope we get enough time to prepare some very nasty surprises for the bastards."

"I sincerely hope we can," said Polomo.

Chapter 17

"So far," I said to the Generals, "we have one hundred and thirteen Mages, and two thousand Guards moved down here. We can't just pull everyone here, because the Demons can open the smaller portals anywhere. We are afraid to pull everything to Kansas, and leave the rest of the country unprotected from smaller incursions."

"Sensible," Polomo said with a nod.

"What I don't know about is what to expect with their incursions," I continued. "Up till now, they came in secrecy. They hid in caverns, and made sneak attacks. I have a feeling this won't be the case anymore. They could open a portal in downtown Atlanta."

"This is going to get very ugly," Polomo said. "We don't have enough forces to protect every square inch of the country, and there are going to be a lot of civilian casualties."

"Yes," I said sadly, "They want to kill us all, now. The only thing that I can say for a certainty is they will come. They will come here at some point. I hope we can have enough defenses in place when they do."

"After such a defeat as they already had here, why do you think they will come back here?" asked Stratton.

"I'm not sure if you saw footage of the portal," I said, "but it was large enough to let hundreds of them cross at a time. They are fast and they came through at a run. Our best estimates were nearly a thousand per minute poured through that thing."

"I see," he said.

"I've seen the regular portals, and they can come across two abreast. If they're sending an army it would take forever with the small portals," I said. "Of course, I don't know how many portals can be open at one time in any given place. All I can give you is my best guess as to what they will do. We will just have to hope for the best and prepare for the worst."

"What can you tell us from the last battle that can help us prepare for what to expect?" Polomo asked.

"The Kresh have some sort of telepathic link," I said. "They have different levels of control with it. The strongest we faced controlled the majority of the underlings. This makes them very dangerous. Communication is not as hard for them as it was for us. But with this telepathic link, there is a weakness."

"Do tell," Stratton said, "because you're scaring the shit out of me here."

I chuckled and said, "When we killed their Demon Mage, their Kresh'Ma'Nar, they all turned and tried to come at us. All of them. If they had scattered, we would have failed to stop them. It would have taken years to hunt them all down, and people would have died in droves."

"But your closing of the gate is what killed them," Stratton said, "wasn't it?"

"Yes, but if they had scattered, and opened multiple small portals all over the place it wouldn't have worked. This may have been part of their plan, before. You can damn sure bet it will be part of it next time. They're ugly, not stupid."

Both generals chuckled.

"What we have to do is hold them together until I can kill their boss," I said, "which may be a hell of a job in itself. I've seen two of these things, and the second was much stronger than the first. They also have many more powerful Mages than these two were."

"If you've only seen two of these, how do you know this?"

I studied the Souls in front of me for a moment and made a decision, "It's not common knowledge with either the Soulguard or the American government, but we captured someone who is from the Kresh homeworld. He was a spy sent to cause trouble in any way he could, but he failed and has traded a great deal of information for his life."

"You know this could cause a great deal of strife between your people and ours if it gets out, yet you reveal it to the two of us. Why?"

"I am a Soullord, gentlemen," I said, "and what that means is I can see into your Soul. I can see the true mettle of any man at a look. And the both of you have integrity, honor, and loyalty laced throughout your Auras. I trust that you will do what is best with the information I give you. We need this man's insight on the Kresh, and we need the information he has given us. As for the truth of what he tells us, I am also a damn good lie detector since I can see the truth in a person's Soul. There are several people, high up in the government who know about this man, and I feel that it's necessary for you to know as well."

I could see the worry in both of them, "I'll probably get in a bit of trouble for revealing it, but I guess it's easier to apologize than ask permission."

"This will definitely bear some thought," Polomo said. "For the moment, let's get back to the battle. What else can you tell us?"

I nodded towards him, "I think the Kresh, or lesser Demons, can probably be taken down with bullets. But you'll need some heavier caliber weapons than the standard M-16, I think. This is something I'm not really sure about. We haven't had much success with gun use until very recently."

"I could see the problem with that fire thing you do," Polomo said, "because fire and gunpowder are a bad combination. How did you get past that problem? I assume that the 'until recently' means you found a solution."

"Part of what a Soulguard is taught," I began, "is to push a bit of their Soul out into the weapon in their hand. This is what makes it look so easy to cut them in the footage you have seen. An imbued sword can cut through steel with enough force applied. And a Guard can apply plenty of force."

"As the demonstration you held showed," Stratton said. "They showed it to all of us when we were sent here. It's shown to each and every one of the Guardsmen who come here."

I continued, "The problem we've always had is that the Guard has to push it out through his hand into the weapon. This would always ignite the powder in the bullets. So guns haven't been part of our training for hundreds of years. Now, though, guns are much more advanced and if we use a Mage, instead of a Guard there is much more that can be done. The problem has always been the small numbers of Mages. But I think we can spare some Mages to imbue some very big guns, such as the ones in the Aircraft we were talking about earlier."

I saw the smile slowly creep across Stratton's features as he thought about what I was saying, "AC-130's, I can see how those can help with taking out a force contained in a closed area."

"I'm thinking it will definitely tenderize them a bit, wouldn't you?" I asked.

"You'll have anything you need to test this and get it rolling," Stratton said. "What else can we bring to the party?"

"I've got some ideas on some ground pieces, but they'll have to wait a bit. I'm thinking we need the air power more at this stage. The thing I need the most from ground troops will be pulling out any civilians and wounded. We can use a lot support in that area. And I could use someone who knows tactics, old style tactics. Infantry, Heavy Cavalry, things like that. We've got a group of Mages working on something like the Heavy Cavalry was used for back in the old days. Soulguard hasn't seen much of the open battlefield in nearly a thousand years."

Both generals were nodding and jotting down notes.

"There are some facilities I would like to put together up by the Gateway. Perhaps you guys would know who I need to meet to get these started as well?"

"What sort of facilities?" Polomo asked.

"I want Guards there when they come through, I'm thinking of underground facilities that I will place a shield around. Something large enough for a good sized force to stay in for a relatively long span of time."

"That can be done, but what are you talking about with shielding?" Polomo asked. "Do you mean like the two spots out near the Gate? You created those?"

"Yeah, we needed somewhere to stage our fight from so I built a shield."

"It's amazing what you people can do," Stratton said. "And they say anyone can become a Soulguard?"

"With the right mental skills, yes. Not everyone can become a Mage, though."

"I foresee a lot of guys coming in from the various Military branches to volunteer for the Soulguard," said Polomo. "If I was a little younger, I might try it myself."

"Age isn't an issue," I said. "If you want to join, anyone is welcome. What happens when you become a Guard can actually reverse the aging process."

"You're serious?"

"Absolutely."

Chapter18

Hillsboro was a small town north of Newton. One of the main features of the small town was the college campus, Tabor College. It wasn't a huge campus, but it had several buildings and a football field. It also had a few tennis courts, and a place for soccer. We had set up in the rec center on campus since the whole campus had been completely evacuated not long after the attack.

Most of Hillsboro had been relocated as a matter of fact, and we were using the abandoned town to house our forces until the facilities could be finished nearer the Gate's location, which was just north of town. The place really bore very little resemblance to the town that had been here before our invasion.

Other towns in the vicinity were evacuated as well, and the idea of evacuating Wichita was being kicked around too. I, personally, thought that was an excellent idea. We may not be able to hold them, and a huge population center like Wichita would be easy targets for the Demon hordes.

"Where are we on the evac of Wichita, Ric?" I began, and turned toward the man walking on my left.

Something slammed against my head, and I flew forward to the ground. Everything was foggy and I heard voices from a distance.

"..under that car!"

"..water tower!"

"Boss!" Rictor was hovering over me, "You hear me?"

My vision was clearing, and I felt a lot of blood running down my face.

"Still here, buddy," I muttered.

"Thank God," I heard him say. "Prada! Clear that building! I've got the tower! You gonna be ok, Boss?"

"Yeah," I said, "go get 'em."

They pushed me up against a car out of the line of fire of the snipers. Ric then sprinted toward a water tower. He launched himself hard enough to crack the asphalt he had been standing on.

Prada also took off in another direction with much the same effect. Then I felt them both Pull, and my head throbbed. That's about the time it sunk in that someone had just shot me.

I heard footsteps, and glanced up to see someone approaching me. He held a very large pistol, and his Soul was the ugly color of one of the Demon blood. My mind was jumping all over the place. I felt sadness, pain, hate, joy, and many more emotions slamming into my thoughts. He pointed the pistol at me, and I saw his finger tense on the trigger.

Then the rage erupted, and consumed all of the different emotions being projected at me. I lashed out with that rage like I had done with the Senator, and the world seemed to stop as my focus was returned. I was moving at Guard speed as I pushed off of the car hard enough to cave in the door I was leaning against. Before he could shoot, I was next to the man.

Before I could even think about it, I had plunged my fist completely through the man, and ripped his spine out of his back in an explosion of blood. I looked around to find a large group of them incoming from all around me. What escaped my throat wasn't quite human, and I was moving.

I Pulled and in moments, there was nothing left but blood and ash, mostly ash.

My vision was now clear, and I was looking around for more of the ugly Souls, but all I could see were the Souls of Guards moving toward me at high speed. The former water tower was a twisted lump of metal, and one of the college buildings was a pyre of flame. The area around me was charred black, except where the first one had met his grisly end.

"What the hell!?" Ric asked as he rounded the car to see me standing with Soulfire burning all around me.

"A couple more showed up," I said.

"Boss," he said, "that was a professional hit team. They set us up to leave you unprotected. That type of precision isn't cheap."

"They were Demon blood," I said, "It wasn't a paid hit. They were doing what their masters ordered. Looks like I need to talk to the ex-Senator again. I need to know how many of these Demon blood are out there."

"Should we have him shipped down here?" he asked.

"No," I answered, "I think I'll go up and bring him down here, personally."

"Not before you have that wound examined," Prada said, looking closer at my head, "The bleeding has mostly stopped but you need to have it checked. It was a graze, though, so it could have been much worse."

"Gonna have to start keepin' the shield up, Boss," Ric said, "They consider you public enemy number one. They'll send more, you can count on that."

"It does tell me one thing," I said.

"What's that?" he asked.

"They haven't given up," I said, "They *will* be back."

"We always knew that."

"We always believed that," I corrected, "Now we know it."

"True enough."

Chapter 19

We were met by a small group as we exited the jet in Montana. The first person who met us was Lyrica. She walked up and looked closely at the wound on the side of my head.

Her fingers touched it softly, and then she hugged me. I watched the play of emotions rolling through her aura- worry, anger, relief, frustration, and love.

As I hugged her back, I realized something that should have been obvious to someone who could read emotions in others. Lyrica had loved me since that day in Tennessee when I had driven up to that country farmhouse. But it had never even occurred to me until now, she was in love with me as well. And that is a totally different thing.

And it was something to be handled at a different time than now. Now I had to talk to that putrid bastard, the ex-Senator.

Lyrica stepped back and said, "Every time I let you out of my sight, you pull some stunt that nearly gets you killed."

"In my defense," I said, "I didn't do this one. It was done by someone else. And I intend to find out who that someone else is."

"You better," she said, "because it's time to put an end to humans killing humans. We have much bigger fish to fry."

Sometimes it's hard to remember that Lyrica is only seventeen. She was raised with the realities of our war with the Demons. There was never a time when she wasn't aware of them, since the day she became aware of the world at all. Something like that makes you much older than your years. I can attest to that, personally. I was raised the same way.

Next in line was my mom. She greeted me warmly, but there was a great deal of worry in her aura as she also looked closely at the fresh scarring.

"That was a close one, Son," she said softly.

"Very close," I said. "I had just turned my head, or it would have been dead center."

"We've got to work on some extra security measures," she said. "We aren't used to being out in the open. We've not been targets like this before."

"I'm working on that," I said. "I've got someone in mind to take up security for us."

"Good," she said.

The next one was Paige, "There's more than you knew about before you left the ground in Kansas."

"What?" I asked with a sense of dread.

"A high ranking Mage in China named Chou Lin was killed a few hours ago," she said, "Chou Lin and fourteen Guards were massacred by men with guns. Several witnesses said that Lin and his Guards fell over with spasms, and ten men stepped from cover and shot them all."

"Son of a bitch!" I said, "I could guess what happened, and I'd probably be right. They were humans like the Senator. They have Demon blood and telepathic abilities."

"Looks that way," she said, "and even worse, the ex-Senator, when asked about the situation, freaked out. We couldn't get much from him except he kept mumbling about shadows."

"He'll talk to me," I said.

"Why?"

"He's more afraid of me than them," I said simply. "I should get to it."

I looked at the other member of our welcome committee, Gregor Kherkov, "I'll give you both a full report as soon as I speak with him."

***

Heltor looked up to see me as I entered the room, and fear rolled across his aura. I hadn't come to interrogate him before now. I had hoped that the fear he learned from our first encounter was enough. I really don't like the side of me that enjoys tormenting others.

I walked over to the camera, and unplugged it. His fear spiked higher.

"I ll only ask you once," I said. "How many of you are here? You told the others there were only ten or so, and I warned you about lying to us."

"Th..There may be as many as fifteen," he stammered.

I was across the room and grasping his shirt front in less than a second, "Then explain how thirty of you attacked me yesterday in Kansas and ten more in China."

His face went completely white, "Oh no, dear God, they've sent the Shak'Tar."

I cocked my head to the side a little, and released my hold on his shirt. He eased back into his seat.

"And who are these Shak'Tar?" I asked.

He took a deep breath and began, "I've been here for forty years. Fairly soon after my group was experimented on, the Kresh decided it was too costly in their Human resources to make people of the Blood that may or may not do their bidding. So the program was ended."

I nodded for him to continue.

"A new experiment was begun. The Kresh have never been much on the use of technology, so their experiments were ugly and brutal. They would inject their blood into pregnant women. The women died but the children, sometimes would survive. A lot more would survive than the numbers in our own groups did. They began using these children to build a force of Humans loyal to them."

My outrage was apparent because he paused, and his fear was growing again.

"These children were raised to use against other Humans," he said, "You see, their telepathy doesn't work on pure Humans. But the telepathy of the Blood works on Humans and Kresh."

"It works on them?"

"Yes, but the Blood doesn't have the sort of strength that the Kresh do. Except, it seems, for you."

He could see the question on my face before I could even ask.

"I've never felt a Lash as strong as the one you hit me with, from Kresh or Human."

"Lash?" I asked, "Is that what you call that?"

"Yes, we call the forcing of emotion or thought on another, the Lash," he answered. "Worthington had a strong Lash, but for long term jobs the Lash can't be used. She was an expert of manipulation using minute amounts of the Lash added to what was already present in her victims. She was quite skilled."

"She almost took down the Soulguard," I said, "I know what to look for now though. I recognized you as soon as I saw your Soul."

"And that is something I never expected," he said. "It is truly amazing what you can do."

"And these Shak'Tar?"

"The Kresh use them on Human worlds to keep the populations in line. If someone gets hard to deal with, the Shak'Tar removes them. They are what the Kresh use to keep those of us who aren't as loyal to them in line as well."

"Then why were you so surprised to hear that they were used?"

"I was under the impression that Earth had been slated for a worldwide purge. But now they send the Shak'Tar. I don't understand what the reasoning behind this is unless the Kresh'Ma'Nar you killed was the head of the faction advocating the purge and another faction has assumed control. This is pretty new to me as well as them. I've never even heard legends of a time when the Kresh'Ma'Nar were killed."

"None of them?"

"None," he said, "Their name, roughly translated, means cherished one, and the race does cherish them. You have upset them dearly by slaying not one, but two of them."

"How many of these Shak'Tar are there?"

"Thousands," he said, "But they're scattered about fifteen worlds. It's feasible that they would have fifty to a hundred assigned to this one for their program. They would be used for assassinations of key people. You say they came for you?"

"Yes, they tried."

"Tried and failed?"

"They tried and died," I returned. "There were thirty of the bastards after we finished counting."

I could see the disbelief rolling through his aura.

"You killed thirty of the Shak'Tar?" he asked.

"No," I said, "Rictor got one and Prada got another. I only killed twenty eight."

His mouth was hanging open.

"I see why they want you dead," he said, "How did you withstand the Lashes of that many of them?"

"I Lashed back."

Chapter 20

I sat across the table from a man I had only seen three times before. Jim Duke, also known as the Whisper in the Night, sat there staring at me. His Soul as black as night. There was a coldness about the man, but in his line of work, it was to be expected.

"Will you consider working directly for us as a Security Consultant?" I asked after I had explained what was going on with the Shak'Tar and their attacks on the Soulguard.

He was silent for a moment, "You know my methods, and I will not change them to suit your Oath."

"You don't need to," I said, "When the security of my men is at stake, we have to defend ourselves. I can't be everywhere and I'm the only one on our side with this mental skill that they seem to possess."

"These men," he asked, "They aren't completely Human?"

"No," I said, "but neither am I."

"How strong are their mental powers? What kind of range do they have?"

"Unknown," I answered, "I think the mental power is limited in range but if its anything like that of a Demonmage, it's at least several hundred feet. Probably farther. When I killed the Mage in Kansas, their reactions spread from the center outward. But I can't give any exact details, I was a bit distracted."

"I can imagine," he said with the calm, even tone he had used from the beginning of our conversation, "I need to be able to pick my own teams, and you probably won't like some of them. Your Soulguard doesn't really approve of the methods of the kind of people I need to work on this."

"You might be surprised at some of the methods I would approve of," I said, "But you have free reign to build your team. Right now speed is of the essence. We lost a powerful Mage and twelve Guards this week. They almost got me as well. I don't think they can get to me now as long as I keep the personal shield up. They can't overload my brain as they did to the guys in China."

"This will be expensive," he said, "We're talking multiple nations and a lot of people to cover."

"We have deep pockets," I said, "And if you find where they are based, they won't be a problem long. They'll have a hard time when I turn the world inside out underneath them."

"I've seen some of the shit you guys have done, and I actually believe every word you just said."

I slid a card across the table, "There are two numbers there. One is a phone number where I can be reached at any time. The second is an account number with the money you will need to get started. The password is Rash'Tor'Ri."

I spelled out the password for him. I would use the name they had given me for more than scaring their children.

"Odd password," he commented.

"They call me that, the Kresh," I returned. "They say it translates as Ender of all Life, or Life-Ender. I like it and I will make them know that they named me aptly."

"I saw the numbers after Kansas," he said, "They named you aptly."

I stood and shook his hand, "Good hunting and remember, the second you find their base, call me."

"I will," he said, "Perhaps I'll get to watch as you work. I saw that you and Hughes were both watching in Knoxville. That isn't how I usually work, but I know Hughes, and you are the ones to tip me on that guy, so I let that one slide."

"I had to see it done, or I would have had to violate my oath and done it myself."

He looked at me speculatively, "I see."

I nodded once more, and exited the room we had used to hold this meeting. It was a back room of a bar in Chattanooga that Jim was a part owner of. I kept my head down so that no one would recognize me, now that I was somewhat of a celebrity.

This plan seemed to me to be the best way to handle the situation with the Shak'Tar. I don't know anything about assassinations and covert operations, so I thought I would put someone who does in the position to try to stop the attacks on our men.

I just hoped he could get set up in time to prevent any more attacks. I had no idea how frequent the Shak'Tar would make their strikes, nor could I guess accurately where those strikes might occur. I was a definite target as well as Paige and several of the Mages that headed up the other Academies.

And Lyrica, she could be a target as well. They had tried to get her as a child, just as they had tried to get me. But she was surrounded by the Mages at the Academy, and I was afraid to bring her back to Kansas yet. Since the healing had started, many people had gone to Montana to see if she could help them. She had many more people around her than I, and it would be much harder to get to her.

And they were welcome to try me again, I thought, and my rage tried to surface. I must have been snarling, because a woman who had been walking toward me turned suddenly to move away from me. Her face was pale and I could read fear in her aura.

I can't help it sometimes. I think I project my emotions toward those around me much more than I used to. Maybe the telepathic skills from my Demon blood grow the more they are used, and I had used the Lash a few times now.

I shook my head a bit to clear the rage, and walked across the street where I could see a restaurant that looked interesting. It was a burger joint named Checkers.

I found that their hamburgers are probably the best burgers I have ever eaten. I bought a whole sack full of them to take back to the plane with me.

As I turned to walk away from the window, a young man stopped a few feet from me.

"You're that guy from the TV," he said, "That Soulguard guy."

I looked around for the ugly Souls but there were none of the Shak'Tar around us.

"Yes I am," I said, "can I help you?"

"How would I go about joining the Soulguard, Sir?" he asked, "I've been to all the Military recruiters to weigh my options, but I haven't found a recruitment office for them."

"That's something we'll have to do something about," I said as I pulled a card from my shirt pocket, "Call this number and ask for an interview. I'll see to it you get one. I can't say they will accept you, there is a very comprehensive background check done on applicants. But I can say you definitely will be given the chance. Give me your name so I can tell them."

"Jackson Kenner, Sir," he said, "I'll surely make that call and thank you."

"Thank you, Mr. Kenner," I returned, "We need all of the recruits we can get. This is only going to get bigger from here out. They have us in numbers, but as long as men like you are willing to fight for our world, we'll always have the edge in quality."

Chapter 21

The darkness closed in on me as the creatures of nightmares died on my blades. I danced with death on the pitch black plain. Creature after creature fell, and I stood atop a pile of dead bodies as they still flooded toward me. I felt blow after blow as they struck me. They seemed to be infinite.

I felt weaker and weaker as the battle continued, but I would not quit. If they took me, I wouldn't be there for my family when the hordes of Demons came. I wouldn't be there for my friends who fought and died for me in Kansas. I wouldn't be there for Lyrica, my little angel.

So I fought on. My strength was fading but my rage was unfaltering. It flowed through me and kept me going.

Suddenly, I felt strength returning to me, and I could see figures to each side of me. It was my Guards. I saw Rictor and Prada, Ramirez and Jacobs. Power flowed through me as the forms fought alongside me, and the horde of creatures poured up the mountain of bodies we stood atop.

The battle continued for ages. Even with my Guards alongside, my strength began to falter once more. At one point I saw Kharl at one side of me and Kyra on the other. But the creatures wouldn't let up.

I went down on one knee after a particularly hard blow from an ogre-like creature, but it too died on my blade as I staggered back to my feet.

The darkness dispersed as a brilliant golden light poured from a form that strode past me to confront it. It was a woman of Golden armor. She shone like the sun, and the shadows fell back from her in stark terror.

One word thrummed across the plain as a huge, golden sword swung in an arc in front of her and the blackness was shattered.

"Mine," reverberated across the plains, and I heard screams behind the darkness as it retreated.

The golden Valkyrie turned toward me, and I couldn't see her face for the brilliance of the golden light.

She touched my face gently, "Rest now, you are safe."

As I slumped in exhaustion she knelt beside me, and I felt a jolt run through my entire being as she placed a kiss on my lips.

As my mind settled into unconsciousness, I heard a whisper that sounded like music, "Mine, forever."

***

I awoke with those words echoing through my mind. It was the dream/memory again. That is what scared me the most about it. Was it a dream or a memory or both? I've spent most of my life without wondering about the afterlife, but my brush with death has put me on a track where I can't help but think about it, now.

I sat up in my bed and rubbed my face, trying to get the memories to return to the unconscious so I didn't have to face them.

"Time to begin building some shields," I muttered to myself.

Today I would place the first shield around the first facility completed out near the Gate. It was a barracks of sorts so that we can keep a force near the Gate at all times. It would house five hundred Soulguard troops and would contain nearly a thousand people for short term, such as while an attack was in progress. It would give us a place to mount our attacks from a strong point of defense.

If all went well, we would have four of these facilities up and running before the Kresh came back. But we couldn't count on that, so we build them one at a time and hope for the best.

Rictor knocked at my door, I could see his Soul through the walls.

"Come in Ric," I said.

"Hey, Boss," he said in greeting, "Jacobs is here to see ya."

"Send him in," I said.

Jacobs stumped in on his one leg and the shield prosthesis we had built and tied directly to his Stream. I could see the excitement rolling across his aura.

"It works!" he was practically jumping up and down, "We took the AC130 up and it worked like a charm. It takes two Mages and they can even be Support Mages."

"Great!" I said.

"Of course, I have some bad news too," he said, "the shielding is a bit more complicated."

"Shielding?"

"Yeah, we were toying with having another Mage putting shields around the plane to protect it from Demonmages. Unfortunately the shields messed up the whole process of flying so we almost crashed the plane."

I raised my left eyebrow.

"I said almost," he said quickly, "We just have to come up with a way to shield without affecting the aerodynamics of the plane."

I thought for a minute. We were trying to come up with things that were able to be done by Mages as well as a Soullord but I had an idea that I may have to do the shielding like I had done with the stuffed bear for Lyrica back in Knoxville. I had tied it directly to the Source and interwoven the shield throughout the bear, making it nearly indestructible.

"I might have a thought on that, Ivan," I said, "You remember Bearguard?"

"Yeah," he answered, "But there's no way I can do something that intricate."

"I'm thinkin' there are some things I'll just have to do myself," I said. "I don't want those planes flying unprotected if there was something I could do to prevent it. If you guys can come up with something easier that the Mages can do, then it's fine. But I'll work on how to do it that way, in the meantime."

"Sounds good, Boss," he said.

"How's Gina?" I asked.

"She got the first loop of the knot yesterday," he said, "it's all downhill from that point."

"Excellent," I returned.

The first loop of the Soulguard knot is always the hardest to accomplish. It's the one where you are working completely on the belief that it can be done. Once you attain the focus needed to do it and you have the faith that it can be done, then you can loop your knot.

After the first one there is a great deal of difference in the physical power of the body and the faith is rewarded. There is so much difference in the belief that an act is possible, and the knowledge that it is indeed possible and already been done. The rest of the loops of the Soulguard knot were much easier. They only relied on the focus of the person doing the knot.

It had been incredibly easy for me, but I had been able to actually see the knots of Kharl and Kyra and I could see my own stream with my own eyes. I never had to deal with the belief aspect at all.

"She'll start weapon training fairly soon, then," I said.

"Yep, and I'll be glad when that's done so she can come back down here," he said, "I know it's a little mushy, but I miss her."

"I know what you mean," I said with a smile, "By the end of the year, we'll probably have the training being done here instead of Montana, anyway. So you may get to see her even sooner than you expect. We don't need to hide anymore so our training doesn't have to be all the way back in the mountains."

I watched his happiness at the thought. It seemed that the incorrigible Ivan Jacobs had fallen in love. Who would have thought it?

Chapter 22

I sat at my desk looking at the sketches I had drawn of how I would like the battlefield to be laid out. If the Kresh waited long enough, I thought we may just contain them. But I knew that if they come back here it would be with a vengeance.

There really wasn't any way to tell exactly what to expect. All we could do was the best we could and hope it was enough. What worried me more than anything else was the fact that the Wraith had said there were seven gates.

If the Kresh did what I would do, it would be to come through at one of the Gates that we know nothing about. But I was counting on their arrogance to send them here, first. I just hoped I was reading them the way they were and not just the way I want them to be. I thought they would be pretty pissed about their loss of a whole army and would want to step on us hard.

The layout I had planned involved four facilities with up to a thousand Guards and Mages stationed inside them on a temporary basis. There would be five hundred Guards on duty at any given time inside each facility. The facilities would hold up to a thousand each. But I was pretty sure that, after the four facilities were finished, that two thousand Guards on duty would be able to hold a line around the Gate until the others in Hillsboro reached them. There were other things I would like to have in place before then, as well, but I had no idea if I would get the time to build the other projects I had in mind before they came.

I had a meeting in two days with an engineer who I was going to go over the specifics of my Soullance. I wanted to make something mechanical that I could assign Mages to. Something that would work much as my shields did to channel my power. If all went well, there was the possibility that support Mages would be able to man, for lack of a better name, their own laser cannons.

Rictor would have a ball with that. He already blames Star Wars for so many of the new things I've come up with. Of course, he might have a point.

I looked up to see Ric enter my office. His face was pale, and I opened my Inner eye to see pain and grief rolling through his aura. There was a great deal of anger as well.

"What is it, Ric?" I asked with a feeling of dread.

"The Shak'Tar hit us again," he said, "Duke stopped two attacks before they could hit us but one got through. Eoss, they got Luis."

It felt like there was a knot in my chest and I could feel the Rage coming. Luis was one of the men who had been by my side throughout my career from the day I was sent to Knoxville.

Luis Ramirez was one of the Guards that had supported me while I was in a Source Coma. He was one of the best Guards I have ever served with and he was my friend.

The rage blasted across my mind as I ripped the Oak desk in front of me in half. I beat the rage back down a bit but it wouldn't stay. It kept trying to surge forward. It wanted to be let out and I think, if I hadn't walked out of my office and out of the building, I might have hurt someone.

Rictor was only steps behind me as I stepped out the door.

"I need a few minutes alone, Ric," my voice was shaky.

"What if they come after you?" he asked, "When you're alone."

"Then God help them," I returned as the rage tried to escape again.

He nodded and stepped back.

I saw the world slow as I shot forward, north, toward the Gate. As I neared the hulking ruins of Gasper's tanks, I let the rage out.

It came with a howl of fury that didn't quite sound human, and power surged from the Source as I Pulled. I blasted the wreckage in front of me and tore at it with my hands, ripping and tearing metal as power flowed through me.

I have to say, I lost myself for a little while as I became the rage. When I found myself standing directly in front of the spot where the Gate had been, the plains behind me were afire and the wreckage of the tanks was scattered in much smaller pieces across a good half mile of fiery grassland.

I stood there a long time, wishing for the Gate to open. I wanted to kill them, I wanted to destroy their world, I wanted them to come at me now. I don't know how to fight these assassins, I know how to kill Kresh.

"Come on!" I screamed at the empty air, "Bring it to me!"

But there was no answer and the Gate remained closed. My friend remained dead, and the war would continue without him.

"One day, I'll step through into your world, you bastards," I said softly, "and when I do you'll learn what Rash'Tor'Ri truly means. I swear it."

"Son?" a voice rumbled from behind me, "Are you alright?"

I turned to find Kharl standing behind me with a whole squad of his new Jaeghernauts. Daphne Cavanaugh stood directly behind him and the twenty of them stood in a v formation, ready for battle.

"I will be," I said sadly, "I needed to vent a little."

Daphne looked at me with one eyebrow raised. She looked back at the burning grassland and the scattered hunks of metal.

"A little?" she asked, "I don't think I want to see a lot."

"I don't either," I said softly, "Believe me, I don't either."

We walked toward the base and Kharl strode beside me, "You wanna talk about it?"

"The Shak'Tar got Luis, Dad," I said, "This has to stop. But I don't know how to make it stop. I need a target. If they can give me a target, I'll end it, but I need the target."

"I see," he said, "It's hard to lose friends, Son. I know, I've lost a great many in the last hundred years. It doesn't get any easier as you get older. And it shouldn't ever get easier. The only thing I can say is that we'll avenge him and when these Shak'Tar are located, we'll all stand beside you and we'll call up hell from below. We'll destroy them just as we'll destroy their masters."

"Amen to that," Daphne said from my other side, "And when you get ready to step through that Gate into their world, we'll be right there with you. One day we'll bring those bastards down."

"Thanks," I said. It was the only thing I could think of to answer that. I knew that the Guard would follow me into the abyss if I chose to go there. I don't really understand why they are all willing to do such, but I know they are.

We met Ric and Prada about halfway back.

"Get me Duke, Ric," I said, "I need details about these Shak'Tar. I may be able to give some insight as to how they think since we share the same blood."

"I already called him," Ric returned, "He's on his way. Be here by tomorrow morning."

"Good man," I said, "Sorry if I flew off earlier. I needed..."

"No explanations needed, Boss," he said, "although you need a new desk and some walls repaired in your office. Probably easier to just move to another office."

"I guess I shouldn't take bad news inside,"

"Probably a safe bet," Prada said.

Chapter 23

"Tell me how Luis died," I said to the man who sat in a chair across the desk from me in my new office.

Jim Duke looked at me a moment, "You knew Ramirez, personally, didn't you?"

The knot formed in my chest again, "He was my friend."

He nodded and said, "He actually wasn't even the target. The target was a Russian Mage named Sergei Ivanof. He is the head of the Russian Academy. The whole hit team was destroyed but your man was killed in the fray."

I nodded.

"The attack occurred close to the Academy and their initial action was much like they used in China. They did something that scrambled the brains of all the Mages and Guards in a certain area and walked in with some heavy bore pistols to unload into the unconscious forms."

"Only, they hadn't planned on Ramirez," Duke said, "He had been out late and was returning at just the right moment to intervene. He ran in at that crazy speed you guys have, and fried all of the Shak'Tar except one who was close enough to slam Ramirez with the telepathic attack. Ramirez was shot seven times by this man but the Shak'Tar was also picked off by one of the initial Mages who was still alive. It was short and ugly but your man saved seven of the ten in the initial group and killed almost a complete hit squad of the Shak'Tar."

At least Luis hadn't gone down easy. I could easily see him intervening in an attack as well. Everything rang true about the whole scenario, but it still called forth the rage in me when I thought about it.

"I need to know where these guys are based, Jim," I said, "Have we gotten any closer to finding the bastards?"

"A little," he said. "They're based over in Europe or possibly the Middle East. I'm narrowing down the choices but it's still an immense amount of territory to search. We're pretty certain they have to come into the country from outside to do their hits here. The ones in Europe always seem to happen before the ones here, and we figure it is a matter of travel time."

"You have no idea how much I want those fuckers," I said with a snarl. "Is there anything I can do to help you? I have the same Demon blood in my veins. I honestly don't know if I could help with how they think, I was raised completely different than they were. The only commonality is the Demon blood."

"Actually, they think more like someone in my line of work would," he answered, "That's how we've stopped several attacks already. We anticipate and meet their teams. Their telepathy doesn't affect a sniper who is several hundred yards away from them and, I'll be honest, some of them are just plain sloppy."

"How so?"

"A lot of the teams rely on the telepathy too much," he explained, "They project to people around them somehow. People just don't notice they're there. But, like I said, a sniper who is several hundred yards away can pick them out with ease. But, as with any force, there are also some that are very good. These use positions like we would and the telepathy is a secondary skill which they use very well."

"I would say those are much harder to interfere with," I said.

"All too true," he said with a nod, "Sadly, my Russian teams were too late. I'm truly sorry about your friend."

"I'm not trying to place blame on you or your teams, Jim," I said, "You guys are doing wonders already, but I just want you to know that I'll help in any way I can. If you need me to look at a group you suspect, I can tell by sight if they are Demonblood. Just contact me if you need me to actually look and see."

"I hadn't really thought of that," he said, "How close do you need to be to see their Souls?"

"Maybe a mile if I'm in a plane looking down," I answered, "Maybe more. I haven't really experimented with that so much.'

"I'll definitely keep that in mind," he said, "It would be quite useful at times."

"Call me with any updates," I said as Jim stood up to go, "and as long as they aren't launching a full blown attack like last year, I should be available to do some distance spying for you."

"Will do," he said as he turned and exited my office.

Part of me still hurt at the loss of Luis but I was also proud of the man. He'd taken out the hit squad before he went down. I also know that it's how he would have liked to go out if he had to go. Swinging with both fists in the act of saving others.

I truly dreaded the fact that I would have to tell his family about his death. He'd had three sisters still living and a whole slew of nephews and nieces. It would be a sad day when I flew down to Florida to tell them. It's not something I wanted to say over the phone. Family deserves more than an impersonal call.

***

The base in Kansas was growing rapidly. When the government actually backed us we could move at a greater speed than before. The first shield was up around the first facility out by the gate and the second facility was in the beginning stages. There was a great deal of construction equipment working twenty four hours a day digging the great big hole that would house a concrete and steel bunker.

There were independent power supplies to each facility in addition to the buried cables that brought in the primary source of power. Ventilation had been an issue when we had begun this project. My shields would sever any tunnels that weren't buried very deep.

When I had sunk the shield into the earth to anchor it, there had been a couple of incidents where my shields had crossed ventilation shafts and cut them off. It wasn't too hard to fix, I just had to actually enter the shafts until I reached a spot where I could see the shield across the shaft. When I had reached that point, I had opened a hole in the shield to allow the air to pass.

I have learned that my Soullord skills allow me to fiddle with almost any flows of the Source. Shields literally are putty in my hands. The first time I had realized this was when I ripped a hole in the shield surrounding Kevin Graves. I had just reached out with my mind and changed the flows of a shield tied directly to the Source.

At the time I hadn't really thought much about it, but the implications were truly astounding. If I can manipulate any flows of the Source, there aren't many things I couldn't do to a person's Soul if I chose to do so. That is terrifying to someone who is constantly fighting a monster that lives inside them, and is always trying to claw its way out.

This day, by some stroke of fortune had left me with some free time, and I was about to use that free time to go into Wichita, and find some quiet restaurant where I could try to relax for a few minutes and enjoy a good meal. Rictor and Prada were both working with Kharl and I seemed to have the time completely to myself.

I walked out toward the area where they kept the vehicles. It seems that we have to be a bit more formal now that we are constantly in contact with the US National Guard. I don't just go jump in one of the SUV's and drive out. I have to sign for one and pick it up at the Carpool.

"What can I do for you, Sir?" asked the woman who had Carpool duty for the day.

"I just need a car for a few hours to go into Wichita," I said, "I haven't signed one out before and have no idea how I'm supposed to go about it."

"Not very complicated, Sir," she returned, "I just need the tag number of the vehicle you want to sign out and your signature. Sometimes an ID is required but everyone knows who you are so it won't be required."

"Ok," I said, "I guess I just need a car or a pick-up or something."

"Will you be needing a driver, Sir?"

"I don't guess so," I said and chuckled, "Those come standard with the vehicles?"

She smiled and answered, "Yes, Sir."

"Nah, I'll drive myself," I said.

"Alright," she said and pointed to a spot on the form, "Sign here and you can take the truck over there."

She pointed to her right at a black Humvee. I'd never driven one of these yet. It might be fun.

I signed on the line and smiled, "Thanks."

She handed me a set of keys and I walked over to climb into the driver's seat.

I drove out of the garage and something was just tickling my awareness, but I paid it no notice. I exited the compound that had been erected at the former college in Hillsboro.

As I turned down the highway toward Wichita, I heard a voice from the seat behind me, "Mr. Rourke, you are a hard man to find alone."

Chapter 24

I looked into the mirror to see a man staring at me from the back seat. Both hands were held up in my sight. I opened my inner sight and slammed on the brakes. Before the man could even move I was out the door, which flew across the road to slam into the side of a building. His door was ripped off the hinges, and my other hand was gripping him by the front of his black uniform.

What I'd seen when I truly looked was one of the Shak'Tar, or someone who had the Demon blood, at the least.

As the Humvee rolled onward, I stood holding the man off the ground in front of me.

I'll say this for him, he didn't panic. He held his hands out with the palms up, and I could see the nervousness in his aura.

"I see how you killed thirty Shak'Tar, now," he said.

This statement confirmed his status as Shak'Tar.

"Give me one reason it shouldn't be thirty-one," I growled with my rage beginning to claw its way forward.

His eyes widened as he felt the buildup inside me, "You're a Bloodborn?"

"And you're Shak'Tar," I said as I beat the rage down some.

"I have information you need," he said, "I came to seek asylum."

Not many things can blindside me because of the abilities I have to see into the Soul, but this was the last thing I had expected. I want to hate them all, but now

I find that some of them are not the evil that they represent, and it was like a slap to the face.

"Asylum..." I muttered, "You want protection?"

"More like an Alliance, Mr. Rourke," he said. "I could talk so much easier without the hand to my throat."

I slowly set the man down on his own feet and let him loose. I needed to see what he had to say, at the least.

I watched his Soul closely, "So talk."

"I belong to an organization that I wish to part ways with," he said.

"Shak'Tar," I returned.

"It seems you know more than is suspected. I was going to approach that exceptionally good security consultant you have, but what I have is very time-sensitive."

"Then you should spit it out," I said.

"Recently," he said, "a full Company of Shak'Tar arrived and were sent after a target here in the United States. A full company is one hundred men. The only high priority/high risk target I am aware of is you. I came to warn you."

"Where are they?"

"That's the problem, they're not here. Do you know who else would be considered this high a priority target?"

I felt a hole form in my chest and my face went white as a sheet.

"You *do* know."

I said one word as I launched myself back toward the base, "Lyrica."

I grabbed my phone from my pocket and punched the first speed dial.

"Yeah, Boss?"

"Drop everything! Get to the plane, we have to go to Montana, now!"

"Yes, Sir!" he didn't ask why or anything. That's Ric.

I ran straight for the airstrip where the Soulguard jet always sat, prepared for take-off at a moment's notice. We kept pilots on duty at all times for just such occasions.

Rictor, Prada, Kharl, and Daphne Cavanaugh all reached the jet at the same time as I did. We all piled into the jet. And the engines began to whine.

"Now! Now!" I yelled to the pilots, "Go! Fuck clearance! Montana at the fastest this heap will fly!"

The pilot didn't hesitate, slamming forward on the throttle. The plane jumped forward before the door had even shut all the way. I may have been projecting my desperation toward them all, because I turned toward the others and their faces were as pale as mine.

Kharl grabbed my shoulders, worry rolling through his aura, "What is it?!"

There were tears in my eyes, "They're going to kill my Angel!"

I was barely in control of what I was feeling and it was projecting to the others as I paced the length of the plane for the longest two hours of my entire life. I've come face to face with what I fear the most. What if I never got to hear that musical laughter again? What if I never got to see her emerald green eyes, glowing with life, again? What if?

As we neared The Academy, I opened my Sight to scan the ground miles below us. The communications to the Academy had been cut off. We'd been trying to contact them since leaving Kansas to no avail.

Then I saw her Soul and my heart soared. She was alive! But I also saw the ugly Souls down below us and they were so close to where she was. The terror swept through me again as I thought we would be there just in time to see her die.

I ripped the seat I had placed my hands on in half as I looked groundward.

Ric placed his hand on my shoulder. He'd felt the hope and the terror I was feeling.

"Boss?"

I saw her approaching the ugly Souls below us. I could imagine what was happening. She was running like she always does, and they lay in wait for her.

I think something broke inside me in that moment. I looked at the pilot.

"Will this thing fly with the door open?"

"Yes, Sir, but you can't just open it like..."

CRASH!

I kicked the damn thing off and grabbed Rictors shirt front, "Don't follow me!"

I dove out the door.

Wind buffeted me, and I spun around and around for a moment as I got myself oriented again. I spread my arms and legs to get myself into position. I looked down and focused on the Soul below that blazed like the sun. Then I turned myself and dove straight down toward her.

I hadn't asked how high we were but it couldn't have been more than three miles. But it seemed like it took forever as the world slowed and my focus was achieved.

I could see the whole thing play out from far above them. I could see the Shak'Tar close in from all around her. Farther out I could see a portal form and Demons began to pour through it.

At that moment, she felt the Demons and opened her sight. Her Soul rippled with the attacks from the Shak'Tar. Emotions flooded across her aura and her mind wasn't able to cope. She didn't have a Lash like I do.

But, by God, she is a Soullord and there is a reason they sent a hundred of the bastards to kill her.

As she began to crumple I saw her Soul Blaze as she did something I have never seen before. She reached out with her mind and ripped the life out of the area around her.

The area within five hundred feet of her died. The grass, trees, insects, animals, and fifty-seven humans that had called themselves Shak'Tar.

Her stream blazed as the Source was sucked into her body. What she had done took a great deal of power and her stream wasn't keeping up. Her Soul dimmed and I screamed as I let my rage surface.

They were still closing on her crumpled form when I Pulled harder than I have ever Pulled. I unleashed everything I had at the circle of forms closing in on my little Angel.

The world exploded around her in a circle as disks of fire slammed into the ground, incinerating the Shak'Tar who were closer than the others. The back lash from my shots was slowing my fall and I fired the rifled fireballer I had created at the Academy. The fireball slammed amidst the group of Shak'Tar on her left and the recoil slowed me even more.

I flipped and slammed into the ground with a bone-jarring thud. Dirt and ash exploded up from the impact, and I released three more disks to slay the last of the Shak'Tar.

I knelt next to her crumpled form and pulled her to my chest. Power flooded up my stream as it flowed into her just as her stream was glowing with the Source pouring into her.

It was only moments until her Soul brightened and stabilized. The relief flooded through me when I saw that my Little Angel would live. Tears were streaming down my face as I realized that I would rather die than live a life without her in it. That must be what it means to be in love with someone.

Her eyes fluttered open and she saw me. Astonishment, relief, and love rolled through her aura and as she looked back into mine, I saw triumph.

Then her eyes closed. She was unconscious.

I felt them closing from the left and I put everything that I am into a Lash. My sorrow and joy, my love and hate, happiness and all of my rage, everything that makes me who I am. I put it all in and I Lashed out toward the horde of Demons that was closing in on us.

Then I bent down and kissed Lyrica's forehead and reached into her stream to turn on her personal shield. I gently lay her back down and turned toward the Demons with my eyes blazing.

They had stopped at the edge of the dead zone. The Demon in the front was enormous. His stream was gigantic and he stood staring at me.

There was some sort of link after the Lash I had released. I could see the emotions rolling through his aura, which I wouldn't have recognized if not for the fact that I could feel them as well.

I'd seen rage and hate before and fear. Now I knew what dread looked like.

It looked at me and spoke with a rumbling voice, "What are you?"

I answered with one word. A word he would not mistake for anything else.

"Rash'Tor'Ri."

With that word I saw/felt his dread turn to despair, and I saw it spread throughout the hundreds of Demons that faced me.

But I also saw something else. I saw a memory roll across the leader's aura. I saw what was unmistakably a female Kresh holding a small one in her arms. And I saw/felt the pain and loss he was feeling, knowing that his end and the end of his clan/family was here.

There are a few life-altering events a person receives throughout his or her life. The first time you know someone has given their life for yours, the first time you realize you would give your life for someone else, When you find that you love someone so much that you will jump out of a plane just on the off chance you can save them before you impact the ground, and when you find out that a Demon can love.

And I had two of those moments in the last half hour.

The flames that had sprang from my body flickered and went out. I pointed toward the portal.

"Take your people and go home."

He stared at me and I could see/feel the amazement in him. It slowly dawned on him that he wasn't going to lose his clan today and relief flowed through him. It was all up to him now.

I watched as the ones in the rear returned to the portal and disappeared. He stood directly in front of me while his whole clan made their way back through the portal.

As the last of them vanished he spoke again, "Why?"

I sent out the emotions he had felt, "You felt this as you thought of your mate. I don't want to kill that."

He looked behind me, "You're mate lives?"

I nodded.

"Good."

"If there are more like you over there," I said, "Keep them off my world."

He looked at me one last time as he stood before the portal. He nodded and stepped through.

"What the Hell did I just see?" a voice came from behind me. I turned to find all four of them standing at my back. Kharl, Daphne, Prada, and Rictor.

"Thought I told you not to follow me," I said.

"I didn't," he said and pointed at Prada, "I followed her."

I smiled and turned to Kharl who had asked the initial question, "What you just saw was hope, Dad. There may be a possibility that we don't have to kill every single Kresh to gain peace."

I returned to Lyrica and turned off her shield. Then I picked her up and we started walking down from the mountains toward the Academy.

We met the advance forces of the Guard halfway down the mountain. Kyra was in the lead and Paige was right beside her.

Chapter 25

"I'm not leaving," Lyrica said, "I have three patients tomorrow and I can't go yet."

"They tried to kill you," I argued, "You're not safe enough here."

"I'll not be safe enough for you anywhere," she answered, "It won't take long to see these patients and they won't be able to be moved to Kansas unless I see them first, anyway."

I sat back and looked at her. She had gotten out of the infirmary bed the minute she woke up and refused to join the Exodus to Kansas. We were moving the trainees and most of the staff down there. The college in Hillsboro was much better suited for our offices and Paige had set in motion the buying of the college and the surrounding area.

The Military had taken the area where the Gate was and it was patrolled to keep people out of harm's way. Surprisingly there were still a great deal of people trying to get into the area, which made no sense whatsoever to me. Didn't they see what the hell happened there?

The locals didn't have the same problem. They'd seen it first hand, and were more than happy to get the hell out of there. But there were a lot of friggin' idiots in the world, and they all seemed to be trying to get to the Gate. I'd seen a lot of end of the world proclamations, and an influx of religious figures claiming to be able to exorcise the Demons and close the "Hell Gate" for us.

Perhaps we should have chosen a better name for them all those years ago. Of course, it was during the

Crusades and they were discovered by a Knight, so they were thought to be Demons at the time.

But none of this was helping me try to convince a teenage Soullord to do what I want her to do and come back to Kansas with me where I could make sure the Shak'Tar couldn't get to her again.

"Colin, I know you want to protect me," she said, "And without you, I would be dead many times over, but I have obligations here, and I need a week to take care of it before I can come with you."

I knew she was right, but I have a hard time equating anyone else to the same importance as I place her. I didn't even know how important to me she was till I thought I was going to lose her and now I didn't quite know how to deal with the repercussions of that. I know I love her but do I have the right to take advantage of someone who has seen me as her hero since she was a child. I really needed someone to talk to about it.

"Ok," I said, "but I'll go with you and help. Who knows? I may learn something as well."

"I'll be perfectly all right without a..."

She realized that I wasn't going to give another inch on this. She can see exactly what I'm feeling, just like I can. And there was no point in arguing any farther on the subject.

"Alright," she said and hugged me, "And thank you for saving me again. I thought I was a goner until I looked up and saw you. I thought I was dreaming. Did you really jump out of a plane?"

"Um..."

She shook her head in wonder, "Ric said you did and I watched his memories as he thought about it, too."

"Just how did that go, by the way," I asked, "They all seem to be avoiding me."

"I looked at both Ric and Kharl's memories and it looked like Ric threw Prada out of the plane, and followed her out only seconds after you went out the door."

"He threw her out?" I asked. "She's terrified of heights."

"Oh, she was at the door, but was having trouble actually doing the deed, you know," she said. "He, more accurately, pushed her out the door. He was in a bit of a hurry and may have pushed a little harder than he would have normally."

"I wonder how hard he would push a person out of a plane, normally?" I muttered.

"No smart-ass remarks from you," she shook her finger at me, "Kharl and Daphne were right behind them. Did you know that none of them had a clue how they were going to survive that jump when they jumped?"

"What kind of solution did they come up with? Like I said they've been avoiding me. I told Ric not to follow me, but I kinda meant all of them."

"Shield parachutes, all four of them made shield parachutes of some sort. It seems the only one who didn't was you. Did you know that the recoil from your weapons would slow you?"

"It hadn't occurred to me until I opened fire," I answered, "I hadn t really planned any of it."

"Jesus, Colin," She said, "You can't just keep doing this kind of crap, and expect to just find the solution before you hit the wall."

I had figured I was a dead man, but the least I would do would be to kill the bastards before they got to her. I don't think it would further this conversation to actually tell her this so I just shrugged.

"That's just how I roll, baby."

She sighed in exasperation and made shooing motions with her hands toward the door.

"Shoo, fly," she fussed, "I gotta get ready for the day in Missoula. Places to go and people to heal."

I left the room knowing that I hadn't accomplished near what I had intended when I entered. But at least I had convinced her to move to Kansas, even if it was going to take a few more days than I wanted. One thing I wasn't going to do was go back and leave her here. No way in hell.

***

"Wait, wait," Lyrica interrupted and I stopped Pulling through the elderly woman's stream, "You're like a bull in a china shop."

She lay her hand over the woman's left kidney and I watched the flow of Power run up the woman's stream but it didn't stop or spread out. It flowed directly toward her hand, focusing the power near the area that was the problem.

The Woman had a kidney that was only working at ten percent of the strength it should have been, and the power Lyrica focused through it would repair it to a state that she probably hadn't seen in forty years.

I had been Pulling the source into her, and letting the body distribute it.

"I see," I said. "You can Pull more to the same spot than would ever distribute there before reaching a level where I would have to had to stop."

"It works like that for any localized injury," she said. "Sometimes you need to do it like you were. Like if you were curing some sort of disease that is throughout the whole body. But injuries or things like this work better if you Pull directly to the spot."

"That would work better on battlefield injuries, too," I said, "I wish I had known this back when I had Pulled for Mom. I really messed up there."

"You didn't know," she said. "Hell, no one even knew we could Pull from another person's stream, at the time."

"I know, but I still feel guilty that I didn't heal her right."

"You saved her life, Colin, never forget that. You can bet she won't ever forget it. None of the Guards on the field will forget what you did there."

She stopped Pulling, and the woman's Soul looked stronger. The spot where her Kidney was had been duller than the other parts of her Soul and it was now brighter than the rest.

"You wanna work on this guy?" she motioned toward a man who they said had an infection that had spread throughout his body, "He'll need a full Pull like you were doing."

"Ok," I said and walked toward the man. His Soul was dim and he was terrified of us.

"You don't have to fear us, Sir," I said, "This will help you."

I Pulled through his stream and his Soul began to brighten. I watched as his fear level began to drop. When I was done I turned to walk away. He grabbed my arm.

"Is this truly the end of days? Are the legions of Hell coming back?"

I really didn't know how to answer him but I tried, "They aren't really Demons from Hell. They're aliens and they're trying to invade our world to destroy us. This is all I know. We'll stand and fight them when they return. And if they come again, we'll do as humans have done throughout history. We'll protect our own. I don't know what the end of days entails, but, if we fail, that very well may be what we're facing here."

"So you two aren't angels?"

I laughed, "I'm no angel. She may be, though."

I heard her musical laughter, and whispered to the man, "Definitely an angel.

He smiled and let go of my arm with a knowing look.

Chapter 26

I heard their voices as I neared Paige's office.

"...dinner?"

I recognized the voice of Kevin Graves.

"It doesn't bother you that you are scared of me?" Paige asked.

"I'm scared of everything," he answered. "I'm used to it. The question is can you handle the fact that I'm scared of you?"

"That's a good question," she said. "Considering the source of that question, I'd love to have dinner with you."

"Seven this evening?" he asked.

"That will be great."

"I'll see you then."

I met Kevin as he exited her office with something besides fear rolling through his aura. There was a flow of triumph and excitement along with anticipation. His eyes grew wide as he saw me, and a shot of fear rolled through him that I saw him push down much like I push the rage down in myself.

"Good morning, Sir," he said to me.

"Hey, Kid," I returned, using the name we had given him when he got to Tennessee, "How's it going?"

"Very good," he said with the return of the emotion he had been feeling before I interrupted him.

"Be careful out there, Kid," I said, "Keep that personal shield up. We don't want to lose you."

He nodded, "Yes Sir."

"And Kevin," I said softly, "She loves Orchids."

His face turned red and I chuckled. Then I turned away from him and entered Paige's office.

"I heard that," Paige said as I closed the door behind me, "and it's not really fair if you tell him. The joy is in the learning."

"True," I said with a smile, "But it doesn't hurt to start a tiny bit ahead of the game. The question is what kind of orchids he'll come up with."

She laughed and sat down behind the huge desk that made her look even smaller than she usually did.

"Is everything prepared to head to Kansas?" I asked.

"Yes," she said, "I've spent the last eleven years here, and I'm going to miss it, though."

"The move makes sense," I said, "now that secrecy is not an issue any more."

"That just tickles the shit out of you, doesn't it?" she asked. "You always complained about it from the first day I met you."

"I guess it made sense on some levels," I said, "but I still think we would have been much better prepared without the secrecy."

"There were issues on both sides of the argument, but, thanks to you, the issues were bypassed quite handily."

"Me?"

"Really, Colin," she said with a small shake of her head, "you're very birth was the thing that set all this in motion. They spent a lot of time trying to kill you, both as a child and an adult. Their failure caused them to send one of those damnable Mages, which you killed quite thoroughly. This sparked the fire that caused them to decide to come in force."

"I think they would have come through anyway," I said. "Perhaps it would have been a bit later than they did. Weapons are progressing to a point where humans can fight them now. I could see a where the weapons at the government's command could really cause a lot of damage."

"I agree," she said, "but they came through early or they would have done a hell of a lot better than they did. I just feel that they were unprepared to face what you put out there in Kansas. I think they'll send more next time and I think there will be a plan in place. These Shak'Tar are dangerous, but they aren't going to succeed any better than the last group of Kresh sent to assassinate you."

"Oh?"

"Your security specialist is getting better and better at stopping attacks," she said, "Just where did you find him? He seems to know where they're going to hit as fast as they do."

"He is quite good at his job," I said, "probably because he's been an assassin for the last twenty years."

"You hired an assassin to be our security?" She was looking at me with a startled expression.

"Who better to stop assassins than an assassin?" I said with a shrug.

"That still doesn't really answer where you actually found him," she said. "It was Rictor who introduced him, wasn't it?"

"Of course," I answered.

"That figures," she said, "I'm not even going to ask why your crazy second in command knew where to find this guy. He is a great success, but some of the people assigned to my detail worry me just a bit. They're a scary lot."

"They're a scary lot? Really?????"

She smiled, "Touche! I guess I don't have any business calling them scary--pots and kettles."

"Exactly," I said.

She looked at the clock and pointed toward the door, "You better get going before you're late for your flight. Try to leave the doors attached to the plane this time."

"I wasn't thinkin' too clearly before," I said with a grin.

"What were you thinking? The others all had some sort of shield parachute devised to slow them down."

"It wasn't fast enough."

"Did you know the weapons would slow you enough to land?" she asked.

If there was one person I could be totally honest with on the subject, I would say it would be Paige.

"Honestly, Paige," I said, "I didn't expect to live through it. But I was gonna make damn sure I killed all of those bastards before they could get to her."

"Jesus, Colin," she said. I didn't need my Sight to see the emotion that she felt. There was almost a tear in her eye as she really understood the words I had just said.

"We can't afford to lose you, Colin," she said.

"Without her," I said as I stood to leave, "I'm dead already."

I don't know where that came from but it felt like total honesty, and I would have kept it to myself if I had been prepared for the feelings that I was feeling.

"Holy shit," she said softly, "You're in love with her. You have no idea how happy that will make her. She's been in love with you since she was six."

"What?"

Paige began laughing, "She swore when she was ten that one day she would marry you. She's been patiently waiting for years. This is too good."

"This isn't good, Paige," I argued. "You've seen what I do. I'm a monster. Do you know what the happiest moment in my life is? When I was in the middle of a hundred thousand Kresh, and free to kill as many as I could. What does that say about a person, that his happiest moment is a battlefield, drenched with blood?"

"You'll see," she said with glistening eyes, "No matter if there is Kresh DNA inside you, you are not a monster. Perhaps, in time, you'll accept the fact that you're better than the blood in your veins. There is also the blood of Kelvin and Rhayne Rourke. And if that's not enough to offset the Kresh, nothing is."

I was silent for a moment.

"Let's hope it's enough," I muttered as I turned and left her office.

I headed down the hall to the elevator. I had said more than I should have to Paige. I know what it is that I feel, but do I really have the right to bring that monster that lives inside me into another person's life? I mean, what would happen if we were to have children? Would they have the same genetic problem that I have? Do I have the right to do that to an innocent life? There are hard questions to ask there, I think. And I just don't think I'm ready to ask those questions yet.

Chapter 27

I turned my MP3 player on and stuck the earbuds in my ears. I formed a small shield to hold them in place as well as another to hold the player on my shoulder. This was something I had done many times. As I practice alone, I like the music to set the beat, and it's hard to keep the wire and earbuds in place while doing the Dance. I let the grind of the guitar flow through me as Seether started ripping from the speakers.

I stood out at ground zero, right where the Great Gate had been. I spend a lot of time out here trying in vain to see some sort of pattern in the flows of power that make this spot unique for the gate. I haven't found anything that sets this spot apart from any other, so it must be something at the other end that makes it open right here.

I began the turning stance I call the Whirlwind, and flowed into the Reaping as the music pounded in my ears. From there I flowed into a defensive stance called Blade Barrier. I don't use defensive stances very often because I believe the best defense is a good offense. If I kill the one facing me there is no need for a defense at all. I use it more in sparring than I ever did in battle. I tend to be quite offensive on the battlefield.

The song ended and another began, this one was from Straight Line Stitch. They were a band that I learned about in Knoxville, their hometown. The beat was different, and my Dance adjusted as well.

I'm not sure how long I spent out there, but it was dark when I finally stopped. Sweat was pouring from my body, so I must have been at it for hours. I had been lost in the music and the dance. It's surprising how much of the tension and rage I can bleed off just by zoning out and Dancing the Blades.

As I made my way back toward the base I saw the sentries who saw me as well. I waved and they returned it. As I walked away from them I heard their comments.

"What do ya suppose he does out there?"

"He probably just stands there waiting for the Demons to return."

"I don't doubt that. I was there when they came through last time. I never saw someone so happy as the Soullord when we were surrounded out there."

"Some folks say he's a little crazy."

"He may be crazy, but it's a good crazy. He was carrying a spine when he came back from one of his runs, and I don't even think he knew it. Bet he can't wait till they come back."

"I can wait, I saw the footage and you guys were in some serious shit. I'd just as soon they give up and don't come back. I could seriously get behind that."

"No doubt but I doubt that's gonna happen, they'll be b..."

I walked out of range. I could have enhanced my hearing, but I'd heard more than I needed already. I hear a lot of comments from Guards that they are not aware of. The consensus, I think, is that I'm crazy and disturbing as it is, a lot of them act like I was the only one out there on the field. I was just one of many and without that many, I'm just a Mage.

I shook my head and continued on. There's not much I can do about it. People will think what they think, and it doesn't matter how many times a person tries to explain it. I made my way past the barracks to see a young National Guardsman slipping out of the door with a dazed expression on his face.

I almost laughed aloud as I opened my Inner Eye, and saw the memory rolling through his aura. Sex with a Soulguard could be quite the adventure for any normal person, and I knew that this one was quite an adventure all by herself. Andrea Prada's face was burned into this man's memory, and I'm not sure he would ever recover from this evening.

He saw me and saluted, "Sir."

"Relax, Son," I said, "I don't have to be saluted."

"Yes, Sir."

"I only have one question," I said, "You're off duty?"

"Yes Sir," he said, "I'm off till tomorrow morning."

"Good then," I nodded.

I was pretty sure that Prada would have made sure that she wasn't causing a problem before she had any sort of assignation with any of the Guardsmen. Our view on sexual relations is a bit different than some. Up till now we had tried to keep it within the Guard, for secrecy, if for nothing else.

Most of the Guard were people who had been attacked as normal ,or seen too much of the real world to stay out of the fight. To most, the Guard was all they had left. There were a few who had more ties to regular people than that.

Like Luis Ramirez. He'd had family in Florida. A lot of family, it turned out. I had gone there, and explained what had happened, and set up his sisters with the stipend every beneficiary of a fallen Soulguard receives. It was an emotional trip, and I found his family to be as likable as Luis had been.

I nodded to the Guardsman and proceeded onward toward the building where they had placed my quarters. I was planning on sharing the barracks with the Guards, but they had built the quarters for me anyway, so I just accepted graciously and moved into them.

Tomorrow I had a meeting with Marcus Stratton and Seran Polomo, Marco and Polo, the National Guard Generals.

***

"There seems to be a lot more young soldiers around than before," I said, "Not that I'm complaining or anything, it just seemed like most Guardsmen were a bit older than they are now."

"It's true," Polomo said, "The National Guard has gone through a lot of changes over the last year. An invasion on American soil will do that."

"As soon as the invasion took place, the President activated the Guard nationwide," Marcus said.

"Which means we can pull forces from any state to put in place here," Polo said, "But the SecDef, Secretary of Defense, decided this wasn't enough. We had to pull in our armed forces from overseas, or we had to make a huge change in the National Guard."

"The Joint Chiefs came up with a plan," Marco said. "The National Guard is now a full Military branch of its own. A lot of men transferred from our other branches, and our recruitment has gone off the charts as well."

"Why didn't you pull in the forces from overseas?"

"Because we have a responsibility to help everyone," Polo said. "America has always been on the forefront of world politics, and that won't change now. Your people tell us there are seven of these Gates and we need forces out there to help back your people up."

I nodded with a smile, "I had hoped for something along those lines, but I expected every military to get their asses home as quickly as possible. We are working with branches all around the world.

Most of that is being done by the Archmage and her staff. It's nice to know that we have you guys backing us as well."

Both men nodded and I continued, "My biggest fear from all this is that they'll use one of the Gates we don't know about and scatter. Casualties would be so high it makes me cringe. I want to be there but I don't know where 'there' is. It's making me crazy."

"Understandable," Marco said, "but you have to understand, you can't be everywhere. You can only do what you can do."

"I know," I said, "but it doesn't help up here."

I point at my head. I wouldn't talk about most of the uncertainty that I feel. I've led men into battle, but I've never been in command of something this big. One wrong decision could friggin' cost us millions of lives. But my allies don't need to see that uncertainty. That is mine to bear and mine alone.

"The price of leadership," Marco said.

"True," Polo agreed.

"I seem to be seeing a lot more youngsters in your ranks as well," Polo said, changing the subject.

"How could you tell?" Marco asked.

"Look in their eyes," Polo said, "The new ones don't have that look like my dad used to have. You can tell they've lived a while by that look."

"You've got a point," Marco returned.

"Our recruitment has jumped, much like yours," I said, "We just brought down all of the Trainees from Montana, after the attack on Lyrica."

"I've met that young lady," Polo said. "She is quite impressive. The first thing she did when she got in was heal several Guardsmen who had been injured in training. It's truly amazing what you people are capable of doing."

"I was talking with a certain pilot yesterday," Marco said, "I have to ask. Did you kick the door off a jet and jump out without a parachute?"

He was the first one who had the nerve to just ask. Rumors had gone the rounds already. One of the pilots had been on his first flight for us and he had quit after that. He had told a lot of people about the incident, and everyone seemed to know. No one had built the nerve to ask till now though.

"Yeah," I said, "It seemed like a good idea at the time."

"That never sounds like a good idea," Marco said with a shake of his head. "I'm ex-Air Force and I have more sense than that. Sounds like something an Army guy would do."

"Hey!" Polo exclaimed, "I resemble that remark. But no, not even an Army grunt would do that. Wouldn't put it past a Marine, though."

I chuckled, "Funny thing is, a couple of ex-Marines followed me out the door."

"See?" Polo said. He shook his head with a sad expression, "Marines. What are ya gonna do?"

I really like the two Generals. They can always lighten my mood, and they both know their jobs and do them well. Both are veterans so they know what war is. Their advice is priceless, and their friendly banter is a nice relief.

We finished up our meeting and I made my way out to head toward the growing facility out by the Gate. The second barracks was almost complete, and I would be building the shield around it today.

I was met at the door to the command post by an ugly, wrinkled mess of a dog. He wagged his stump as he saw me and followed along as I walked toward the north. Ric and Prada were going to meet me out there. I looked back at the dog. How the hell had she sneaked the dog onto the plane?

"At least she gave you a bath," I said. He wagged his nub faster and his tongue hung out of his mouth, "You're still the ugliest damn dog I ever saw, though."

Chapter 28

"Come on," Ric muttered, "You're still mad?"

Prada glared back at him.

"Really? How long can you hold a grudge?"

"That's a dumb question, Ric," I said, "She's a woman, they hold grudges forever."

The glare turned toward me and I hastily added, "But she's got a point. You did throw her out of a plane."

"It was a small push," he returned, "and she needed a nudge."

"A nudge?" she asked. "I flipped three times, head over heels from your *nudge*."

"Everything worked out alright, though," he answered.

I heard her musical laughter from behind us as Lyrica joined our little group. With her came Mattie and Trent.

"She still givin' ya hell bout the plane?" he asked.

"Constantly," Ric answered.

"What do you expect?" Mattie asked. "You threw her out of a plane."

He sighed and our little group all laughed. In his defense, he did just push her because she was having a bit of trouble making herself jump. She was at the door with every intention of jumping. She was just having trouble actually doing the deed.

But she couldn't give up the opportunity to give Ric a hard time.

There was a good sized crowd out where the football field had been for the college. It was now a training ground for our newest Guards. Except for today. Today it was where we intended to make twenty new

Mages. There were twenty new volunteers who wished to do as Jacobs had already done.

I wouldn't risk it with anyone with less than twenty years of experience in the Soulguard. Anyone with trouble at focusing was excluded automatically, but there weren't many Guards who couldn't focus. It is the prime skill needed to become a Guard at all.

As we reached the center where our volunteers awaited, Kharl walked up. He looked at Ric and Prada.

"She still pissed cause you threw her out of the plane?"

The look of utter dejection on Ric's face was priceless, and the laughter once again made the rounds.

"It was just a nudge," he muttered.

"Sure it was," Kharl said and turned toward me. "You doin' this one at a time or gonna do the whole group? How many supports you want?"

"I think I'll try five at a time," I said, "Lyrica can help keep an eye on things, while I'm Pulling. You, Ric, and Prada should be enough support."

"Good enough," he said and turned back toward the group of volunteers, "Five at a time. First five line up right here."

He was pointing directly in front of us. As they lined up, I lit my Stream up, and showed them the tendril I wanted them to form to channel the power.

"You all know what I want here. Steer the power out the tendril. All of it," I said, "Anyone wants to back out now's the time to do it."

"We're good, Sir," returned Malcolm Hendrix.

He was one of the Guards who had come in from Denver with the Kid. He was also one of the few black men I had met who had been in the Guard long enough to be a veteran of twenty years. There were quite a few black men and women in the Guard, and there were more now as trainees than there had ever been before. It wasn't as if they had been unwelcome in the old days. It was just that the African Academy was the place they mostly served to blend in with the population.

Malcolm was one of the best Guards I knew with a sword, and he had created his personal shield with a lot greater ease than many others. I didn't expect much trouble with his ascension.

I nodded back to him and watched the tendrils form from the five volunteers, three men and two women. I had met all five of them over the years. Actually, I had met all twenty as they cycled through Knoxville over the years.

"Ready?" I asked and received nods from all.

I Pulled gently and felt hands from my supports land on my back and shoulders. The Source flowed up five Streams and all five turned it aside into the tendril.

I could see the amazement rolling through auras as they felt the Source flowing up toward them for the first time but none of them lost any focus.

"All right," I said, "Here it comes."

I Pulled hard on their Streams and fire shot heavenward in great gouts. The spectators were stepping back and the emotions were running from excitement to fear. There was always the fear.

After a few moments, I stopped Pulling through Selina DeReus' Stream. Lyrica was nodding as I did so. Some people can take more stress to their stream than others, and I was getting the sense that hers was as far as it was safe to go.

I continued for a few seconds more and stopped on Allen Rhode's as well for the same reason.

It went on like this for a time until the only one still going was Malcolm, who's stream was showing no stress whatsoever.

When I finally stopped, his stream was as big as Gregor's, which was bigger than the previous Archmage's stream had been.

"Careful, Malcolm," I said, "When I stop, you're gonna get a hell of a jolt. Don't even think of Pulling it."

"Yes sir," he answered.

I stopped and the enormous stream began to feed his body. He gasped and his hands shook. I could see the whites of his eyes as they widened when the power of his new stream entered his body.

"Just be still a few minutes and get used to the feel before you try to move, Mal."

"Jesus Christ!" he said, "You feel this all the time?"

"I don't," I answered and pointed toward Gregor, who was standing out in the circle of spectators, "He does."

"How friggin big is it?"

"About two feet in diameter," I answered and held my hands in approximately that big a circle.

"Don't even think of Pulling till you get in some classes. Just a tiny nudge on that thing will burn you to a crisp."

He nodded quickly, "Yes Sir, fried to a crisp. Definitely not the outcome I want."

He followed his fellow volunteers toward the edge of the crowd where several Mages were waiting to start giving them the introductory lesson. The next five stepped forward and we continued. There were no incidents, and we ended up welcoming our twenty new Mages. None of them were as powerful as Malcolm but there were none that were less than ten inch streams.

I think I could probably take support Mages and turn them into powerhouses like Greg and Paige if we tried, but I can only do so much at a time and Lyrica has a pretty full schedule already with her Infirmary. They were setting up schedules to bring people from all over to see her. Plus her classes with Pickney as he taught her everything he could think of about his field.

As we finished the last one, I turned around with fire dancing across my skin from the Source rolling through me. It felt awesome as it rolled around inside me, but I knew I had to release it before it hurt me. So I channeled a great gout of fire into the sky.

As my eyes settled back to the level of the crowd, I found myself looking at the largest man I have ever seen.

He stepped forward with astonishment rolling through his aura, and what an aura it was. He had a Soulguard knot that was enormous. His Soulstream was at least eight inches and it had the look of iron cable. This was the first time I had ever seen a Soulguard so old his hair was grey. How many friggin' years would that actually take?

"Merlin?" he asked in astonishment.

"Merlin?" I asked in return.

He shook his head as he heard my voice, "Nope, not Merlin."

Then something seemed to run through him as he realized something important, sadness to begin with, then a burgeoning excitement.

His laughter rumbled across the clearing for a moment. Then his eyes crossed the crowd behind me and grew wide as he saw someone.

"Dad?" I heard from behind me. I could swear it had been Kharl's voice.

I saw the whole cycle of emotions flood the big man's aura. He strode past me as if I wasn't there, and I turned to see him meet Kharl with an embrace that would have broken anything less than steel.

"God, I thought you were dead, Boy."

"I thought you died a hundred and thirty years ago," I heard Kharl return.

Someone cleared their throat behind me, and I turned to see the most beautiful woman I had ever seen. She was a Nordic Goddess. She was six feet tall, and would reduce any man to a puddle of goo in seconds.

And she was furious.

"Father," she said, "Can you explain why this man just called you Dad, and I haven't a clue he even existed?"

Chapter 29

"I wondered from the moment I saw the news reports," Dietrich Jaegher said, "just what it would take to cause the Demons to come in such force."

I was being pointed at by thirteen of the fifteen people sitting around the table at yet another Hooters. This one in Wichita.

The rumble of Dietrich's laughter rolled through the room.

"I figured as much as soon as I saw the boy. You may not be Merlin but you're damn sure a direct descendent. No one looks that much like someone without genetics," he said and turned to look at Lyrica, "And you, young lady are the spittin' image of Jillian Kent. What are the odds that both bloodlines would come into power again after the purge?"

"The purge?" Lyrica asked.

"Yes, after the death of Kent, The Demons went on a rampage. They hunted Kent's family down and destroyed them, or so they thought. And none of us even knew Merlin had any children. But I guess you can have many children in a nine hundred year lifetime. He never made it known that he had any children at all."

"I have to ask," I said, "The same Merlin that the legends are about? King Arthur and all?"

"That's him," Dietrich said. "He told us stories of his earlier attempts to fight the Demons only to fail. He was in China when the hordes came, and wiped out his 'Knights'. He came back to find everything lost. But if Merlin was anything, he was dedicated to fighting them. He later found Kent and showed him what he was. Kent began the Soulguard, and they fought the Demons for two hundred years."

I was stunned by the fact that there was an actual Merlin. But the fact that I was a descendent was amazing.

"What happened to them?"

His face went a bit somber and I saw the sadness in his aura.

"I was a new Guard at the time, and I was assigned to Merlin. We were in the south of France when the hordes came for Kent and the Soulguard. We felt the Pulls from hundreds of miles away and when we returned, we found everything destroyed. I've never seen any but one as powerful as Greyson Kent, but whatever they sent across destroyed everything that was there."

"And Merlin?" Lyrica asked.

"Something broke in him when yet another friend and ally died while he was away. He blamed himself for not being there when they came. About a year after that he told us he was going through the next portal that opened and take his vengeance. He charged the remaining Soulguards to continue Kent's mission and protect our world. Then he left us and never was seen again."

"The purges started soon after that, they killed whole villages where any of Kent's descendants lived. We thought that the Kent line was gone and I find, not only his, but the line of Merlin lives as well."

"And I have no doubt that you are the reason the whole world is about to see a war on a scale they have never dreamed of before. And since my daughter has decided to join this battle, I find that I have returned to the Soulguard, and I offer all the assistance I can."

"I had sworn to stay out of Soulguard business," he continued, "and then I heard of the death of Kelvin Rourke and the supposed death of my son. There was no reason to ever contact them again after that. Then there was an invasion, and all she could talk about was the duty of every human to take up arms and protect our world. Sounded like her mother, and I knew there wasn't any arguing about it so I came as well."

"Speaking of a certain angry woman," I said. "Are you still upset with him?"

"Of course," she answered, "Twenty years and he never even told me the Soulguard exists."

She had a thick Russian accent. I could guess where Dietrich had been for the last number of years.

"Women," Rictor said sadly, "they're grudge holders. I mean, you push a woman one time and ya hear about it for a month and a half."

"Out of a plane," Prada said with narrow eyes that would have sent chills down anyone with any sense's spine. But Rictor doesn't have any of that, so it didn't bother him too much.

"And it was a pretty hard shove, I'd say," Daphne added.

"Almost would be classed as throwin' her out of a plane, wouldn't it?" Kharl asked innocently.

Rictor was looking from one to the other with a completely hurt expression. His gaze finally turned toward me and he pointed straight at me.

"It was his fault," he said. "He said not to follow him, and I had to have someone to follow."

He pointed at Kharl and Daphne, "Both of them are too strong for me to throw out of the plane so that left Prada or a pilot."

"Told you he threw me out of the plane," Prada jumped on Rictor's choice of words.

Dietrich's laughter rumbled as he had turned to each one as they spoke, "One hundred and thirty years and still no one has taught a Mage any common sense. They were all crazy before and they haven't changed."

Kyra laughed, "Every one of them used to be such good, solid, average everyday Soulguards until he got ahold of them."

Once again the finger was pointed at me.

"You, too?" I whined, "Everybody wants to blame the Soullord."

I turned back to Dietrich, "Don't let em fool you, every one of them was nuts before I showed up. If I hadn't come along and displayed such a grand amount of skill with calm, calculated planning, it's hard to even think where they would be."

Musical laughter exploded from Lyrica, "Planning? Really?"

The laughter kept coming from all around the table.

"Humph," I said with a sad expression and reached down to my plate for another wing.

"Can anyone tell me," Irenia Nevara Jaegher interrupted, looking straight at Andrea Prada, "*why* you were thrown from an airplane? Parachuting isn't all that bad. I've jumped a couple of times."

"Honey," Prada said, "No one said anything about parachutes."

***

"Oddly enough," Jim Duke said, "We managed to stop three more attacks but there was one we weren't in time for I'm afraid. The odd part is that someone else stopped it. We found nine bodies at what we suspect would have been an attack in Scotland."

"Nine?" I asked, "I was thinking they used ten man squads."

"Maybe we've killed enough of the bastards to make them short-handed. I don't know what to think about it yet. All of them were killed at close range with blades. Everything points to two attackers with knives took out all nine in a very short time."

I suspected who had been behind the deaths. I figured it was probably my mystery visitor from last month. He had seemed like a pretty capable sort. I really wished he'd show back up. I really wanted the whereabouts of a certain headquarters housing a bunch of telepathic assassins.

"I really needed to talk to you about something that happened a month or so ago, anyway, Jim," I said, "It started when I found this guy in the back seat of the car I signed out."

Chapter 30

Over the next week, my Mage squad began to show up. Lennox had found eight of them from various parts of the world to volunteer for this. I hoped I could get along with them all. Mages are harder to deal with than Guards. They are used to being in command, and most of the Mages I have met seem to feel a bit well...entitled.

The first three were waiting outside of the barracks for me. I walked out to find two men and a woman standing patiently outside.

"Colin," Lennox Flynn said, "this is Galen Stone, Reyna Sereno, and I believe you've already met Len Yueh."

I reached out and clasped Yueh's hand, "It's good to see you again."

I hadn't seen him since the funeral rites after First Kansas.

I moved to my right to find myself facing a solid woman of about five and a half feet. She looked like a body builder.

"Good to meet you Miss Sereno," I said.

"Reyna, please," she said with a husky voice, "Is that Rictor Hughes back there?"

"Yes," I said, "He's my second in command. I take it you know him?"

"He was a lowly Marine when I met him outside Laos," she said with a smile, "Maybe you should ask him about his last mission as a Marine."

"I'll do that," I said. My curiosity was definitely peaked.

I continued to my right and shook Galen's hand, "Nice to meet you Mr. Stone."

"We've heard a great deal about you sir," his British accent was unmistakable, "I'm looking forward to learning if any of it was true."

"Probably not," I said. "Things tend to get blown out of proportions along the rumor trail."

"Don't let 'im fool ye," Flynn interjected, "The odds are 'e did more than 'e's bein' credited with."

"I may have done some of it," I admitted.

The three of them smiled and Flynn laughed, "Each Mage has brought ten Guards as their squad. We can introduce them as soon as they get settled."

"That's fine," I said, "As I said, Rictor Hughes will be my second in command, and each Mage will report directly to him. I have one other Mage from here who will have a squad as well. Andrea Prada will join us later today. She's training with Gregor at the moment."

"Isn't Hughes a relatively new Mage?" asked Stone. I could see the uncertainty in his aura, "We were told not to expect too much in the way of traditionalism, but I have to ask."

"Yes he is," I said, "but more importantly, he's been my second for the last twelve years, and he knows how I think and what I'll want when I order something you may consider ludicrous."

"I see."

"He is also one of the most capable people I've ever had the pleasure of serving with in the Guard. As most of you were warned, the new Guard is not as traditional as the former. We have four Soulguards on the Archmage's Council, if that tells you anything at all."

"Don't take it wrong, Sir," he said. "I'm not casting aspersions toward Mister Hughes. I was just looking for a bit of clarity on the subject."

"Not a problem," I said. "If any of you have any questions, feel free to ask me at any time. If you want to know why I'm asking you to do something in training, ask. But when we are on mission I want no hesitation. I'll be asking for things you don't normally do, and I won't be able to wait until I've explained everything to do it."

All three nodded, as well as Flynn.

"Feel free to get settled in," I said, "or you can come see the new facility receive its shield."

"How many Mages will you be using for this shield?" Reyna asked, "I've only seen one shield tied to the Source before. There were twenty Mages working in unison to do that one."

"'E does these shields by isself," Flynn said with a knowing smile.

"This I absolutely have to see," Stone said.

"As will I," Said Len Yueh.

"I will also come see this," Reyna said.

"Alright, then," I said, "let's head out to the Gate and set this one up. I hope they got the ventilation shafts deep enough this time."

"Tis a fact, that," Flynn said.

It wasn't long before we all stood next to the newest facility the government had installed to house another rapid response team. Our RRT's had grown a bit but they remained the same. They were ready at a moment's notice to hit anything that came out of the Gate.

"How do you raise a shield without the help of the other Mages?" asked Reyna, "I know the mechanics and it's hard to believe you can channel the power it takes to hold the Source back as you do the final stages."

"It's not really a matter of power so much as a matter of timing for me," I said. "Since I can see the power flows, I just need to disconnect at the right time."

As I was talking I was crafting the shield around the facility. When it was finished, it was a dome that was fed by two twelve inch streams. The two streams were hovering above the ground ready to be sent into the Source when I was ready. I concentrated and lit the whole construct up. Power flowed up my stream as I did so. It takes a little power to light things up for others.

"Bloody Hell," muttered Stone.

"Now I will push the other side down and just before the power hits me, I'll do the other and disconnect from the construct."

"That just seems incredibly dangerous," Reyna said.

"It's not so bad after I did it a couple of times," I said.

I pushed the far side down into the Source, and the power of a twelve inch stream surged through the shield. Just before it reached my end, I slammed the other end down. About a second later, I cut my tie to the shield as the power joined and the shield blazed to life.

"Bloody Hell," muttered Stone.

"Ye said that, already," Flynn said with a smile.

"I really meant it," Stone answered.

An engineer approached with a frown on his face, "Sir, I hate to say it but we got one of the shafts a little high."

"Damn," I muttered, "time to be a groundhog."

"A groundhog?" Yueh asked.

"Yeah," I said, "now I get to crawl down an airshaft to open a hole in the shield."

"How do you open a hole in the shield when it is already tied to the Source?" Yueh asked.

"Something I discovered fairly recently is that I can manipulate flows of power all around me. Lyrica can do the same. She actually ripped the life out of a five hundred foot circle in Montana because she can affect power flows the same way."

"You talk of amazing things," Reyna said, "as if they are an everyday occurrence. I think our new job is going to be quite exciting."

"It's part of the whole Soullord thing, it seems," I said. "We both discover things all the time. Sometimes I don't seem to be discovering things fast enough. I find out things as much in the thick of battle as not. That's part of the importance of this unit. I need everyone thinking about new things we may accomplish together. I've got a pretty good imagination, but I think it'll help immensely to have other viewpoints working toward a common goal."

"We know next to nothing about what you can do, Sir," said Stone.

"I intend on spending the next week with you guys, after the others show up, to show you what we've discovered so far. Then I hope to get some new ideas and we can try some of what Prada calls 'crazy shit'."

"Tis actually an apt name for the things I've already seen," Flynn said.

As we had been talking, we had followed the engineer down to an access hatch to the ventilation system.

"Anyone wanna come crawl through the vents with me?"

For some reason there was a great deal of looking around at the inside of the room.

Reyna Sereno yawned with a good deal of exaggeration, "I think we all need to get settled in with our forces."

"Right, I think I told my Guard Captain I would meet him at," he paused and glanced at his watch, "three thirty-five."

"I see how it's gonna be," I muttered as I crawled into the vent. There were a few chuckles behind me.

Chapter 31

"Let's dance," Lyrica said and grabbed my hand to pull me to my feet.

"I can't dance," I said. I heard a snort behind us where Trent and Mattie both sat. Prada actually laughed aloud and I heard Ric choke on something.

I turned back to them, "What? I never danced with anyone before."

"What do ya call that thing where you run around the battlefield with a pair of swords? Seems like it was called something with blades," Prada said, "Oh yeah, the Dance of Blades. If that's not dancing I don't know what is."

"Yeah but I don't want to kill anyone," I started.

"Silly man," Lyrica said, "just go with the flow. You just dance like you want to be close to someone instead of try to kill them."

I followed her toward the dance floor where there were crowds of people dancing to a tune I'd never heard of.

She started to move with the music, and was into my arms in a flash. I began to mirror her moves, and it *was* a lot like the Dance, except there was no rage. Soon, people were pulling away from us as we began to move together. I could see her Soul blazing, and I could actually feel what she was about to do. So I was always there when she changed.

We flowed across the floor like we did while dancing the blades, and we never even noticed when the song changed. We just flowed into it like we had been dancing together for years.

As I had told Paige, up until this very moment, my happiest moment had been on a battlefield, drenched in the blood of Demons.

But, now there was something else. A new moment and there was no rage. Nothing of the monster inside, and it was as joyous a moment as I could conceive of ever happening.

As the song ended, she was in my arms, and I was staring into those deep pools of emerald fire. We were only inches apart, and I was falling into those pools of fire when I felt them arrive.

I felt the Shak'Tar, and my happy moment was gone as the rage flooded my consciousness.

Lyrica's eyes widened as she saw the rage flood my aura, and she was twisting around toward the direction I was looking. I could see the portals opening on her stream as she readied weapons for an attack.

Then I saw him and clasped her arm, "Hold on, he's the one I told you about. Give me a minute but be ready, there are five more outside."

The crowd that had been rapt as they watched us was heading away from us now as fast as they could. I guess two people who seem to just catch on fire would send most people backing away. I may have been projecting a bit of rage as well. They tell me it's a bit overpowering when I do that, and it makes me a bit frightening.

I could see the disappointment in her aura, "I'll leave you to business then. If you need me, I'm ready."

She backed toward the others, "And we really need to talk about some things, Colin."

I nodded, "That we do."

She had seen and felt all that I had projected toward her while we danced. She knew exactly how I felt about her, and I knew what she felt about me.

I turned to walk toward the man who had saved my Angel's life. I owed him a debt. One I would repay, whether my allies agreed or not.

"I came at a bad time," he said with a nod toward Lyrica. "She was the target?"

"Yes and if you hadn't come forward, I would have lost her," I said. "I owe you a debt that I probably could never repay. I will make sure your Asylum is granted."

"I am happy that you can keep your love," he said. "I lost mine before I even knew what the word meant."

I saw a memory flow across his aura. A woman held between two men and a Kresh ripped her apart. It ate her right in front of the man standing before me, and I could feel the emotion that ripped through him. His pain and helplessness, and then his bottomless rage. A rage I know quite well.

"I'm sorry that had to happen to you," I said. "To do that right in front of you is monstrous."

Suspicion flooded his aura, "How would you know that?"

"I just watched it in your Soul."

"How is something like that possible?"

"It's something I can do," I said. "Before we continue, are the five others outside friendly or are we about to have a problem?"

"They are part of the reason I have spent this much time before coming back to meet with you. I have been pulling them out of their teams as they get assigned. They also wish to escape from the rule of our Masters."

"How many people are you trying to pull out?" I asked. "The longer we wait to hit that base, the bigger the chance of more losses."

"That is why I am here," he said. "I still have a few to pull out, but they just brought three companies across. There are close to five hundred of the Shak'Tar at the base, and I think they plan to use overwhelming numbers in their strike teams. I had to move before I was ready."

"Then we need to hit that base," I said, "right now."

I could feel a burn beginning inside me. My rage was beating at the walls, and I felt a great anticipation. This I could do. Give me a target and I can bring more force to bear than they would believe. I don't even know the limitations of the power I can wield with enough support. And I intended to use everything at my disposal.

"The base is in Romania," he said. "All I can ask is to let me go in, and pull out my men before you hit it. I will understand if this is too much to ask. We all knew the score before we chose to head down this path."

"If there's any way to allow you this, we'll do it," I said, "but that base is going to be wiped from the face of the Earth. Count on it."

He nodded, "I have the coordinates for you here."

He handed me a paper with longitude and latitude coordinates written on it.

"Bring in your group," I said. "We are heading for the base to set up the movement of my troops."

I strode back to my friends who could probably guess what was coming by the look on my face.

"We got a target, Boss?"

"Damn straight, Ric," I said, "a base in Romania."

I watched the relief flood his aura. He had been as frustrated by the waiting as I was. Ric is a warrior and the cloak and dagger stuff gets under his skin as much as it does mine. I think there will be a great deal of happy Guards and Mages, both, when we could actually hit back at these assassins.

"'Bout damned time," he stood and headed for the door. "I'll start callin' in the troops. How many you want to use?"

"Every Mage we can get, Ric. I want overwhelming force, and I want as much power as I can get available."

He smiled and hit the door.

"Looks like our night out is over," I said and looked at Lyrica, "but not our last night out. We'll talk when I get back from this."

"When we get back," she said. "I'm not sitting here while you blow up Romania. I'll be right there with the marshmallows."

There's no use arguing with a woman who you can already see won't budge. I can see it in her Soul, and it would be useless to argue the point. Not to mention, I like knowing she would have my back when I try something this big.

I nodded and we headed for the door.

"See, you big ox," Mattie said, "that's how it's supposed to be. No argument, no fuss."

"You'd blow up if I didn't argue with you," he said. "It would absolutely kill you."

"Would not."

"Of course it would."

I heard Lyrica's musical laughter and it cascaded through my mind. It was beautiful and I was very happy that it was back. For a time it had been gone, and I hadn't realized how much I would miss it until then.

Chapter 32

"Kel'Sin'Deres."

This was the answer I received when I asked if Touran Gorvelis knew who the Kresh was who I had met in Montana.

"He was the Kresh'Farrara'Ti in charge of this world for the last one hundred and fifty years. He was pushed out around ten years ago."

My eyes narrowed as I realized that I had let my parents' murderer return home. At least he had to have been the one responsible for the orders.

"Farrara'Ti?"

"There are many levels to the Kresh who control things," he said. "The Farrara'Ti are the rank above Kresh'Ma'Nar. Some control many Ma'Nar, some few, depending on the power of their minds. The Ma'Nar control what you call Wraiths. The number depends on the power of their minds. A weaker Farrara'Ti who controls multiple powerful Ma'Nar may have more forces at their disposal than a strong one controlling weaker Ma'Nar. A lot depends on chance and they compete fiercely."

The plane lurched and Gorvelis' face paled a little. We were on our way to Romania to meet with others that were in route. Flight seemed to be a relatively new experience for the man.

"And this Kel'Sin'Deres?"

"He controls fourteen powerful Ma'Nar. His clans are large, and when they pulled out of the competition for control of this world, many were surprised. He left the Hub and took all of his clans with him. It puzzles me as well, I know he is different from most, but his power should have assured that he would regain his place over this world. He had lost a lot of his authority when he failed to kill you multiple times."

"And he's the one in control of the Shak'Tar?"

"No," he said, "I am not sure why he was in Montana. He hasn't been the one running things for some time. His forces have been in Hub for the last ten years. His failure to kill you when you were relocated pushed him even farther out."

"If they knew how badly he failed the first time," I said, "he would really have trouble, then. His clan is the one responsible for the Kresh DNA I carry."

"Did you use the Lash when you faced him?"

"Yes."

"That would help explain why he didn't choose to fight in Montana," he said. "He could sense one of his own bloodline."

That may explain some of the feelings I had seen and felt from the giant Kresh I had met. It may not all have come from my reputation. He may have recognized his own bloodline when I lashed out at them with my mind.

"So he is my ancestor as well as Merlin," I muttered, "My life is so weird."

"I have heard this name, Merlin," he said, "His is one of the bloodlines that is hunted down and destroyed."

"Do you know why?"

"He and several others caused so much trouble when he lived that he was deemed too dangerous to remain. They say he may have been the one who destroyed the So'Doran Gate Facility nearly five centuries ago."

"So'Doran?"

There are two facilities that house the gates to each world. They are located in Hub. Hundreds of years ago, according to legend, a human walked through one of the gates in the So'Doran facility. There were hundreds of thousands of Kresh there, and it was unclear as to what happened. There were very few survivors, and the So'Doran facility was destroyed. There is a great crack in the world there now. I've seen it and sometimes I wonder what sort of man can leave so much destruction, alone?"

"A Soullord."

"And this is what you are?"

"That and a bit more, thanks to the efforts of Kel'Sin'Deres. I have Kresh DNA, unlike my ancestor. What I don't know yet is what that will truly mean. I have to fight this thing inside me all the time."

He looked at me with confusion rolling through his aura for a moment until I saw some sort of realization roll through it.

"You can't fight it," he said, "It is a part of who you are. You must embrace this part as a piece of yourself, or you will end up falling into insanity. I've seen it happen before. It is something we are taught as children, before the DNA truly begins to change us."

"I can't accept that," I said. "I've seen what I become when I let it out. I can't, I won't accept that I have to be that."

***

I stood in the darkness atop a mountain range looking down at a massive facility in the valley between two large mountains. The valley was more like a canyon, a box canyon at that. There looked to be only one approach to this place, unless you're a friggin' Soulguard. I know I can scale the rock face if need be.

That wasn't part of the plan though at the beginning. I just intended to use the power from three hundred and twenty two Mages to melt the whole place to slag.

"Plan A isn't gonna work."

"Why not?" asked Reyna. "That place is perfect for that sort of attack."

"There are people down there," Lyrica said, "And by the looks of their placement, they're prisoners. All of the regular Souls are in one place."

"Shit!" Ric exclaimed. "Why can't it be easy?"

I laughed softly, "You know better than that. It's never easy."

"So what sort of plan B have ya got in mind?" Kharl asked, "You do have a plan B don't you?"

"Of course I do," I said, "It's a lot like the last plan B."

"So you're gonna make some shit up," Prada returned with a nod, "Got it."

"While you make your plans, may we go in and pull out the rest of our men?" Gorvelis asked.

"That will go nicely with the plan I have in mind," I said, "You get your people and meet me at the prisoners. When everyone is there I'll raise a shield. Then I'll call in the rest on coms and they can blow the hell out of the place."

He looked at me with one eyebrow raised, "You plan to walk into a facility with five hundred telepathic assassins? With no training in how to hide your mind-glow from them?"

"Not exactly," I said, "I'll be coming from above, and I'll land directly on top of the prison."

"I'll wait until you get there before I jump and things will, most likely, go to hell as soon as I raise that shield, anyway. Shouldn't need to hide anything by then."

He shook his head, "It never ceases to amaze me what your people have become. There is no other colony that has come close to what you people have."

"One day we may just have to do something about that."

"I don't even doubt that you will," he said.

I turned to Ric, "When I send the signal to come in, you all come fast and hit hard. I don't want them to have time to use the telepathy. But not before I give the signal. I may have to adapt the plan as I go and I don't want to waste any lives if it looks like we can't keep going with that strategy. You know how things tend to go for us."

"Yeah," he said, "the enemy tends to screw up our plans pretty quickly."

I ran left toward the crescent of mountain ridge that surrounded the facility.

I tested my throat mike, "Test."

"Clear," Ric's voice returned.

I bounced along the top of the ridge until I was looking down on the facility. I worked around a little bit further until I was as close to the prison as my ridgeline reached. Then I scaled the cliff face downward toward the buildings below.

I stopped about halfway down the wall, "I'm in position."

"Acknowledged," came the voice of Gorvelis, "we are on approach."

I watched their Souls as they entered through the front gates. They moved at the speed a returning patrol would have, and split up a bit inside the perimeter, as if to head to their various barracks.

I watched patiently as...who am I kidding? I don't even know patience. It's a virtue I just don't possess. Yet I did wait. I saw the others approaching the prison. There were now twelve of them. I knew it was them because I could recognize Gorvelis' Soul at the head of them.

I was just about to launch myself when the clearing right beside the prison twisted with the darkness I have only seen with a portal. A big damn portal.

One of the seven Great Gates opened right below me and several forms walked through it. The one in the lead was huge. It was the size of Kel'Sin'Deres, and I knew it was a Farrara'Ti. My group of Shak'Tar stopped dead in their tracks, and I saw fear roll through them all. There was despair in the aura of Gorvelis, and I knew that the Farrara'Ti detected them right off.

He released a roar that reverberated across the box canyon and every Shak'Tar in the valley turned to face my guys. The clearing before the gate was full of Shak'Tar.

I launched myself out into the air as the world slowed to a crawl.

Chapter 33

As I sailed through the air, I drew from the Source and opened all of the weapons at my disposal. I needed time to open a shield around the prison, and my guys weren't inside yet. I can't offer to be allies and leave them to die.

The time I would need was swiftly dwindling away so, as Prada had so eloquently put it, I made some shit up.

Much as I had done in Montana, I formed a Lash. There were so many Shak'Tar down there I didn't think a simple emotion would do so I used everything that made me who I am. I used my joy and my sorrows, my hate and my love, my honor and duty, everything that made me who I am. All of that nestled inside a great big nest of rage.

As I landed directly in front of Gorvelis and his men, unleashing a roar of my own, I launched my Lash with every ounce of my being.

I could see the effects of that lash roll through all of the Shak'Tar. It blasted through their Souls like a savage wind. I could almost see pieces of their Souls blasted away.

That wave rolled across them all, and reached the huge Kresh and the five others that followed him.

I swear there was a force to that Lash. I saw pieces of their Souls seem to shatter from the power. It was one of the most exhilarating moments I had ever had, and one of the most terrifying. No one should be able to do things like that to another being's Soul.

Everything simply seemed to stop as the effects of my Lash rolled through.

The huge Kresh grabbed his head with his hands and screamed. I could feel him as well as see the utter terror he felt, and the rage and hate he felt for me. He began to shake all over, and fell to his knees. With great roars of rage, he smashed his head into the ground, over and over. Then he stopped and looked directly into my eyes as he brought his clawed hand toward his face.

I could see the unbridled hatred in his Soul as he ripped his own throat out.

"What the hell?" I muttered.

Like a wave a movement began across the Shak'Tar. All of them dropped to their knees. The wave didn't stop there, the other Kresh that had followed the Farrara'Ti knelt, as well.

I turned around to find Gorvelis, and the others kneeling behind me. Gorvelis' shoulders shook, and I thought he was weeping but his head came up and the tears were from the laughter he was barely holding inside. As he saw the utter confusion on my face, he couldn't hold it back any longer, and his laughter rolled through the silence.

"You have no idea what you just did," he asked after a moment, "do you?"

I shook my head, slowly. I was still stunned because I could feel them all now. I could feel the Shak'Tar. I could feel the Kresh behind them, and I could feel seventy three Romanians from inside the prison. I could not only see them, I could *feel* them.

"You have given us all your Mark," Gorvelis said as a stood back up.

He seemed to be examining something. Something from inside himself, and he was smiling. "It is a Mark that will be a joy to carry. The first Human Mark. No one has ever had the power to Mark other humans, much less a Kresh."

"I take it the fight is over?"

He laughed, "Very much over."

I clicked my coms, "Come on down guys, it seems there won't be a big fight, after all."

"Why do you sound so disappointed, Boss?"

"You'll just have to see it when you get down here."

I looked at Gorvelis, "Can you explain this to me, please?"

"The Kresh are telepathic," he said. "The way they establish authority is through their Mark. The Farrara'Ti are the only ones who can mark a Ma'Nar. The Ma'Nar marks his underlings with the Mark of its ruler, and the Mark passes down to the lowliest of the Kresh."

"The Farrara'Ti are the rulers of Kresh, and there are a limited number of them. Each Marks as many Ma'Nar as they can until their Mark weakens. The Farrara'Ti over there was Sol'Kor'Vanas. He ruled five Rash'Tar, Life Clans and the Shak'Tar, or Night Clan."

I nodded slowly as the words he was saying began to sink in.

"Are you shittin' me?" I asked, "I just took his clans?"

"We are all yours to command," he nodded toward the Kresh'Ma'Nar near the gate, "including them. The second they return through the gate, your Mark will spread down through the ranks, and they will all be your Clan."

"Holy shit," I muttered.

"What the Hell do I do with five hundred telepathic assassins?"

"Five hundred?" he asked, "You are now the master of all the Shak'Tar. The second we enter the gate your Mark will spread from us as well. We are all yours, and we are ready to do your bidding."

I stood there as all of this was registering. The link has to go both ways, my honor demanded it. I can't just let my own responsibility to them be denied. If what he said was the truth, and according to my Sight, it was, then I'm responsible for their well-being as much as I have the right to receive their loyalty.

In a split second I had become the Liege Lord of God only knows how many Demons, and an unknown amount of telepathic humans. Why does everything have to be so complicated?

Rictor came around the corner of the prison followed closely by Lyrica and the Mages filed into the clearing. Rictor looked at the kneeling Shak'Tar, and then his eyes landed on the kneeling Demonmages.

He looked back at me with one eyebrow raised. I shrugged.

"Can't take you anywhere," muttered Kharl as he took in the strange sight.

Lyrica shook her head, "Well *I* just brought home a dog."

***

"You're sayin' this Mark is a template for others to mold themselves into?" asked Ric.

"Exactly," Gorvelis answered. "Not a forced match, it's what each one of us knows the Master wants. The Mark is everything the Master wants us to be."

"And you used yourself as this template?" he asked me.

"I didn't know that's what it was when I did it."

"Can you imagine thousands more of him?" Prada asked. "That's just crazy."

"Friggin' insane," Ric answered.

"Hey, I'm standing right here," I complained.

"At least it's not forced on them to be another him," Kharl said.

"Thank God," Daphne Cavanaugh said.

"Right here," I said, "I'm right here."

Lyrica's musical laughter brought the smile to my face as I heard it.

"In all seriousness, Boss," Ric said, "Have you got any idea what you want to do here?"

I had spent the last day talking with both the Shak'Tar and the Kresh'Ma'Nar. When they go back through the Gate the countdown would begin. My Mark would spread through the Rash'Tar that currently controlled the Gates to Earth. But within days, those clans would be attacked by the others as abominations. I could only think of one solution to that issue. I would have to send them to Kel'Sin'Deres. He was the closest thing to a human I had seen from the Kresh.

My new Clans would be much closer to human as my "template" spread throughout the clan, and I had no idea where that would really go in the end. Perhaps the fact that his bloodline is mine, and his closer resemblance to what I would call human would be enough for him to protect the five clans.

I couldn't keep them here. When the Gate closed it would sever their Streams and they would die. I didn't have the forces to go through and hold the Gate facility from the attack of a whole world's population.

"The Kresh will go to Kel'Sin'Deres," I said. "I'm really not sure what to do with the Shak'Tar."

"Let me take them back through the Gate," Gorvelis said. "We will spread your Mark throughout the fifteen worlds, and remove the Shak'Tar from the control of the Kresh. We will begin the revolution."

There was an iron conviction to him. This is what he'd waited all those years. A chance to fight the tyrannical masters he'd been forced to serve all of his life.

"So be it," I nodded and he stood proudly.

It was five hours later when we watched the last of the Shak'Tar approach the Gate.

Gorvelis stopped in front of me, "We'll make you proud, Sir."

"Don't get killed," I said. "A dead freedom fighter finds no victory. And don't try to come back through this Gate. It won't be a very good place to step into."

He nodded, "I will send word through other portals when opportunity allows."

"Good luck," I said and shook his hand.

He stepped through the Gate. Dun'Fil'Resaf approached.

"We will do as you have commanded," his voice was part growl and part speech, "This alliance you suggest is not something done by Kresh but Kel'Sin'Deres is not a normal Kresh. He is different, and we will do this. The only other choice is death of our Rash'Tar."

"Show him all that happened here," I said, "and give him a message from the Rash'Tor'Ri. Tell him I said 'Protect my Rash'Tar as if they were your own...Grandfather'."

I said the last word bitterly. He was the cause of so much of the pain in my life, but he was also one of the sources of my bloodline. And he was different from the others. Maybe he would be different enough that they would survive.

With a nod the Kresh turned, and walked through the Gate followed by the other four.

As the last one disappeared I heard Reyna, "Never, in all my days, would I have thought I would see such as this."

"The lad as a way of stirrin' things up in a new way," Flynn returned.

"Now," I said, "we close this Gate for good."

"How do ya propose we do that?" Rictor asked.

"Oh, now we're going back to plan A."

It took another hour to get everyone out to the ridgeline in front of the Facility. My new Romanian subjects, included. I wish they hadn't been affected but they were and I am responsible for them now. It's something I'll have to figure out after we leave here.

"You ready?" I asked Lyrica.

"You've tested this?"

As my memories flashed back, she laughed. Apparently, it was quite humorous to see me blow myself off the top of a mountain in Tennessee.

She began forming a massive shield somewhat like a cupped hand. I did the same thing with one that looked like the opposite hand. They were huge shields but they weren't solid. We pushed them into the mountainside on each side of the complex.

We each had ten Mages crowded in close. They placed hands on us to be support if we needed it. The shields were now in place.

"Set?" I asked.

"Yep," she answered.

"Pull," I ordered.

Three hundred Mages Pulled from the Source. They felt that Pull back in Kansas, Paige had told me after we had returned home.

Half of the Mages had steered their Pull to the spot where I would take it, and the other half to where Lyrica would use it.

Together we poured the power down the huge tendrils with which we had fed our shields. The shield flared with power, and it surged down into the earth to fill the area inside the shield. It was solid rock.

I had found that this would have a very explosive result some years back.

Nothing happened for a moment after we stopped and Reyna said, "That was a little anti-climactic. I thought it..."

It felt like the whole Earth lurched as the two sides of the mountain slammed together and about a million tons of mountain fell on the Gateway.

"Madre de Dios," Reyna said.

"Sian ger han Deros," muttered one of the three remaining Shak'Tar. I don't know what it meant but it sounded a lot like what Reyna had said. Mother of God.

Chapter 34

"I told you to be careful with that particular skill," Paige said.

"I know," I said. "I had no idea what I was doing, and seventy-three people are messed up afterwards. You can't berate me any more than I already do myself. It's something I'll never do again. And these people will be taken care of for life. I doubt I could feel worse than I already do."

She still wasn't happy but she didn't say more about it.

"I have some other news for you," she said, "Your pet Senator tried to escape, and he left three Guards in the Psych ward."

I sat forward quickly and I felt the rage begin to build.

"I'll take care of him," I said. "He was warned."

"No need," she said. "He ran into Kevin and I as he was leaving. Those mental attacks are awful. I was unconscious almost immediately. When I came to, Kevin was holding me, and the Senator was dead. I asked Kevin what happened. He said 'The fool tried to use fear on me.' The Senator went nuts after we asked him what it meant to be marked, after the report you sent in to me. I wanted to know the effects this was going to have on those people. We're all responsible for them, not just you. The Soulguard will help them, as well."

And I thought I couldn't feel worse.

"I'll take a look at the Guards in the Psych ward," I said. "Maybe there's something I can do to help them. I have three of the Shak'Tar with me, and they know more about these types of attacks than anyone. Maybe I can fix, at least, this part of my mess."

"Your skills removed the Shak'Tar, and actually turned hundreds of thousands of Kresh into allies, Colin. There is an up side to this thing. That is a great accomplishment. It's just that with most great accomplishments, there is a great price. This one is paid by seventy three innocent Romanians."

I had found that these Romanians were farmers, and that their families had been captured by the Shak'Tar and the Kresh. Their farms were destroyed, and many family members had already been killed. They had nowhere to go when we left the base in Romania. I brought them back with us.

The Mark didn't make them completely change who they were, but it placed my imprint forever in their minds. They know me like I had been with them forever. The children would run to me as if I was their father, the older ones treated me as if I was a long-lost friend. All of them were from many different families, yet, they were one family now. My Mark made them pull into one family as if they had always been one.

There were benefits for them when this occurred. All of them had lost family and friends but now they had more to lean on. There were ten children who had no one left at all, and they were pulled into this family as if they had always been there.

No matter how much good my Mark does these people, it was put on them without their consent, and I will have to pay for what I did. Because there was harm done as well. They aren't exactly who they were, and it all boiled down to the fact of consent. They may be in better shape than the Kresh would have left them but it wasn't my right to force it on them, however unwittingly.

"Where are your wayward Romanians?" she asked.

I know where they are at all times, I can feel them. Another part of the Mark that I have discovered.

Just as I can feel them, they can unerringly point out where I am.

"Wichita, for now," I said, "I asked them what they would want to do now, and the majority of them want to farm as they did before. Several of the younger men and women want to join the Guard, as well as several of the older ones. Three of them were soldiers in their youth, and have a good bit of experience."

"And your plans?"

"I had Warren buy a big chunk of land in Oklahoma. It's close enough to here that I can go there pretty regularly, and it's far enough away to be out of immediate danger when they come through the Gate. This knocked a big hole in my fortune but there's enough to set them up nicely. The ones who want to join the Guard will have to pass the testing as any other has to. If they pass I'll sign off on them to join and put them in training."

"It sounds as if you have things in hand there," she said, "but you have to be careful with this telepathy you have. Things could have been so much worse than they turned out."

"I know, believe me, I know."

***

"They love you," Lyrica said.

We watched as Talib Yarrow inspected the new tractor that had just been delivered. Children ran in circles around us yelling. I couldn't understand what they were saying but they were very exuberant.

"They didn't really have a choice in that, now, did they?" I replied.

"We are in a far better place than where those monsters intended for us to end up," a voice came from behind us.

I turned to find Terena Isora standing behind us. She was the closest thing to a leader the Romanians had. While they were in the prison, she was the glue that had held them together, and afterwards she became somewhat of a Matriarch to the seventy three members of my new "family".

"One form of slavery is much the same as another," I muttered.

"One thing that has been made quite clear to us is the fact that we can go or do as we please. We choose to stay together, and we choose to consider you as our leader, whether you like it or not. If there is one thing that we know it is that you are a good man, and one worthy of the loyalty we choose to give."

"How do you know that doesn't come from the Mark?" I asked. "Would you feel the same if things had been different?"

"We would have stayed together because we all lost a great deal inside that place. We saw loved ones slaughtered and eaten. Children left without their parents. What you did gave us a reason to live on instead of giving up. You see it as a violation of our rights, perhaps our minds?"

I nodded.

"We feel that you have set us free from the despair that comes from the loss of so much. Yes, we are a little different than before. But Romanians have always been believers in family, and we are no different. We lost our families and you have given us all another one. We owe you a great debt for what you have given us, and we will repay this by helping you in any way we can. Our warriors are your warriors, our farmers are your farmers, and our children are your children."

I really didn't know what to say or even what to think so I did the best I could.

"I just hope I can prove worthy of what your people offer," I said.

"When I close my eyes, I can see you there," she said with a smile. "We already know you are worthy. You just have to come to understand that yourself."

"We've been trying to tell him that for years," Lyrica said. "He'll figure it out one day."

Terena smiled and turned to walk away, "There will be a Feast and a dance tonight as a celebration of the second home to be finished. You both will attend?"

"We wouldn't miss it for the world," Lyrica said.

It seems that seventy or so people can build houses at an astonishing rate. Three weeks after we had come back from Romania and the third house was begun. It helped that the materials were readily available. I was told that the planting season would still be several months away so they were concentrating on getting homes for all of them built.

It's nice to be a part of building something instead of destroying them. Lyrica and I spent a couple of days in those three weeks here helping build homes. It was quite relaxing and I could almost see myself as a carpenter in another life.

Chapter 35

"What about a link from our streams to yours?" Cristof Damaris asked.

We were trying to come up with a way for them to support me when I needed it. It was a bit crowded when ten Mages were trying to reach me at one time.

"That may just work," I said.

"Also we would not be constrained by the distance," Adaya Tovah added.

Cristof had come in from Greece with his squad of Guards and Adaya was an Israeli Mage. There were also Alexei Rostov from Russia, Alec Brighton from Australia, and Asante Xhosa from Nigeria in Africa. Each had brought their own squad of ten Guards. Flynn had brought together this Company from all over the world. Reyna was from Argentina, Stone came from England, Yueh from China, and Flynn from Scotland. Prada, also had a squad, and Rictor was in command of the whole lot. He was very familiar with this position, anyway, much like he had been as a Guard Captain. He was second in command under myself.

"If I build the links and we put a portal at your end, then you can keep from being hit by the drain at a bad time. It might just work," I said. "Shall we experiment a little?"

"I bet I know who the test subject gets to be," Rictor grumbled.

"Of course," I returned, looking at Prada, "You know how much he likes to try new stuff."

"It's a shame you're not throwing him out of a plane," she said.

"Still harpin' on that?" Rictor asked, "I swear, it never ends. Throw someone out of a plane, one time, and you never hear the end of it."

Adaya laughed, "I have heard some others talking of this. I must say you have a novel approach to bypassing orders.'

"Never start a mission without a plan to circumvent stupid orders that should never have been given," Rictor said. "No tellin' when you're gonna need to do it. Always keep some sort of backup plan in mind."

Rostov chuckled, "It was a serious lack of planning on your part when you chose a woman to throw out of the plane, Friend. I have found that men will forgive much faster than a woman. They hold grudges forever."

"So true," Rictor agreed. "All right, Boss, let's get to it. Experiment away."

I built a hollow tendril that sprouted from my back to fasten on the side of Rictor's Stream. A rush of power from his stream ran through me as if my Stream had grown again.

"I felt that," he said, "My stream feels smaller."

I built the portal on his end of the tendril and closed it.

"That's better," he said.

"I just put the portal in," I said, "Let me light it up for a minute so you can see where it is."

As I lit up his stream and mine, I felt power flow up my Stream into me. No huge torrents, just a gentle flow. He located the portal and opened it. A flow of power ran down the tendril to me as my body sucked it up to hold the streams visible. I shut it off.

"Now, close it," I said.

He concentrated for a second and the flow stopped, "Got it."

"I think we just solved the problem with supporting."

I looked back toward Cristof. He was a short, dark haired man with a dark complexion. His aura was showing that he was impressed.

"'E tends to do tings fairly quick when the idea starts," Flynn said with a laugh, "'Ow close do ye 'ave to be for the link ta work?"

"Head out from me, Ric," I said, "I think the link will stretch out."

He started across the field and the link didn't break. It stretched farther and farther. As he kept going, the link was getting smaller.

"I think it'll stay but the closer you are, the stronger the link," I said while keying my throat mike.

"Got it."

I turned back to the others, "This is another of those volunteer things. You can pull out of the unit at any time. This is probably going to be standard for this company though."

"You specified open minds," Adaya returned, "so go ahead."

I repeated the link like I had made to Ric with the same results. I placed it in the exact position I had used with Ric.

"I'll try to get it in the same position on each of you. So it's easy to remember where it is."

"I'll go next," Reyna stated and stepped forward.

One after another, they all stepped forward for the link. The last was Alec Brighton and he had reservations. He was slow to make up his mind, and I didn't have to be a mind reader to know why. He took a dislike to me from the beginning. I'm not sure why but it was there, nonetheless. After a moment, he stepped forward and did as the rest.

"Alec," I said before making the link, "Do you have some sort of problem with me? I don't expect everyone to like me, but I feel there's something more with you."

"I'm not here to like you," he said, "But I have to trust you. And I'm having a bit of trouble with that."

I appreciated his honesty. He knew I could tell if he lied to me so he didn't bother. All of them knew what I could see in their auras. Emotions, memories and truth.

Rictor's aura flooded with anger and Prada's was much the same. I held my hand up toward them before anything could be said.

"Can you tell me why?" I asked, "Trust is the most important thing with a unit like this. If it's not there, then we'll fail."

He was quiet for a moment, and I could see the war of emotions in his aura, "I had a friend when I first joined the Soulguard. His name was Ramirez. He was killed by these Shak'Tar bastards. These bastards that you let walk back into a portal free and clear."

I was surprised. But I guess it was a reasonable complaint. I'd kept my DNA issues out of the common knowledge of most, but, if I was to ask them to trust me I would have to trust them as well.

"Luis was a close friend to me, as well, Alec. You have no idea how much it pained me to hear of his loss. But these Shak'Tar aren't the same people they were before our trip to Romania," I said, "I have my secrets and I don't suppose I could ask for your trust and not give you mine."

"You even brought three of the bastards back with you," he said bitterly, "How can you say you're a friend of Luis and ally yourself with the ones who killed him?"

"I guess we should start with the day I was born," I said, "My mother managed to kill fourteen soldiers who had entered our home. She did this while in labor with me. During the battle, she was wounded badly and some of the Kresh blood got into her bloodstream and, through the umbilical cord, into the unborn child-into me. She died that night after my father had returned, and I was left in the care of his two most trusted Guards."

He was staring at me with utter astonishment rolling through his aura. I think he expected an excuse. This was a lot farther from his expectations than he was expecting.

"You've all been briefed on the Shak'Tar. They were experimental subjects raised by Kresh to be used against humans. They have the DNA of the Kresh inside them, and it gives them a degree of telepathy like the Kresh. I also have that DNA, and the telepathy that comes with it. But I was raised by Kharl Jaegher and Kyra Nightwing, not Kresh. And I most certainly was not raised to be used against humans."

"What happened in Romania was as much a surprise to me as it was to them. I'm still discovering what I can do with the telepathy, and I did something while I was there that I cannot ever do again. I altered the minds of all of the Shak'Tar, all of the Kresh that were there, and even the Humans in their prison. They aren't the same people they were before that Mark I put on them. You ask how I can ally myself with Luis's killers?"

"After what I did to them, I can't do any different than I have done. I'm responsible for them all now. I don't know how far the Mark would push them to do as I ordered but I think, if I ordered one of them to do it, he would walk into fire and burn. What terrifies me is that he would do it happily if I asked it. What else am I supposed to do?"

All of them watched with different reactions to what I had said. Rictor showed no surprise and neither did Prada. Flynn wasn't surprised much, I think he had figured out quite a bit of it already. Len Yueh didn't show anything. His aura was behind that shield like his brother, Tien had around his. I couldn't see the emotions or memories in his aura because of it.

The rest of them had various emotions rolling through their auras. It would take a little while for some of them to accept what I had said, and there may be a few vacancies in the company. It might be hard to accept that the man you are following is part Demon.

"I had my suspicions after what happened in Romania," Reyna said, "After we found out about the Shak'Tar and their DNA, it was a small step to realizing that anyone who could do what you did there had to have the same."

"Some people have known for years and it's hard to fight what lives inside me. I'll understand completely if any of you want to resign from this unit. There'll be no repercussions if you choose to do so. Take the evening to think about the decision. We can't function without trust."

I turned and walked away. I hoped none of them chose to leave. I could see some real promise in these Mages. I really wanted this to work out but if not, I knew two hundred or so Mages who would follow me into hell. It would be disappointing if they chose to leave, but I would be damned if it would stop me from being prepared to fight this war when the Kresh returned.

Chapter 36

"You think any of them will leave?" I asked.

"I doubt it," Ric answered. "They're Soulguard and they're the best of the best. After they think about it a bit, they'll come to the same conclusions as we did. You showed us what's inside you in Knoxville. Did anyone request transfers? If anything, it made us appreciate the willpower you have to keep that under control."

We were sitting near the practice field, watching the new trainees do weapon training. Irenia Jaegher seemed to be the center of attention. That's not hard for her to do. She's probably the most beautiful woman I have ever seen. Worthington had been a beautiful woman before the burns, but her Soul had been hideous. Irenia's Soul was as beautiful as she was.

Dietrich may not have told the girl about the Soulguard, but he'd taught her how to fight. With her knot in place, she was hell on wheels in the practice ring.

"I know Flynn will be ok," I said, "I think the others will too, except maybe, Brighton."

"He'll be there, Boss," he said. "Damn that girl is good."

"I know. I haven't met a Jaegher yet who isn't. Seems like it's a family business."

"True."

"Hey, when Reyna first showed up, she said she'd met you once before. Back when you were a lowly Marine. Got me wondering a little, so, what happened?"

He was quiet for a moment as I saw memories of a jungle flashing through his aura, "It was back in '68. My company was stationed in Laos. We ran across a village that was completely empty but there was blood everywhere. There were a lot of atrocities in that war but this looked bad. We trailed the force that had done it for a day and a half."

"They were leadin' us deep into the jungle, and the Captain figured they were playin' with us. Somethin' just didn't seem right about 'em. They hit us out of the darkness. They moved so fast, we only saw shadows. Over about three hours, they destroyed a whole company of Marines. We got a few, and when we saw what they were, we knew we were in trouble. They weren't human."

"There were only fifteen of us left when the jungle lit up off to our left. She walked out of the jungle and it looked like she was on fire. Behind her came twenty men, and women with swords of flame. It was the kind of thing I expected to see if I was losing my mind. It really pissed off the forces that were hittin' us. They came out of the shadows quick."

"You can imagine what we witnessed after that. Soulguards are impressive to normal people, and I was very impressed. After all was said and done, all fifteen survivors of my company became Soulguard. Been tryin' to kill all of the Demon bastards ever since."

"I see," I said. "I guess we all have something like that in our past."

"Just about all of the Guard came from that sort of thing," Ric said. "These new Guards will be different. In some respects, better, some not. They'll fight like soldiers, but they have families and friends who they'll return to eventually. They'll serve shorter terms, and they'll want to go home. I can't say that's a bad thing."

"True enough," I said. "They have people they fight to protect. Most of us fight for the memory of people. I never met my parents, but I fight for their memory. My true family is the Guard. I have nothing else."

"It's the same for me, Boss. The Guard's all the family I got," he said. "Things are gonna be different from here on out."

"That's what I told Paige the other day," I said. "Of course it's gonna mean a whole new thing when you say veteran after this. Over time there's gonna be a lot of people who don't work directly for us anymore, and yet have the power they gain from the knot. There's a lot that we need to work with in dealing with that. But that's something Paige has to worry about. We only need to worry about several million Kresh bent on destroying our race."

"Oh, is that all?"

"Yeah, we'll leave the big decisions to the Archmage."

He laughed and gripped my shoulder, "We'll take care of the little things then."

"Yep."

***

"What was he like?" I asked Dietrich.

We sat at a table at the Hooters in Wichita, once again. It seemed to be our unofficial meeting place now. Every week a group of Soulguards would descend on the place, and try to eat all the food. They tried to convince the girls to go home with them as well. Some had been successful, like Jacobs. But mostly, the girls who worked there were immune to the advances of soldiers and Soulguards. They had to be to still be there, I suppose.

"Merlin?" he said, "Honestly, no one knew much about his personal life. He was one scary bastard, though. When I met him, he was close to nine hundred years old. He would say things that sounded ridiculous to most folks about things that had happened so long ago. But then we would meet a Demon army in the field, and he would blow up the world around us. I've seen some pretty impressive displays of power in my life, but he was at the top. Our world was small, we knew there was more, we just couldn't get to it all. I think he had gone to places most of us had just dreamt of."

"I guess you could cover a lot of the world in nine hundred years," I said.

"No doubt. He was fond of something I saw you do on some video footage. The huge vortex of power you held over the field in Kansas. He would do that, and just rip giant gouts of fire down onto their heads. If we'd been there when they came for Kent, things would have been different. Kent was awesome by himself, but, together they were something totally different. I saw them destroy an army of Demons together. We were just there to feed them power. They left the ground so hot it was flowing like water. It was beautiful and the most terrifying thing I have ever seen."

"It's hard to believe they could send something over here that could kill one of them. But they had something and they used it. There was nothing left after that day, only the Guards who weren't there. We started over and Merlin disappeared. For a while I couldn't understand his leaving. But a hundred years ago or so I did the same."

"I was tired. I'd spent so long killin' and fightin', and my stubborn son decided he had to join the Soulguard too. I left and then I heard he had died with some Mage they called the Demonkiller, and I swore never to return."

"Then I started a war," I said, "And another of your stubborn kids was gonna run off and join the Soulguard."

He looked down the table at Kharl, who was laughing at something Jacobs had said, "I'm not gonna make that mistake again. Never let your pride make you leave the one's you care for, Boy. Sometimes there ain't a miracle that can bring them back to you."

***

My office door opened, and I saw Alec Brighton standing in the entrance.

"I'll never really trust them, the Shak'Tar," he said, "but I'll give you my loyalty. I've spent the last week talking to every person I could find about you. What you did out there, tying yourself to the Source. You didn't expect to survive that, did you?"

"No," I said, "but my Guard would survive. That was enough for me."

"And that's why I'll follow you."

"Thank you, Alec."

He nodded and turned away. I watched his Soul as he walked down the hall. There was one thing that truly bothered me about how the Guard has given me so much loyalty. Was I forcing it on them with the telepathy, or did they truly follow of their own free will. Alec helped in dispelling that worry. He chose to follow. I had stayed away from the company as they decided. I wanted to be sure I wasn't affecting them by being there.

Over the last few days, they had all come and given me their decisions. All of them stayed. Alec was the last of them to come see me. I could see his point with the Shak'Tar. I had a serious hate for them myself. But when I Marked them, I became responsible for them. It wasn't their choice, and I could have just killed them, but they looked to me for direction now.

And after the explanations, I felt there was no choice. The Shak'Tar were still out there killing humans, and if I sent them back across, that would stop. No choice at all, really. I'm not sure my oath to protect humanity can just cover those on my own world. There are fourteen other worlds of humans out there, and they were under the rule of the Kresh. That's unacceptable, and I will cross into their worlds one day.

Then I will end their rule.

Chapter 37

They hit New York in November. It was the biggest catastrophe ever seen by that huge city. Right in the center of Broadway and 174th street, a portal opened and Demons charged through. Other portals formed nearby at several intersections. They poured through the portals for some time before the National Guard and the Soulguard could get anywhere near the place. It was estimated that there were close to five thousand Demons loose in the largest city in the U.S.

They poured into the congested population of New York, and killed everything they could find. It was absolute chaos.

It was 8:45 PM when our plane landed at LaGuardia. My company exited the plane to be met by a Military Liaison.

"Sir," he said, "we need to get your men over the river, and to the staging ground in Central Park."

I looked at the map in my hands, "You got enough helicopters to get us all over there?"

"No sir," he said, "We'll have to take three trips."

"We'll get there faster on the run," I said and turned to Rictor.

"Ric, we're hittin' this Parkway," I said, pointing at the map, "at a run. Form everyone up."

"You're going to what?!" the Liaison asked.

I looked back at him, and my rage must have been very close to the surface because he stepped back quickly, and tripped to fall on his backside. I reached down and pulled him to his feet.

"Take more NG's on the Helos. We'll get there faster on foot," I said.

I didn't have time to explain better than that.

"Ready, Boss," Rictor said behind me.

I turned and the world slowed as I shot across the runway at seventy five miles per hour. I leapt the fence with one Soullord, eleven Mages, and a hundred Guards hot on my heels. Traffic was backed up on the parkway, but it didn't even slow us as we ran across the tops of cars in the heavy congestion. We followed that road through several name changes until we reached the turn toward the bridge. I had wanted to return to New York someday, but it definitely was not under these circumstances. I could only imagine the death toll already. I cringed and poured on more speed. Traffic on the Robert F. Kennedy Bridge was completely stopped, and people were pouring across the bridge on foot.

We hit the top of vehicles once again, and never slowed down. On the other side of the bridge, it was much the same so we ran across cars and leapt to open areas. Once we even launched ourselves to the top of a building to get past the crowds of people trying to escape to the other side of the East River. We stayed on Martin Luther King until 8th Ave where we headed south.

The staging area was in the big open area at the Northwest corner of the park, Cathedral Parkway. I could see the darkness of Demons to our Northeast, and the rage was clawing at the walls.

We reached the mass of soldiers before the first helicopter made it. I stopped in front of a surprised soldier.

"Where's HQ, Private?"

"The big tent there in the center," he said quickly.

He had already met a few Soulguards this day, and our speed hadn't affected his response time.

"Thank you, Private," I glanced down, "Swann."

"Ric, Lyrica, with me," I looked to the others, "I'll be back with targets in a moment. I'd suggest looking over your maps for the time being."

I headed to the central tent where a guard stood outside, "Colin Rourke, Soulguard."

"Go ahead, Sir."

I entered to find several Officers arguing over the map stretched across the table. One of them looked up, and I recognized General Gasper.

"Good!" he exclaimed as he saw me. "Welcome, Mister Rourke. Welcome indeed."

"What's our situation, General?" I asked.

"It's bad, Colin," he said and pointed at the map, "They showed up here, and we got slaughtered in there. This is part of the densest population in the whole city. Your guys and the NG's have the top along 181st pretty well stitched up, but they poured south killing everyone they find. There's still more pouring through those damn portals, and there are thousands of people in these areas. Last report says the Kresh are into Harlem already, and they're destroying anything they can."

"Where are our lines?"

"Across 138th. They're stayin' to the roads, so we set up in intersections to hold them. Damn these bastards are tough."

"That they are," I agreed. "OK I'll put my guys along 138th at the intersections, and start advancing to the North. We need everyone we can get pulling people out of the occupied territory. I can't open up with innocents in the line of fire. We clean this area of civilians, and we'll bring hell down on the bastards. You get any information you think I need, we're on frequency 32 on the coms."

"Got it," He said. "Good luck, Colin."

I left the tent with my whole body vibrating. I'd been waiting to get at the bastards for nearly two years, and my walls around the monster inside me were getting thin.

"You heard the man, Ric," I said. "I want our guys on that line, and I want them working North to pull people out. Lyrica, you're with me."

"They have injured here," she started.

"I need you on the top of a building," I said. "I need to know when this area here is clear of humans."

I was pointing at the area that was about the center of the island about halfway between the two lines of NG's and Guards.

"This is the kill box," I said, "When I give the order, I want everything we have hitting right here."

She looked at me with narrowed eyes. There's nothing slow about that woman's mind.

"Just how are we going get them into this 'kill box'?"

"They'll be going there soon," I said. "They'll have an irresistible urge to go there."

I could see she was pissed.

"It's the only thing they want more than to slaughter the human race."

"What the hell are you saying?" Prada asked from behind me.

"He's going to be bait," Lyrica said with a snarl.

"Now I want everyone on that line," I ordered, and turned away from the worried faces of three of the people I cared about most in this world, "so let's get this done."

With that I headed back North along 8th avenue. The Mages and Guards followed silently, and when we reached the lines where the National Guardsmen had fortified the intersection, Rictor started barking orders.

Each Mage went either right or left to join the NG's at the other intersections.

"I need you here, Ric," I said, "You need to run things from here, and me and Lyrica are heading North. She'll be on that tallest building there. She can steer you guys to pockets of civilians to pull out."

"You're determined to do this?" he asked.

"I don't see any other way, Ric."

"At least take a squad of Guards with you."

"They're all needed on the line," I said, "Don't worry about me, I can outrun them if I need to."

"I wouldn't know," he said, "because I've never seen you run from them."

I chuckled, "True enough. I will if I need to."

The "kill box" was the area between 145th and 149th streets, hopefully between Broadway and St. Nicholas. I intended to try to get them to focus on that area in an attempt to limit the casualties from this point out. Right then they were scattered from 138th to 180th Streets all across the island. The bridges were all closed off but the Kresh weren't trying to cross them anyway. They were satisfied in the crowded areas of Hamilton Heights and Washington Heights. They had gotten into the northern-most parts of Harlem before the NG's had established the lines where we were now passing.

Lyrica and I leapt over the NG's and headed into the war zone. I pointed to the left at the tallest building I had seen.

"That one should do it," I said.

She grabbed my arm as I was turning toward the darkness I could see ahead of me. I turned and she was abruptly right there, close. Our lips met and she kissed me. There was a surge of something through my entire being, and I really didn't want to stop, but duty called. We parted and there was a smile on her face that I know was mirrored in my own.

"Please, be careful," she said softly.

"I'll do my best," I said, "You watch yourself, too."

I nodded toward the building, "Let me know when you're set on the top."

"OK," she returned and ran toward the building.

She didn't bother entering the place, she just went straight up the wall in a flash, reminding me a good bit of another comic book hero I loved as a kid. He scaled walls with ease, and swung through New York on strands of webbing.

I smiled at her, and turned toward the area I had chosen. Then I leapt forward, and scaled a building side as she had. In moments I was leaping from roof top to roof top.

Chapter 38

Just south of 145th Street I saw two groups of Souls. One was a cluster of probably seventy that had fortified themselves at the intersection of 144th and Amsterdam, right at the edge of the "kill box". They seemed to be all right at the moment. The other was a small group of Souls in an alley a little ways to the East of the others. There were the dark ugly Souls of Kresh near them. I leapt across another gap to close on these. I hoped I could get there in time.

"I'm set on the roof," Lyrica's voice said over the coms. "Andrea, one block north, take a left and the second building on the right has about twenty people in it."

"Got it."

"Alec," she said, "the building straight in front of you has a group hiding in the basement. There are some Kresh scattered through the area around the corner. It looks like a lot more heading toward you from the East."

"On it."

She continued steering the others toward targets, but I didn't have time to really pay attention to the others. I had come within sight of my own target. My eyes crossed the scene in an instant.

What I saw in the alley was a young black woman holding one child, perhaps two years old. Huddled behind her were four others that looked to range between seven or eight and three.

Facing down the alley toward them was a Soldier Demon. Just behind him were the crumpled remains of seven Lesser Demons. Standing directly in front of the Soldier, surrounded by discarded weapons, presumably empty, stood six and a half feet of concentrated violence.

That's what the man's Soul looked like to me. Concentrated violence. In his right hand was a gleaming blade. Apparently, this man had already killed seven Demons before the Soldier arrived. But no normal human would stand a chance against a Soldier.

All of this I had registered in my mind in an instant. The next instant, I was airborne once more.

The Kresh pointed toward the woman.

"Mine," It hissed and without a word, the man moved.

He was fast, maybe the fastest person I had ever met who wasn't a Guard. The Soldier stepped away from the blade, and started to laugh. That's when the sword I had hurled as I leapt, slammed into its side.

The Demon was slammed right down to the pavement, where my sword pinned it for the half second it took for me to land right behind my sword. My fist ripped through its neck, and its head flew from its body in a gush of Demon blood.

I turned to find the man right beside me, ready to plant the knife if needed.

"Hi," I offered, "can you tell me where the nearest Starbuck's is located?"

He looked at me with one eyebrow raised. I seem to find that look everywhere I go. I'm beginning to think it might be me.

"Quite a ways south," he said in a deep voice.

I chuckled, "There's a group of people a couple of streets that way. They seem to be fortified in an intersection. If you guys will follow me, I'll make sure you get there safely."

He nodded and motioned toward the woman and the children. One of the little boys never looked anywhere but at the man. His eyes seemed glued to him.

I sheathed my swords, and stuck my hand out, "Colin Rourke."

"Khalib," the man said and grasped my hand. "This is Dreanna and... well, a bunch a kids."

"Let's get moving," I said and headed toward the end of the alley.

I saw a spot toward the left where a whole group of people had been literally torn to pieces, so I angled right to prevent the kids from seeing it. There was a great deal of blood through the streets, but most of the bodies were gone. Quite a few were just partially gone, and my rage kept clawing at the walls. These were my people, these were the people I had sworn to protect.

We rounded the corner to see to our south, a bunch of cars parked as a makeshift blockade. Atop the cars and behind them were crowded a group of people. I saw National Guard uniforms, police uniforms and a good many others who held guns at the ready.

"Friendlies incoming!" one of the Guardsmen yelled, and we headed for the cars.

As we crossed into the fortified area I heard one of the men who was probably a gang member.

"Check out that..."

"Shut up man," the guy beside him interrupted, "Dat's Mr. Khalib. I give you one guess who she is."

"Shit, man, you think he heard me?"

There was a genuine fear rolling through the fellow-more like terror.

I glanced toward Khalib, and caught the smile as he looked away from the two guys. After seeing the body count the man had left in the alley, I had a feeling the gang members had a right to be scared of the man.

I headed for the NG's, "What's our situation, boys?"

"Who are..." the first one said until he saw me closely, "Holy shit, you're the Soulguard guy."

"Colin Rourke," I introduced myself.

"Trevor Simms," he said, "Sir we got caught inside the zone. I hope the lines get back up here but, for now we're just trying to protect as many as we can. We got thirteen cops, twelve Guardsmen, and eighteen civilians who are armed. We can hold off small numbers of the damn things, but a serious group of em will tear us to hell."

"How many civilians?"

"Fifty seven unarmed civilians, Sir."

I clicked my coms, "I got a sizeable group of civilians close to the Box, here. Intersection of 144th and Amsterdam. If all goes right they'll be OK. I'm heading north from here in a short while to get their attention."

"Everyone is kinda pinned at the moment, Colin," Lyrica said. "You've got a big force heading down Amsterdam straight at you. Couple of hundred at least. I'm heading toward you."

"Negative, stay there until the box is clear."

I could imagine the grumbling she was probably doing right then.

"Copy," she said and I could hear the anger in her voice.

"Don't worry, we got this," I said.

I turned to the Guardsmen, "We got company inbound from the north. Everyone who has a gun needs to form up."

"Yes, Sir."

I headed back out where the cars had been parked, and grabbed the side of a Buick.

"Killed my friend," I muttered and flipped the car to the side, "Murdered all these innocent people," I slammed into a Chevy on the right and it flipped that direction.

I had cleared out a good sized area in front of the barricades well within range of the guns.

"Been waiting for this for two damn years," I said.

I could see them flooding down Amsterdam.

"Waiting for what?" Simms asked. He had followed me out.

I drew my swords and the Soulfire flowed across the blade, "My turn."

"Anything gets past me, shoot it...a lot."

"Y-Yes Sir." I think he had seen the horde coming down the street. He ran back to the lines giving orders.

Chapter 39

I walked forward, and they grew nearer and nearer, so I let the beast out of its cage, and rage washed over me. The lead Demon roared, and I roared right back. What I said didn't sound human. It was one word, in a language unknown to natives of my planet. It was a word that all Demons knew, and it was guaranteed to draw the attention of each and every one of them.

"Rash'Tor'Ri!" echoed through the street, and I saw the reactions of rage and hate as they heard it. I was surging forward, and I was amongst them. Then the Dance began. My blades were everywhere, and I blurred as I swept across the front of the packed Demons.

Once again, I came to realize that this is what I was made to do. It's the place where I can be free, where I don't have to cage a piece of myself or hide who I am. This is where I belong.

There were gunshots as the men behind me picked off several that had gotten past me. There were precious few of those, but there were some.

All too soon, they were gone. There was nothing around me but piles of dead bodies. I spent a full minute, standing there, coated in blood. It took that long to beat the monster back down and push it back into its cage.

"A-Are you ok, Sir?" Simms had returned to where I was. I turned to find him staring at me in terror. He was keeping it in check, but it was there. It was always there.

"I'm fine," I said looking around at the bodies, "but they're not."

I clicked my coms, "Lyrica, are there any hostiles between my position, and the lines directly south of us?"

"Not that I can see," she said, "They're to your north and east, for the most part."

"Ok, I'm sending a group of civilians back toward the lines. See if you can't steer some of the good guys toward them, please."

"And the other two groups of Kresh heading in your direction?"

"Two?"

"Yes, one from the north and one from the north east. Both about the size of the one you just had."

"Ok, we'll deal with 'em. Just steer the civilians out. I'm sending some Guardsmen with 'em. I'll get you the frequency in a sec."

"Copy."

I turned toward Simms, "We got more incoming, and we need to get these civilians out of harm's way. There's nothing between here, and the lines to the south. I need you guys to get these people out."

"Sir," he said, "You're going to need some backup. I'll send half my guys with the civilians. We'll stay and watch your back."

I stared at him for a moment. I could see the fear in his aura, but there was an iron core in him of duty and honor. He wasn't going to leave me here alone.

I nodded, "All right. Get 'em started."

I turned back to the body strewn street where I had met the last group. There was Demon blood running in the streets towards the storm drains. I felt a sort of satisfaction at the sight, then cringed as I felt that satisfaction. What kind of monster was I becoming?

I waded back to the center of the piles of bodies, and formed a shield wall on each side of me. It was about thirty feet long and ten feet high. Then with the strength of a Soulmage I slammed it to the sides and pushed everything up against the buildings on each side of me. I stepped forward and repeated the action to clear a decent sized swath of street for me to fight in.

I turned back to the lines to find Simms arguing with one of the gang members. As I approached they both shut up.

"What's the problem?" I asked.

"Some of the civilians won't leave, Sir."

The gang member stood straight, a steady look in his eye, "We ain't civilians, today."

"You want to stay?" I asked.

"My bro told me a long time ago how'ta survive on dese streets," He said, "He said ta find the baddest mutha in the city and stand behind him."

He looked at the piles of dead Demons up the street, "I think you be da baddest mutha in the city. And I plan ta stand behind you. We got yo back."

Funny how things work out. One day you're the lowest of the low, dregs of society in the eyes of a lot of people. The next you're standing on the firing line, protecting those same people who would have looked down on you from certain death. The world seems to have a way of setting things straight.

The other gang members were nodding and I saw several old men digging through the pile of weapons stacked in the center of the barricades. They both started checking loads and preparing the weapons like experts.

I saw memories flash through both their auras of a dark jungle and machine gun fire.

"You can take the Marine out of the fight, Sir," the closest one said, "You can't take the fight out of a Marine."

"Hoorah," the other one said without even looking up from the rifle he was prepping.

I smiled, "Hoorah."

I turned to Simms, "You heard 'em. They ain't civilians, today. Get the others movin'. The rest of you, get ready. We got two more groups heading our way, and I want these people heading to safety.

I walked toward the area I had cleared, "Simms, set to thirty. I'll have someone guiding you out."

I clicked my coms, "They'll be on thirty."

"Copy."

Simms relayed the information to another NG. I didn't think Simms was leaving. He had sent the other half with the civilians.

The civilians started heading down the street. Khalib pointed south and said something to the woman. She shook her head. He pointed toward the children, and she grudgingly agreed and headed south. The same little boy never took his eyes from Khalib as she herded them along with the others.

Khalib shook his head in wonder, and turned to set himself up behind a Buick. He saw me watching and nodded to me. I smiled and turned to the cleared area, drawing my swords.

"Same as before, boys and girls! If anything gets by me, shoot it a lot!"

I stepped to the center of the street as the Kresh poured into sight. There were more soldiers in this group, and there were probably four to five hundred of the bastards.

I let the beast back out of its cage, and I think I was actually laughing as I leaped into the air and landed in their midst.

"Rash'Tor'Ri!" echoed down the street as I roared my battle cry.

I tore into their ranks with a joy, I admit, and that scares the shit right out of me. No one should enjoy this as much as I do. For a while I just lost myself in the rage that filled my awareness. I heard gunfire as several made it past me, and I glanced right to see a soldier closing on my men. I hurled my left hand sword that slammed the soldier to the wall.

Another was right behind that one and I threw the right hand sword through its head. Weaponless, screaming in fury, I dove into the midst of that horde and ripped Kresh apart with my bare hands.

Then there were no more and I stood there in the midst of the carnage pushing the monster back down into its cage.

"That definitely got their attention, Colin," Lyrica said over the com. "Looks like your plan is gonna work. They're heading toward you from everywhere."

"Is the area clear?"

"The folks with you are the only ones left."

"Guards pull back," I ordered, "Mages to the front. I'm going north on Amsterdam. When you get inside the 'kill box' unload everything. Buildings can be repaired. No more innocents die today."

"We'll be closing from the north," A familiar voice sounded on the com.

"Hi Sam, how the hell are ya?"

"Better than I was. There are five Mages in the north and we'll follow suit."

"Good man," I said. "They should be concentrated between 145th and 149th soon. We're gonna try to contain 'em between Broadway and St. Nicholas avenue."

"I'm goin' out on a limb here and guess you used yourself as bait?"

"Seems to have worked," I said.

"Seems so, we're inbound."

"Copy."

I turned to Simms, "Once I head up this street, I want you guys moving South. I want you down past 138th. You shouldn't have much trouble. They'll be coming after me with a vengeance."

I looked at the others, "All of you."

I saw them nodding. They weren't about to argue after seeing what I had just done.

"Yes, Sir," he said, "we'll move out immediately."

I turned and began walking, calmly up the street. I could see the darkness of the Demon presence closing from the North, East, and West. In an instant someone was walking beside me. I didn't even have to look to see who it was. I could feel her with my mind.

Her hand brushed against mine and I reached out to clasp it in my own hand. We walked together, hand in hand, straight into the horde of Kresh pouring down the Avenue toward us.

Together we Pulled and we kept walking, as everything around us was reduced to Rubble and ash. I've Pulled through another's Stream but this was something different. Our streams had intertwined and become some sort of twisted cable of power. I can feel the Source at the other end of my Stream, and I can feel how much power I Pull when I do. But it seemed there was so much more power available than I had ever felt before. I think, maybe, two Soullords, together can Pull like tenfold what they could Pull alone.

There was so much power flowing through our Streams, we had to release from within several times so the power didn't build too high in our bodies. That amount of power was like a high from a drug, and we were lost inside our meld for a while.

I heard a familiar sound as we neared the intersection of 147th.

"Hold up a sec," I said and we stopped Pulling for a moment as explosions rocked the block from down 147th street. Then a screaming Banshee swept past us leaving nothing but ash in his wake.

"Kevin?" Lyrica looked surprised and I realized that she had never really seen him in action before.

"The Kid," I said "Something to see in action wouldn't you say?"

She smiled and motioned forward up the street at the Horde of Demons pouring down Amsterdam, "Shall we?"

"Oh, we shall," I said and we strode onward with discs firing in every direction.

Chapter 39

"There's a place for you in the Soulguard if you're interested," I said.

Khalib looked toward the tent that had been set up for the excess of injured people. Lyrica was busy inside, and I could see the Soul of the young woman who had been with Khalib when I had found him.

"Transportation is provided," I said, "to you and your family."

The word "family" struck a chord in the big man. I could see the longing in his Soul. I sensed he was a solitary person, and may not have known a family at all. He stared at the tent for a few moments and nodded to me. He turned and headed toward the tent.

I walked toward the command tent where Gasper ,and the Mayor of New York hovered over the map I had seen Gasper using the first time I was inside the tent. The Mayor looked up as I approached.

"I understand you're the man who just destroyed a rather large chunk of my city?"

"That would be true," I said, "though I didn't really have much choice in the matter."

"Yes, I heard the command when you gave it. 'Buildings can be repaired' I think it was."

"No more innocents die today," I added, "That's the most important part of that quote."

"Right you are," he said, "We owe you and your Soulguard a debt."

"We're just doing our jobs," I said, "the best way we can."

"Mister Rourke," Gasper said, "it looks like all of the portals are shut down. Will you be staying here for any length of time?"

"Doubtful," I answered. "What they sent here is a drop in the bucket to what can come through the Great Gate in Kansas. I'll be heading back there soon. It appears the wait may be at an end. They'll hit there again sooner or later. I pulled in another hundred and fifty Guards to help get things here back in order, but they may be pulled at any time if another city is hit. NG's will be the ones doing most of the cleanup after our mess, it seems."

"The new National Guard handled itself pretty well today," Gasper said. "Some thought it was a mistake to put so much into them but I think they'll work out fine."

"Nothing wrong with those boys," I said, "and I have the utmost faith in them. I've worked with quite a few, back in Kansas, and they have as much dedication to protecting this country as anyone I've ever met. Thanks to the new structure of the National Guard, they're receiving the same training as any other branch of the Military."

"I just wish we had some way of knowing when and where the bastards will hit us," he said.

"I know," I said, "but so far, all we've had to go on is best guess. This hit wasn't what I was expecting, but you can't expect the enemy to do what you want, I guess."

"That's why they're called the enemy."

"True," I agreed and nodded to the Mayor, "It was good to meet you, although, I wish it had been under better circumstances."

"We're glad your people were here, Mister Rourke. Without your Soulguard this would have been much worse."

I turned and walked out of the tent to find Rictor waiting for me. He motioned toward the tent where Lyrica was healing injured.

"How long we gonna stay and let her do her thing?" he asked, "She could be here a damn year, and never heal all the people in this city that need it."

"I think we can give her a few days, at the least."

"You know, a couple of us are goin' down into Manhattan for some food at one of the restaurants in a few hours. They're tired and a few are injured. You know, the ones who weren't out holdin' hands, and havin' a romantic stroll through the city."

"I don't know what you're talking about."

"Yeah," he said with a smile, "Didn't think you would. You and the other one who probably doesn't know what I'm talkin about want to join us?"

"I'd say, most likely a yes to that."

"Good."

He turned and headed toward the rest of my Company. I had a feeling I would hear about that little stroll for a while. I can't ever do anything and have the good luck that they would forget it.

***

I watched the various Guards as they boarded the plane. I saw several people look my direction as they too approached the airstrip.

I recognized several gang members who had stood at my back in that little altercation on Amsterdam. The one who the others seemed to be looking to for guidance approached me.

"Yo Mistah Rourke," he said with a nod of his head, "What I got to do to join yo Soulguard?"

I was watching the man's aura and he was completely sincere. I think he expected me to say he couldn't join.

"What's your name?"

"C-Train."

"Your real name-" I said with a touch more force than I really intended, "-you join my Guard, you leave all this behind. There are no more rival gangs. No more preying on another human. You've seen what we fight. You have to be willing to fight that fight for total strangers or the man who was your most hated enemy yesterday. This is the dedication I require from my soldiers. If you can accept this, you're welcome to join."

"Mah name is Cordell Fortrain. I'll swear to yo oath. Dis be much biggah than any gang."

I pointed toward the plane, "Board the plane, Cordell. I'll see you in Kansas."

"Yes, Sir."

I looked to the men who had followed him, "Same goes for all of you. I'll hold you to the oath and I'll deal harshly with anyone who breaks it."

There were nods all around and they all headed toward the plane. I shook my head in wonder as they made their way to the line of men and women boarding the plane.

"That was unexpected," I muttered.

I looked to my left and saw Mr. Khalib and his small group standing there looking at the plane. He said something and turned to walk toward the plane.

The boy who was always staring at him stood beside Dreanna. There was utter despair rolling through his aura.

Khalib stopped about twenty feet away and looked back.

"You coming?"

I felt a lump in my throat as the little boy was off like a rocket. He had started running before Khalib had even finished his question. There was a small smile on Dreanna's face as she followed at a slower rate.

Khalib reached down and caught the boy as he ran right into his arm. He lifted the child up, and I saw the complex emotions rolling through his aura. He was amazed and a little bit dazed. I think he was feeling things he had never had the opportunity to feel before.

He turned and walked toward the plane with the boy in his arms. Two boys and a girl followed in a row, and the beautiful black woman with another child in her arms bringing up the rear.

That lump in my throat is why I can place myself in between them and the enemy. There are so many people who are deserving of a life that doesn't include the Kresh and their evil plans. People who crave a family, need that someone who completes them. I want to give them a world where they can have that. If I could figure out how to stop what was coming I would do it. I would do it in a heartbeat.

As it stood, I intended to stop the bastards, but as they had shown us here in New York, it was going to be bloody. There were millions of people in the cities in just the US. If they had chosen to hit all over the world at the same time, the death toll would be unimaginable. This is the dread that I live with. They'll stop trying to focus on us and come out everywhere.

The only thing I can think of is to make sure they know I am in Kansas. They hate me so much, it may cause them to come at me, even if it makes no sense. It's, maybe, not the brightest plan but it's the only thing I can think of to do. I have to be the bait that keeps them coming somewhere we are, at least partially, prepared for them.

Chapter 40

"Have you seen their criminal records?" Paige asked, "This one is suspected in the murders of over thirty people."

"Yet they stood between innocent people and held their ground. Soldiers aren't saints, Paige."

"I've killed over forty people, Paige. I'm a killer. I'm still here. I told them to come here and join me. I told them what it would cost them and I saw their Souls. They'll make better Guards than you think. We recruit soldiers from war zones. New York was a war zone, and these men proved their metal to me. That's enough for me."

She looked at me for a long moment. I could see in her aura that she didn't agree. But I saw her accept that I wasn't giving an inch on the subject.

"They're in," she said, "But if this blows up on us, it's on you."

"If they don't follow the oath I'll remove them personally."

I'm not sure Paige would ever understand my reasoning in bringing back my motley crew of gang members to Kansas. She hadn't seen those same men stand with me as the horde of Demons came crashing down the street. They stood their ground, even when they had no idea what I could do out in the street in front of them. When all they saw was one insane man standing in the street with a pair of swords--that took courage.

A large part of their previous gang life was based on loyalty to their respective gangs. That, in its own way is a code of conduct, a source of honor. I would give them the opportunity to show that honor I had seen in those men to the world.

I also knew who she said was suspected in the murders of thirty men. Khalib. I had done some research after returning to Kansas. There had been a gang in Harlem called the Bone Dogs.

It was suspected that they crossed paths with Khalib at some point. Over a three year span, thirty Bone Dogs were found in various places around a certain area in Harlem. The Bone Dogs no longer existed long before the Demon attack of New York. Mr. Khalib was suspected of their destruction.

I had seen the raw fear in several men back in that street when they were told that the man they were looking at was Mister Khalib. I believed the suspicions about Khalib were right. But I was sure that there was a story behind that as well, and I intended to get that story before anything else. I was pretty sure Dreanna Whitaker would probably be able to shed some light on the subject,and I would ask her at my earliest opportunity.

"There are so many ways this whole thing could go sideways, Colin," Paige said. "I hope you're right, but I can't help it if I have misgivings about it."

"To be totally honest, Paige, we need everyone we can get in this. Someday, they'll really cut loose on us, and it's gonna make what's already happened look like a walk in the park."

"Somehow, I get that same feeling," she said.

***

I watched the dark Soul of one of my remaining Shak'Tar as she walked toward my office. It unnerves people sometimes when they find that I can see through solid objects when looking at the power flows of the world. I'd known I could do this for years. The Shak'Tar didn't seem to be phased by much. I guess they had seen so much in their lives, most of which would boggle the minds of someone on my planet that had never been exposed to the same type of surroundings.

Pelin opened the door and stepped inside, "I have news from Touran Gorvelis, Master."

"You don't have to call me master, Pelin," I said, "Colin will do."

She nodded. They were still getting used to the new order of things. I wondered if they had second thoughts about changing sides in this war. I'm not sure if they had a choice with my Mark on them.

"A new leader has come forward to take over the handling of this world. He is called Kin'Sol'Ramas. He is also called Yas'Fari, 'The Butcher'. His mind is strong and you will not be able to Mark his followers as you did against Sol'Kor'Vannas."

"Just as well," I said, "I won't be using that particular skill any more. It's too much like slavery. I can't do that."

"But it is the way it is done, Mas...Colin. Without the Mark, we have no direction."

"It's called freedom, Pelin. One day, I hope to show all of you what freedom truly is. The ability to choose your own way, your own fate, your own future."

"You are an odd being, Colin Rourke," she said, "Yet I find it easier to mold myself toward your Mark than it was to mold to the Mark of Sol'Kor'Vannas."

"Will the majority of the Shak'Tar feel the same way, do you think?"

"Some will find it more difficult, some will find it much easier. Some of us found it easy to be the hands of our former Master. Some of us found it difficult. We were left with not many choices."

"There is evil in all of us, Pelin. The true test is keeping the evil at bay and do what is right. I keep a dark monster caged in here."

I pointed at my head, "I can't let it out except when I am in battle. I'm afraid of what it will do. It's my evil and I fight it every moment."

"You must let it be a part of you, Master," she said with a startled look on her face, "if not it may consume you. Insanity lies there. We've all seen it."

I'd heard Gorvelis say the same thing. But I don't really understand what they are talking about. It is part of me. I know this but I can't let it control what I do, I have to control it.

As I was pondering her words something occurred to me. Her Soulstream, like any human, led around her and into the ground. Down into the Source. How was that possible? She was from another world, it should have led to a portal and into her own world.

How had I not seen this before? I guess I can't think of everything at once. It was the same for Gorvelis and the rest of the Shak'Tar. I hadn't really noticed before. Maybe because I saw human Soulstreams all the time.

Why did the Demon streams have to flow through a portal and the human streams didn't? Their Source must just be on the one world, and the Source of human life is on all of them. That's something that needs to be explored at some point.

"All I can do is the best I can about the evil in me," I said.

"That is all any of us can do Mas...Colin," she said with a slight bow of her head. She turned and exited my office.

Chapter 41

"I've got some questions, Dreanna," I said. "I hope you can help me with them."

"I'll try my best, Mr. Rourke."

I could see no fear in the young woman as she faced me. She had witnessed what I was capable of and still had no fear of me. That was a rare thing for me.

She spoke clearly, unlike so many of the people who were raised in the area she had grown up in. So many of the black men I had met in New York spoke their own dialect. She had a northern accent but none of the local dialect in her speech.

"It's about Mr. Khalib."

"You've looked at his past, I take it?"

I chuckled, "I've seen some speculation about his past. I'm not interested in whether he committed thirty murders. I'm interested in why."

She looked at me in surprise.

"Ma'am, I've killed people. I know why I killed those people. I would like to know why he would do something similar."

"Mr. Rourke, I bought the protection of that man when I was seven years old. I didn't know that's what I was doing at the time. I just thought I was helping a homeless man on my way to school."

"He was slumped beside a bench near my bus stop, and I think he was awful near to death. I walked up to him, and gave him my lunch that my momma had packed for me."

"I bought that man for a peanut butter and jelly sandwich and a juice box."

I smiled as I watched the memories of the girl handing her lunch to the big man.

"Several years later there were a lot of break-ins in my neighborhood. Every one of those break-ins resulted in a death or rape. One morning they found four bodies in the alley behind our apartment building. There were scratch marks on our door. My momma was at work at the Diner, so I had been the only one home. I was twelve."

I nodded.

"Three years after that, I was workin' the Diner in Momma's place. She was sick, and we needed the money. There were five of these gangbangers in the diner, and they took a liking to me. I avoided them but they were loud, and very graphic about the things they wanted to do to me. I was not and am not an innocent, Mr. Rourke, but those men were scary."

"I left work and headed home after closing. Almost to my home I heard them coming out of the alley. They were making rude noises and whistling. I know exactly what was going to happen, and I reached in my pocket for the knife I had brought from the Diner. I would not be an easy target for those animals."

"Then the noises became something else, and there was screaming, and a lot of sounds I don't want to think about. After a while there was just silence, and I could see one huge shadow in the darkness."

"I turned toward my door and stopped. 'Thank you, Mr. Khalib,' I said to that shadow and I went home."

"Rumor was those boys were in a certain gang. That gang announced that they were coming to my neighborhood to take me. There had been too many witnesses in the Diner. Over the next week, twenty-three of those gang members turned up dead. The survivors threw away those colors, and no one wears them in Harlem anymore."

"You ask me why he did what he did?" she asked, "All I know is that gang would have killed and probably raped me. Then they were gone. I don't know why he chose to be my guardian, but he did. And I will give him anything it is humanly possible. He's my knight in shining armor, my hero, and my savior. That is enough for me, Mr. Rourke."

"By God, it's enough for me too, Miss Whitaker," I said.

***

I looked out at a crowd of expectant faces. I had no idea what to say. The new recruits were all lined up in the field in front of me. How the hell had I let them rope me into giving a welcome speech?

"I see a lot of new faces here today, and each and every one of you is welcome. We need you. Your world needs you. To join the Soulguard is not something to take lightly, ladies and gentlemen. Be sure of your decisions before you take the Oath."

"The Oath is the most important thing you will ever do in the Soulguard. When you swear it, you are no longer going to consider another human your enemy. To swear the Oath means you will from this day forward stand as I stand. You will stand in that place between the darkness and the light. You will be the first line of defense between that darkness and our world. Always and forever more you will place yourself between Humanity and the darkness. You may serve for ten years or forty, but this never changes. We stand, until the day we walk that road to Paradise, between the Kresh and our world."

"This isn't something to swear lightly. No more do we fight amongst ourselves. When the Oath is taken, we leave our old enemies behind. We declare ourselves as Defenders of all Humanity."

"There may come a time when you have to place that Oath above your own safety, above your very life. There may come the day when the end is come, and there is no hope left. On that day, we will stand our ground, and we will die with honor. We do this because we are Soulguard."

"This is what my Oath demands of me, and what your Oath will demand of you. Do not take it lightly. When you take this Oath, take it with pride, for you join my family. You become my brothers, my sisters. And you will have thousands of brothers and sisters throughout our world who will stand beside you. You will never have to face the darkness alone, and that is why we will win this war. This war we didn't start. This war we shall damn sure finish."

"Welcome."

I turned from the mass of recruits, applause following me as I left the stage, and walked toward the headquarters building. I hope the speech was halfway decent. I hate speeches, and I probably suck at it. All I could do was say what I believed. That's all anyone can truly do.

I met Rictor as I entered HQ.

"Good speech, Boss-" he said, "-short and straight to the heart of things."

"Thanks," I returned, "and how are things with our Company?"

"They're working smoothly with each other," he said. "We really need some more time working directly with you, though."

"I know," I said, " but I'm having trouble with the time to do everything I need to do. I still have to shield the planes, and that is gonna take a bit of time. Plus all the shit that's coming down after New York. Did you see that news report yesterday?"

"They had the gall to actually say 'the cure could be as bad as the disease.' Referring to us, of course."

"I know we destroyed some real estate when we cleaned the bastards out," I said, "but what did they want? Leave all the buildings intact, and let more people die as we worked our way through them?"

"That's exactly what they want," He said with a frown. "If it had been a little farther south where the wealthy citizens lived, I bet they wouldn't be bitchin so much after we saved their asses."

"Yeah, I'd say so," I said with a touch of the rage surfacing, "and then again, maybe they'd be complaining about how we did it, regardless of how things went. It's the nature of people to armchair quarterback everything."

"True enough, Boss," he said. "Have you put any thought into what you're gonna say tonight at the interview?"

"I'll try to just stick with the truth. It's what I always try to go with. It could get ugly, though. It all depends on who does the interview. I wish Alstead could do it, but she's with another network. We may have to do another one with her to counter this one if it gets too ugly. I'll try my best but I'm not gonna sit and take too much crap for doing our job."

"It's all you can do," he said.

Chapter 42

"The short answer, Mr. Forrest?" I said in response to the latest of the asinine questions that had been thrown at me in the interview. "The short answer is that one single human life is worth more than every bit of property damage that was done in New York. One single life, you sanctimonious prick--even yours. You want me to be held responsible for the damage done in a city under attack by an alien race bent on our destruction. When you can stand on the front lines beside me, I'll put some credence to your opinion. Until then you can shut your damn mouth you useless, sniveling shit. This interview is over."

I stood up and tossed the mike to the side. Then I walked off of the stage to the applause of a pretty large live audience. The cameras followed me until I strode out the door. I was seething inside after Forrest kept digging about the damage done by the Soulguard in the area where we had destroyed the invaders.

We had led them out of populated areas and killed them in a relatively small area. I don't know what else we could have done to clean them out. There's really no telling how long they would have stayed focused on me instead of scattering again. The death toll had been over a half a million people. There had been nearly that many people wounded, mostly from other humans. Demons tended to kill any they actually got a hold of.

The problem had come when the actual property owners had raised a stink. No one who owned property there really lived there, and we had destroyed a good bit of property in the "kill box". The government was sending humanitarian aid to the people of New York but this wasn't helping the ones who were raising hell about the damage.

I exited the building with rage flowing off of me in waves. Several people simply turned around and headed the other way. Others froze in place, staring at me in fear. I tried to put a stop to it but it was just beneath the surface and I was having trouble pushing it down.

Jesus, I gotta stop letting shit like this get under my skin. There had only been one question that the man had asked that may actually have done some good. They'd probably cut it from the finished product. But the live audience heard it.

"What can the American people do to prepare for another incident such as this?" Forrest had asked.

"Each and every person should get a weapon. Buy a gun and protect yourselves. We will come. We will stop them, but we can't be there until we can get there. Every American, hell, every human being begins shooting the bastards, and they'll have to think twice before they do this sort of thing again."

Not really likely but still preferable to just rolling over and dying. Not everyone is a warrior, but there is one thing about the human race. We are not just victims. We are the top of the food chain for a reason, and we won't fold because another race wants us dead. They'll have to, by God, work for it.

"That coulda' gone better," Rictor said as I slid into the back seat of the Humve.

"No doubt," I said. "Perhaps I shouldn't be allowed to do interviews anymore."

"Ya think?" Prada asked.

I chuckled. I could feel the rage easing off after I was back with the two of them. They were my friends, and both knew me as well as any other person in the world, except maybe Lyrica. She'd spent a lot of time traipsing around in my head when I was in the Source coma. She hadn't talked to me much about what she'd seen in my head, and I hadn't asked. The things in my head are not for the light of heart. I don't even think what she did would have been possible without the telepathic abilities I had gained from my Demon ancestry. That telepathic link had allowed her truly into my mind.

"Let's get the hell outta here," I said. "When we get back to Kansas, Paige is gonna rip me a new one for that outburst. I keep telling her she shouldn't let me out in public. It's her own fault."

"Oh, so now you're blaming the Archmage for that catastrophic interview on live television? It must be a man thing. He blames you for the circumstance where he throws me out of a plane, and now you blame the Archmage for this interview."

She shook her head, sadly, "Men."

"That was live television?"

"Yeah," she answered, "We watched it as you called him a sniveling shit. The whole damn country saw it. Of course, that's exactly what he is. But you probably shouldn't have called him one on live TV."

"So who we gonna go insult next, Boss?" Rictor asked.

"Probably be safer to just head back to Kansas,wait-" I said and turned my head to the right, "-is that a Checkers?"

It was one of my favorite hamburger joints. They were in the South, and we were in Georgia.

"That's all you ever think about," Prada said.

"That's not all I think about-I think about pizza a lot, too."

"So sad," she mumbled as she pulled into the drive through, "How many do you want?"

"Ten."

"You're joking."

"Nope," I answered, "and get whatever you guys want, too. I'm buying."

"You seriously want ten burgers?"

"I need some for the flight home."

"I'll take two," Rictor said, "and see if they have that Cajun burger. If they still have that I want two of them."

"I forgot the Cajun burger," I said, "so get me five of each. The Checker burger and the Cajun burger."

She shook her head and started ordering.

I ate three before we reached the airport, and took the rest with me on the plane. There were still a couple left when we got off the plane in Hillsboro. There hadn't been an airstrip in Hillsboro until we pretty much took over the abandoned town and made a Soulguard base out of it. It was one of the first things we had added after we got established.

"You got another of those Cajun burgers in that sack?" Rictor asked.

"Yep, you want it?"

"I think I do," he said with a grin.

"I got another one in here too," I said to Prada, "You want it?"

"Yeah," she muttered.

"See, I told ya ten was about right," I said as I crumpled the empty bag up into a ball after giving the last burger to her.

"In the last five hours you've eaten eight hamburgers?"

"I guess I did," I shrugged. "I can't face the wrath of the Archmage on an empty stomach."

"You were right about one thing," she said, "these are definitely the best hamburgers I've ever eaten."

"True," I agreed. "I'll meet you guys later to work off all of 'em. Gotta meet with Paige and then Marco and Polo."

"Did you just call our two National Guard Generals Marco and Polo?" the voice came from behind me and it was a bit frosty.

"Hi Paige," I said and smiled broadly as I turned around, "how are things on the home front?"

"Just once," she said, "I would love for you to just do what you're supposed to. There's a place for this sort of thing, and it is not on live television. Everyone wants to say that sort of thing, but they don't do it. You cannot be calling people sniveling shits on TV. Or sanctimonious prick, for that matter."

"Ma'am, in Knoxville, we didn't let him out much," Rictor said.

Her glare turned to him and I winced, "Don't you even start. You're as bad as he is."

"I thought you might reign him in just a little bit," she turned to Andrea, "but I guess not."

She turned and stomped away.

"She's so cute when she's angry," I muttered.

"Oh my God!" Prada exclaimed. "That woman could blow up half of the state, and you think it's cute when she gets mad? What the hell is wrong with you?"

"Well, she is cute when she's mad," Ric agreed.

Prada followed after Paige muttering things I don't think I want to repeat.

"Guess I get to go meet Marco and Polo earlier than I was planning," I said.

Chapter 43

"There are two thousand Guards in the four facilities out near the Gate. We have five thousand more here in Hillsboro. Some of those are instructors for the trainees, but the majority of those are troops ready for any action taken. If they hit more cities, we will lose some of those numbers as reinforcements for the local garrisons."

Marco nodded, "How many Mages do we have stationed here?"

"Three hundred, but just like the Guard numbers, strikes in cities will decrease the amount here."

"And are we situated with this Code Alpha thing you've been talking about?" Polo asked.

"Everyone is familiar with the Code Alpha scenario," I said. "It may be hard to actually get a situation where we can use it, but we'll all be ready for it if the chance to use it arrives."

"We need a command staff for this," Polo said. "We can supply Staffers for the campaign, but we need to establish who will be the head of the whole thing. I assume that you intend to be out in the thick of it."

"Yes, and I have someone in mind for that position if you don't have any qualms about your men under the command of a Soulguard. We need the flow of orders to be as smooth as possible. The guy I have in mind has fought more campaigns than any other human being alive."

"You're talking about Jaegher, aren't you?" Marco asked.

"He's truly six hundred years old?" Polo asked.

"Six hundred and forty five," I said. "I'd say there ain't much the man hasn't seen. I'll send him to you after this meeting. You'll need to work with him some to get things flowing smoothly."

"We have seventeen thousand National Guardsmen here, as well, Colin," Polo returned. "They'll be thinner, too, if the Kresh hit more cities. But, at this moment our numbers are close to that. We'll be backing your forces up, and we'll pull out injured as we can."

"I just hope we can hold them in. We've never really had this sort of battle before us. First Kansas was pure luck. If the closing of the Gate hadn't killed them, we would have been bled much worse than we were already. I've never heard of calling the loss of a quarter of your command good leadership qualities."

"From all that we've seen and heard from those of you that were here, Colin, it was amazing that four hundred of you could do as much as you did," Polo said. "I saw footage of the thing in New York as well. I saw one of your Mages in both sets of footage. I was under the impression that you guys are limited in the amount of power available to your Mages."

"Most of us are," I chuckled, "but you must be talking about the Kid."

He looked at me with one eyebrow raised.

"He was sent to Knoxville when I was the Mage Captain there. He was young and untried. We came to an understanding, and he learned to use skills that most of us just don't have. We've called him the Kid ever since. He's a machine, and we keep him protected as he plows a hole in their ranks. But even the Kid can only do so much."

"The footage is pretty amazing," Marco said, "I saw what the two of you Soullords did in New York as well, and it was pretty spectacular."

"They weren't there in the sort of numbers we'll see here,' I said. "I think there were just several thousand in New York. The problem was that they were in the most densely populated area in the city. Just the massive numbers will make this hard as hell to hold."

"Have you figured out how to shield the planes yet?" Marco asked. "I hate to think those boys are completely unprotected as they circle up there."

"I've experimented on some small planes," I said, "but I'm having an issue with tying a shield around the moving parts of the plane. I think the best I'm going to accomplish will be to shield the main fuselage and wings. The various moveable parts will have to remain unshielded, unless I figure something out. I may be able to build shields into each piece, but the amount of time will be immense so I may not get the sort of protection on them I want. I'll certainly get as much as I can."

"Just the fuselage and wings will be an immense amount more than they had, Colin," Marco said. "If we get more, it will be welcome, but we all know there's only one of you, and you're doing your best."

"We wouldn't dream of complaining too much anyway," Polo chuckled, "cause you might call us sniveling shits."

"Or sanctimonious pricks," Marco said.

"On live Television or something," Polo returned.

"I didn't know it was a live broadcast," I said, "and I figured it would get censored out of it."

"Really? The show is called Samson Forrest Live."

I shrugged.

I stood to leave, "I'll send you Jaegher. You try picking on him, and see what it gets you."

Both of them were chuckling as I left the conference room. I really liked them. I'm glad the government had done things the way they did. The National Guard was just a little bit more laid back than the other military branches, and they were much more like the Soulguard in that. A lot of us come from military backgrounds but the Soulguard isn't as formal as their previous careers. We were more like a family of sorts.

That was something that was changing now, and I can't say I liked the idea too much, but it comes with the amount of growth we were going through. Much like the National Guard, we were having some growing pains, and we were sacrificing some of that laid back attitude. But it was expected as well, so I have to just deal with it.

I headed out of the Headquarters building, and headed over toward where several trainee squads were practicing maneuvers. Kyra was watching them, and I could see the disappointment in her aura.

"Not going so well?" I asked.

"They don't like taking orders," she said, "I was afraid it was going to be difficult to deal with these fellows you brought back from New York."

"How bad is it?"

"They're born fighters, but they won't work with others. We have to be able to mesh with any squad or company we end up in. They aren't meshing worth a damn."

"Mom, these guys are from a totally different culture than most of the trainees. It may take some time to get them to the point where we need them. Can I make a suggestion?"

"By all means."

"How's Khalib doing?"

"He's the damndest thing I've ever seen. The man is a master of nearly every weapon known to man. Now he's got the speed and power of a Guard. He's nearly unbeatable in a fight of any kind by anyone even close to him in power. It takes a Mage to get to him."

"He killed at least two Demons with a damn knife before that Soldier showed up," I said, "I knew he'd be good."

"He'll be leading a squad before long," she said.

"My suggestion would be to put Fortraine and his boys under Khalib. They'll be afraid not to do what he says, and it will get them into the habit of taking orders. It may take some time to get the effect we want but I think Khalib will pull it out of them."

"Why him and not someone else?"

"They have been raised with the fear that Mr. Khalib would come after them, Mom. He's the boogeyman. I just about guarantee they'll follow that man's orders. They may actually make quite a squad."

"I'll try that," she said.

"If it doesn't work, at least Paige can tell me 'I told you so'. She's just dying to tell me that most of the time, anyway."

"I could always have you go out there and call them sniveling shits or something."

"Et tu Brute'," I said acting as if I had been stabbed.

"Hehe, I always hated that bastard anyway."

Chapter 44

"We need to talk about shields," Lyrica said.

We were sitting out near the first Ac-130 I was going to shield.

"I'm listening."

"In New York you didn't even turn on your personal shield. You devised the damn thing to make it safer for us in a melee and then you didn't even use it. What were you thinking?"

"I wasn't thinking, I guess," I said. "All I could think of was getting to them."

"It's getting harder to keep the rage under control, isn't it?" her arm slipped around my waist. I put mine around her shoulders and she nestled into my side.

"Yeah, it's harder. Mostly, I can keep it down until they show up. Then I lose my friggin' mind, I guess. I know I should have used the shield but I wanted to, I don't know, feel it, maybe. There's something wrong with me, I know it. I just don't know how to fight it."

"We just have to do it together," she said. "Together we are much more than we are apart. You felt that in New York, too, didn't you? I can feel the limits of what I have available to Pull. But when we walked up that street there was so much more. It was like it became limitless while we were together."

"I know," I said. "Dietrich told me that when Merlin and Kent worked as a team they could do things neither could do before. Maybe this is something like that. I hope they weren't holding hands like we were to do it, though. That would be awkward."

Her musical laughter flowed across me. I love to hear her laugh. It rings through me and, hell, I don't even know how to describe it. It's joyous.

"So, what have you figured out with the shield for the plane?"

"Back when I put the shield into Bearguard, I interlaced the shield through the material he was made of. That doesn't work so well with metal. So I'm gonna put, basically another skin on the plane made of energy. It won't strengthen the metal but it will give another layer for anything to have to go through. With the small plane I was able to put a couple of inches of shield without affecting the flight of the plane to much. I'm gonna try to put six inches of armor on the AC-130. If it doesn't work I can thin it down afterwards."

"Perhaps the shield doesn't need to be thicker. Maybe you only have to put bigger feeders and the shield can stay thinner and still be as strong."

"You got a point," I said, "The thinner the shield, the less air resistance. Maybe that's the solution. All we can do is try it. Wanna join me?"

"Sure," she said. "You wanna try on something small, or do you wanna just jump right in like you usually do?"

"It's worked so far, why change something if it works?"

"I figured."

"What say we do an inch thick with about ten or twelve inch feeders?"

"Sounds good," she said, "I'll start on the left side of the plane and you take the right."

I went out to the right wingtip and began forming an incredibly tight weave of one inch tendrils around the wing. I carefully tried to keep the same shape as the original wing so as not to change the way the machine would fly. I carefully worked my way around the flaps that steer the plane, leaving them unaffected by my shield. After a while I reached the main fuselage of the plane and began working my way down the length of the craft, carefully avoiding the moveable parts.

It took close to an hour before we had the shield shaped to both of our satisfaction.

"Ok, you plant yours first," I said.

She thrust her tendril into the Source and cut her tie to it at nearly the same time. I watched the flow of power across the vessel and as it neared my feeder tendril, I slammed it down into the source and cut my tie. The shield glowed with power.

"That looks good," I said, "We'll have to wait a bit while they test it before we do the others."

"Good," she said with a smile, "then you can come help in the infirmary while they test it."

Three hours later we stood watching the AC-130 taxi back into its normal parking spot. Three NG's exited the back of the plane.

"Just a little more sluggish than before but definitely flies better than our earlier experiment," one of the pilots said with a laugh.

"Just how strong are these shields you make, Sir?" asked the second NG. She was a tiny woman, not much more than five feet tall.

I'd seen this group of pilots before and heard about her already. She was said to be fearless. When they needed something tested, they called Carol "Stick" Jackson.

"They're strong," I said and turned toward one of the shielded spots of the plane and Pulled.

I launched a fireball at it and the shield absorbed the power. I don't know what it would do with a disk but it held back a fireball.

The two others had been startled by the fireball but Stick hadn't even flinched. I liked her, already. I could see the emotions rolling in her aura. She'd really been startled, but she had a reputation to live up to so she never showed any of that to the people around her.

I heard Lyrica's musical laughter behind me. She could see everything I could.

"I like her" she said, "my kinda girl."

I chuckled and said, "Some of the moveable parts are unshielded so it certainly isn't as protected as I want."

"That's a shitload better than we had before, Sir," Stick said. "We thank you."

"You're welcome," I said, "and when that gate opens up, I want you to blow the hell outta those bastards."

Stick nodded, "Yes, Sir. Blow the hell out of them. Understood."

I smiled as I thought of the rain of fire that the plane would put forth. I wanted to see it, and would wait anxiously until the day that Gate opened once more.

"Let's get the shields on the other two planes, shall we?"

"Let's do," Lyrica said and we started walking to the next plane, "What do you think about going dancing tonight?"

"I'd love to," I answered.

We both turned as a Soulguard came tearing across the landing strip toward us.

"Shit," she muttered.

"Looks like bad news," I said.

"Sir," Janik Verona said, "They hit in Chicago and Atlanta an hour ago. Simultaneous hits, Sir."

"Damn," I cursed, "Janik, scramble my company, and tell the Kid to get ready with his. We'll take Chicago. Tell Rictor to get two ready companies to send to Atlanta. He's got the watch at the moment, so he'll know which companies are ready to go."

"Yes Sir."

Lyrica started to follow me toward the base.

"Honey, I need you to finish the planes for me," I said, "One of us needs to be here in case they open the Gate."

She stepped in close to me, and I was staring into her emerald eyes, "Be careful Love, cause you always get in trouble when I'm not there."

I kissed her. It felt like an electric shock rippled through my whole body. I didn't want to stop but I had to.

"I'll be careful," I said and stepped back with a sigh, "I have to go. Rain check on the dance?"

"Definitely."

I turned and ran for the base.

Chapter 45

Chicago was hell. The Kresh had been loose, and ripping through the city for hours before we got there. The same sort of plan worked there as we used in New York but they hadn't come out on an island this time, and the casualties were even higher than New York's had been.

I saw the worst in people that day. I saw people trampled by other people, and I saw people attacked by others for the chance to escape faster. The depths people will go is a sad thing to witness.

But I also saw the best in people that day as well. I saw a woman push her children behind her, and she jumped on the Kresh that was coming for them. Self-sacrifice is one of the best traits I can find in Humanity. The willingness to give one's life to protect others. I wasn't in time to save that woman but I was there to save her children. She delayed the beast long enough for us to get there.

I saw men and women standing and firing into their masses to give the people behind them time to flee. The hordes rolled over these brave defenders, but we were able to reach the ones they had protected in time. Hundreds of similar actions took place in that city, and I salute those brave souls. Once I did get their attention, the Kresh came for me with a vengeance. I'd taken a squad of Guards with me this time.

Their single minded hatred for me is their greatest weakness, I think. They stopped their attack and came for me. We killed them.

After we were done and we were boarding the plane, an NG came running across the runway toward the plane.

I turned from the ramp I had just started up and walked down to meet him.

"Sir!" said and took a deep breath, "They hit Los Angeles, Sir!"

I clicked my coms back on, "Thank you Private. We'll be on our way to LA then. I hope we can get there in time to do some good. No doubt, there will be forces sent from Kansas as well."

"Yes Sir," he said.

I headed back up the ramp, and went straight toward the cockpit. I passed Rictor on the way.

"Los Angeles," I said as I passed.

"Shit," he muttered and turned to the Mages and Guards who were getting settled in for the flight back to Kansas.

"No rest for the wicked!" he yelled. "We're goin' to Hollywood!"

I entered the cockpit, and the pilot turned to me. I had seen this guy before. He was the pilot who had flown us to Kansas the first time we had gone. He still wore that crooked ball cap on his head.

"We need to change flight plans, boys," I said, "cause they just hit LA."

"Sir," the pilot answered, "You want both planes redirected?"

"Yeah I think so."

"Roger."

"What?" asked the co-pilot.

The pilot chuckled and began steering the plane toward the runway.

I looked at the co-pilot with one eyebrow raised.

He stuck his hand out, "Roger Dekland, Sir."

I shook his hand, "Colin Rourke."

I turned back toward the back with a smile on my face. Roger...heh heh.

As the plane taxied to the runway, I found my seat and eased into it. Los Angeles, New York, then Chicago, and Atlanta had been hit simultaneously. I had the sinking feeling that they were up to something underhanded. Somehow I still felt that Kansas would be a target. Our preparations would slow them down, but we would need to do something drastic to win a battle there. We had a hell of a lot more people there now, and if things went fairly well we could hold them. The bad part was the pulling down of our forces to meet these small incursions.

I believed that was exactly what they wanted, reduce our forces in Kansas as much as they can. So when we were several hours into the flight, it came as no surprise when I jerked awake with Soulfire covering my body, and the rage trying to claw its way out of its cage.

"Bloody Hell!" Galen Stone exclaimed. He was the one sitting right next to me.

I had come to my feet with every weapon open and ready to fire. My seatbelt was ripped apart, and I was looking for an enemy.

Then I got control of my reactions. The Gate had opened in Kansas.

"Friggin' Gate just opened!" I heard Rictor as he approached from the back of the plane.

"Yeah," I said through clinched teeth, "Gotta go redirect the plane again."

I shut the portals on my weapons and walked toward the cockpit.

"I think a bloody wet myself," I heard Galen mutter.

"We won't tell anyone, Mate," Brighton laughed.

I heard some laughter behind me as I headed toward the front with a smile.

"Boys, we have a problem," I said as I reached the pilot. "The Gate in Kansas just opened. I need you to fly over the base there, and drop some of us off."

"Sir, we don't have any chutes on board," the pilot said, "I won't have fuel enough to land and take back off and still get to LA."

"Not a problem," I said, "Just fly over so I can jump off with my Mages."

He shook his head, "Roger."

"What?" said the copilot under his breath.

I chuckled and turned back to the men in the back.

"Mages," I enhanced my voice to be heard over the noise of the plane, "in two hours we are going to unass this plane, and join the forces in Kansas. The Guards on the plane will continue to LA, and report to Graves when you get there. You know the drill, save as many as you can."

"What exactly do you mean when you say unass the plane?" asked Prada suspiciously.

She looked over at Rictor, who had a wide grin on his face.

"Ah, hell," she cursed and looked at me with a frown, "I hate you."

I laughed and returned to the cockpit

"Send a message to the other plane" I said. "Tell them to continue to LA as before. Tell them my Guards will be there with them shortly. The rest of us are dropping off in Kansas."

"Yes, Sir," the copilot said.

I went back to the rear and paced the length of the plane for nearly two hours. The whole time, the rage kept clawing at its cage.

"At least Lyrica is there if the opportunity to use Alpha pops up," Rictor said from behind me.

We were back at the cockpit by then.

"Alpha?" asked the pilot.

"Hell on Earth," Rictor answered.

"All right, Sir," the copilot said, "Five minutes till drop zone."

"Roger," I said.

"What?" he asked.

I chuckled and headed back to the door.

Two minutes out, the ramp lowered and the wind ripped through the plane. My eleven Mages lined up to jump. Prada was in the front, and I could see the whites of her eyes as she fought the fear in her aura with discipline. She hadn't lost that fear of heights.

The light turned green and Rictor kicked her out the door.

"Fuuuuuuuu," I heard her scream as Rictor followed her out, laughing like a maniac.

Rostov was next and he couldn't hide the laughter. I shrugged and he jumped. The rest jumped and I leaped after them.

"Soullord One, Incoming," I reported on coms.

"Copy," I heard the voice of Dietrich Jaegher, "Command channel 32, Sir."

"Copy."

"Rictor," I said on my regular channel, "assemble at the command center."

"Copy."

"Command channel 32."

"Copy," answered a chorus of voices as my squad heard me. The Command channel would be the channel they would receive orders from Jaegher as he performed his duties. He was the conductor of our little symphony of destruction. He had so much more experience in open battlefields than anyone else alive. He was quite good at it, and I had no doubt he could do the job well.

I was studying the ground below us as we plummeted toward it, "Chutes."

I opened the portal on the shield chute I had created not long after my last incident with a plane.

It was two o'clock in the afternoon and the scene below us was straight out of nightmare. There were thousands and thousands of Demons. They had pushed our lines so far back already, I was worried they would break out. I knew what was planned if that happened. Massive bombing and if all else failed, nuclear bombs. On American soil.

That might stop the bastards, but it would destroy a sizeable chunk of the country. We would be doing their job for them. Destroy ourselves and they wouldn't have to.

I saw a wave of destruction plowing through the horde of Demons on the right flank. The Jaeghernauts were at work. There were only twenty of them, but they plowed a row of destruction through the ranks two hundred feet wide.

I think there were already more of the Kresh on the field than the whole first attack had been altogether. They looked endless. More poured out of the Gate.

I was seventy five feet above ground, and closed my portal to drop the rest of the way. I had steered to land near the command center. It was a fortified building with a flat observation platform at the top where Dietrich had stationed himself and his staff. I scaled the side of the building instead of going inside. It was much quicker.

As I landed beside Dietrich, he said, "Welcome to the festivities, Soullord. Thought you weren't gonna make it to the party."

One of his staff muttered, "Doesn't look much like a party to me."

"Wouldn't miss it for the world," I said. "What's our situation?"

"We're holding at the moment," he said, "but that's not gonna last much longer unless we can get an Alpha situation."

"Are the AC130's ready?"

"They've made two runs already," he said, "They're reloading ammo right now."

"They do any good?"

I watched his memory flash across his aura of one of the planes circling the area, and it looked like it unloaded pure hell into the packed masses of Demons. It was beautiful.

"That has to be one of the best ideas you've had. The forts were too close to the Gate, though. They pushed us out past them in the first hour."

"Damn!"

"We learn as we go," he said, "If we live through this, we can build more, further out."

Suddenly he was looking to the right, "Reinforce Delta team."

The second of his staff began speaking into his com to send a squad to the far right flank.

"Jaeghernauts," Dietrich said on Command com, "Make a run up the right flank and give Delta a respite."

"Copy," I heard Kharl respond.

"When this started, we had a group of civilians out by one of the forts. They had a squad of trainees doing Guard duty. It was close but they got out just in time. They're over there on the left, workin their way out."

"Your boy, Khalib and my daughter are part of the Guard. Your reporter and some engineers were out there. Looks like they're out now though."

"Good, trainees have no business out in that," I said.

I was watching the Gate and what looked like a huge dome of evil came through and stopped not far from the front of the Gate.

I could see the power roiling in that dark mass. Demonmages. It looked like a whole group of them.

"That looks like trouble," Dietrich said just as the twisted blackness erupted with a hail of what had to be fifty of their ugly black and purple fireballs.

"Son of a Bitch!" I cursed as the wave of fire swept a swath of destruction across the left flank. I had just located the small group of civilians when it had happened.

Demons flooded through the hole in our ranks and the party of civilians was right in their path.

"No," I heard the whisper as it escaped Dietrich.

Chapter 46

From the outside of the battle zone swept a large group of men and women. In the lead was my mom, and she was followed by nearly every trainee that had managed to tie their knot. The lines were ragged but they never faltered.

"Damnit, Mom," I muttered.

"Ric," I spoke over coms, "take our Company and reinforce those Trainees! Close up that hole!"

"Copy."

My group of Mages shot off at close to seventy miles per hour.

"I'm going for the civilians," I said. I could see the worry in Dietrich. His daughter was out there in a desperate situation.

"Send the Jaeghernauts to meet me, there."

He nodded and began spouting orders again.

The next instant I was air born.

I'm pretty sure that movies will be the death of me. I saw a movie a few months back about a man who had been transported to Mars where there was a whole civilization of people. Due to his denser structure and the lighter gravity on Mars, he could leap hundreds of yards at a time. Special effects have inspired me to do a lot of things, and this was another of those inspirations.

I flew across the ranks of Soulguards and landed near the lines. Then I was air born once more. As I started down the backside of the arc I opened my weapons and launched everything. Disks of fire blew a great hole in the horde of Demons directly in front of me.

Unfortunately, the backlash had me land in another spot where there was maybe a thousand screaming Kresh.

My swords blurred and arcs of power slammed through the Kresh around me. Then I was air born again. At the apex of my arc I could see the group of civilians. There were ten civilians, twelve NG's, and ten Guard Trainees. They had settled in a diamond formation of sorts.

The way a squad of Guards is divided is Three Guards per team, three teams per squad and a squad leader. At the four points of the compass was stationed Guards. Three to the south, I didn't recognize them. Three to the east, Irenia Jaegher was the team leader and two others on her flanks. On the west was Cordell Fortraine, and I recognized two of his fellow New Yorkers on his flank.

There was only one Guard facing north, directly into the face of the enemy. Six and a half feet of concentrated violence, Mr. Khalib stood with his swords blurring. He was adept with any weapon made by man before he tied his knot. In three months, the man had proven himself to be nigh unbeatable in a fight.

National Guardsmen crouched just inside the Soulguard lines, and their weapons spat fire as fast as they could.

I released arcs of power to clear my landing and was back into the sky again. Two of the trainees were down and the Kresh were closing in. I saw Alstead grab a rifle from one of the fallen NG's, and start firing into the horde.

One more leap and I would be there. I crafted a shield that wrapped around me and anchored to my Soul. On the right side I built a thirty foot long blade that hooked toward the back. It was sharp as a razor and about chest level. On the left was a sloped shield to turn the bullets that were flying. I wasn't sure if they would stop shooting in time so I figured I'd be careful.

I landed on the east, almost directly in front of Irenia. I was about twenty feet out in the horde, and the second I landed I opened the portal on my shield. At nearly fifty miles per hour, I made a complete circle around the group with a huge arc of Demon blood exploding into the sky.

The civilians were looking at me with the strangest looks. It may have had to do with the fact that I might have been laughing the whole time I was slaughtering the Kresh. I made another complete circle as the others cleared out the circle around them.

I pushed the animal back down. That was the source of the laughter. I closed on the group and slammed out a shield around them.

I stopped and saw crumpled forms on the west side one of which I recognized immediately. I could see it was too late for Cordell Fortraine. He was Lying in a pool of blood and it hit me hard. He shouldn't have been here. I brought him here just to die in the dirt. I knelt by him as I saw him reach feebly toward me. He smiled through bloody teeth and I heard his last words.

"Stood...my...ground."

He died there and his Soul slipped down into the earth to join the Source. I reached down softly and closed his eyes. I squared my shoulders and stood back up.

"That you did, Cordell," I said and let out a large sigh.

I began forming tendrils at the beginning of the shield and the end to tie it to the Source. I pointed toward the south where I made an arch glow.

"There's the door," I said, "Guard it till you can get these people out of here. The first chance you get, pull these people out."

Mr. Khalib nodded, and I opened the door. He planted himself there, and began swinging those swords in a form very near what I always called the Blade Barrier. I turned back to the shield, and slammed the ten inch tendril into the Source. In seconds, I slammed the second one down and cut my tie. The shield thrummed with power and shimmered. I had used large enough tendrils to feed it so nothing would be breaking through to the people within.

Alstead approached me, "Why leave a door at all? Can't you take it back down later?"

"If I'm still alive when this is done, yes."

Her face paled as she realized what I had just said.

"Jesus," she muttered.

I turned back to the others and went to the wounded. The first one had a nasty cut down his arm. I lay my hand on his arm and he gasped in pain. Then I Pulled straight to the wound. The blood stopped flowing and the skin began to draw together where I was holding the cut closed.

I had to stop before it went too far. Lyrica had told me it was dangerous to do too much at one time. He would be fine to reach the infirmary if they managed to survive what was going on around us.

I could feel the ground shaking as I looked up to see a great wave of destruction plowing through the horde toward us. The Jaeghernauts exploded through the mass of Kresh to form a circle around the outside of the shield.

"Dad," I greeted the huge man standing in front of me on the north side of the shield, facing out toward the horde of Demons flowing through our area.

"Looks like you got here all right," he said. "I saw the grasshopper act. I could have been wrong about that particular subject. Seemed to work pretty well."

I grinned at his back. Very seldom will you get an "I was mistaken" out of him, and I have to relish them when they make an appearance.

Another volley of black and purple fireballs arced out of the shield. Most of them were blocked with shields as there were more Mages in the area they were launched toward.

"I'm about sick of that," I said, "so I think it's time to put an end to that shit."

"Too true."

"That will be our target in a minute," I said, "but first I've got one more injured man in here."

I knelt beside Keith, the camera man. His leg was dislocated at the knee.

"Sorry Keith, this is gonna hurt."

I twisted and shoved his leg back into place with a pop. His face went pale but he held up pretty good. I Pulled through his stream toward the knee and I could see the pain in his aura diminish.

"That should do you, Keith," I said and stood up.

That was the moment that no matter how I try, I will never forget.

The line of Trainees, along with Rictor and my Mages stopped the advance of the Kresh. The lines weren't in far enough yet, but they were stopped at least.

I was facing southeast when I stood up, and I saw the whole thing in slow motion. Another volley of Demon fireballs arced toward the Trainees, and with a novel sort of response, Rictor was slamming disc after disc into the fireballs. He broke them up that way, except the last one.

His disc just disappeared as a twisted darkness began to form about a hundred feet in front of him, about thirty feet from my mom and a group of thirty trainees.

The incoming fireball also disappeared from the other direction and a huge jagged bolt of energy shot out of the forming portal.

In less than a second, Rictor was airborne, and he landed feet from the energy spewing portal. He slammed a shield out around him and the portal. Then he opened his portal on the shield, and slammed outward with everything he had. The shield impacted the Trainees and Kyra, throwing them sideways, away from the center where he stood. There were Mages and Trainees tumbling through the air and the portal exploded with a force that literally shook the ground under my feet.

Chapter 47

There are many things a person takes for granted. Fourteen years he had followed me into caves, into hordes of Demons. He had never even been seriously wounded in all that time. Somewhere inside my mind I had believed he was indestructible.

I saw my friend's Soul just...cease to be and something broke inside of me. Something important. I thought the ground was still shaking, but it was me shaking as the walls I had so carefully built around that monster inside me crumbled, and that beast came roaring from the darkness.

"Rictooooooooor!"

My voice began as a scream of despair, and ended as something not human. Rage, hate, and pain flooded my awareness, and my head snapped to the north where my enemy was hiding inside its black shield. All that rage was driving me, and I was moving before I had even finished screaming my friend's name.

There was no door to the north but I ripped a hole in the shield as if it weren't even there. Out that hole I plunged with an inhuman roar. I was on the other side of the Jaeghernauts before anyone even knew I was moving.

"Oh shit," Daphne said as I shot past her into that mass of Demons between me and my prey.

I discovered something in that mad charge into the abyss. I learned what makes a Soullord so devastating to their enemies. There was no focus, no planning. There was rage and there was power. I was Pulling harder than I have ever Pulled before and the power wasn't being steered into my weapons. It was flowing through me in torrents. Soulfire ripped out of me in massive arcs. Gouts of flame spewed into the throngs of Demons. Every ounce of that power was channeled through my body instead of around it. That's the Soullord's gift. A body that can channel as much power as he can Pull.

At Morndel I had hurt myself some. Mostly from holding the massive well of power inside me instead of channeling it through me.

I was screaming incoherently as I plowed through the Demons in front of me. I was hit, and the massive well of power healed me as fast as I was wounded. I lashed out with arc after arc, and bodies literally exploded in front of me. It was the most terrifying thing I had ever experienced. I wasn't in control and all I could do was hold on as my monster reveled in its glory.

I speak of the monster inside me as a separate entity, but I know it's not...not really. It's the part of me that does the awful things that people should not do. When I let that part of me out, I am still me, but I am something else, too. More and more I find that part of me growing and becoming stronger. Never more than that very moment.

What scares me the most is that I enjoy it. I'm free.

The shield was getting closer, and I was sending gouts of fire toward it. I could see it bowing under the pressure but it didn't break. I threw both my swords at it and they pierced the shield to the hilt.

I sent discs from my launchers into it with no more effect than the attacks that came before.

A group of Wraiths shot between me and the shield and I charged right into them. As I reached the first one I jumped over its head. My hand grasped the upper jaw below me and I ripped the top of its skull completely off. My flaming left foot slammed through the chest of the next one and my arm came around with the skull top. I poured fire into it and let it fly. It exploded through the chest of another Wraith, and embedded itself into the shield. There were two more Wraiths between me and my target, so I went through them. They exploded in a mist of Demon blood as my flaming form impacted with them.

Everything I had thrown at the shield had been stopped. But I reached out as I had done with the shield I had started from and ripped the damn thing apart. Apparently, my skill with power flows extends right across the board. No doubt, due to the Demon blood running through my veins.

I was inside the shield bubble and the end where I entered became a flaming patch of hell as I erupted in Soulfire.

I could finally see the Demons inside the shield, and there were ten Demonmages. There was also a Farrara'Ti. He was twice the size of the Mages, and his stream was well over two feet in diameter. They were all about to launch fireballs at me, so I did something completely unexpected. I reached out with my mind, and ripped the Souls right out of their bodies.

My hand was outstretched and the Soul of the Farrara'Ti was sucked right into my grasp. The second I touched that Soul my whole world went crazy. I felt their Source and it was massive. In that moment I knew I could use it as I used the Source on my world. I was whatever they would call a Soullord of their Source as well as my own.

But, as with anything, there is a price.

Pain ripped through me as something inside me spasmed. I thought I had felt the extent of what rage could be. I hadn't felt near the limits until this moment. I absolutely went berserk.

The Kresh had no idea what they were creating when they come for my mother. I am descended from the mightiest Soullord to ever walk the Earth. His blood is in my veins. The blood of one of the most powerful of the Farrara'Ti also flows through my veins, creating the bridge it took for me to be on the level of their "Demon Lords". I am Rash'Tor'Ri, the Life-ender. I am a Soullord of the Blood, I am the Bloodlord, the only one of my kind. They created their own Hell on the day when they slaughtered a pregnant Soulguard woman in New Mexico.

I am the Demon that crawled up out of that Hell.

For some time I was lost in the maelstrom of hate, rage, and pain that my touching of that Soul had triggered. I knew without looking that the empty spot inside my Soul was no longer empty, and I had let something into me that I was not going to be able to just get rid of. There would be a price to pay for the power I had just used.

God only knows what that price will entail.

When I regained some of my senses, I found the whole battlefield eerily quiet. I was inside a circle of Jaeghernauts. Kharl was standing in front of me, and there was fear rolling through his aura. It was something I had never wanted to see. Never before had Kharl been afraid of me.

I realized something else. I could feel what my Dad was feeling as well as see it. I felt relief as I could tell that he wasn't afraid of me. He was afraid for me. And with good cause.

I felt something squirm in my right fist. I looked down to see the tattered remains of the Soul I had ripped from the Farrara'Ti. I had ripped it to shreds.

I looked back up to see everyone and everything looking silently at me. Some in horror, some in rage, some with stark terror. That was both human and Kresh alike.

"Damn, Son," Kharl said softly.

I was still shaking with the pent up emotions roiling inside me.

"Initiate Code Alpha," I heard Dietrich's voice on coms, "I repeat, Code Alpha."

"Copy," returned the voice of Lyrica.

"Copy," I said hoarsely.

"Five supports!" Kharl ordered and the five strongest of the Mages around me stepped back inside the ring. The others closed up the ranks in one fluid movement.

Code Alpha. This is what we were waiting for. The Demons were no longer trying to escape the lines. The Mages were free to give me the power to do the damage needed to end this.

"On your command, Soullord One."

"Standby," I answered, and looked out at the seething hatred rolling through the thousands of Demons outside the circle.

I raised that tattered Soul high into the air.

"You want me?!" I roared, "Come get me!!!"

My challenge ripped across the massed Demons, and they returned a roar that literally shook the ground.

"Oh, shit," Daphne repeated her earlier assessment of the situation.

I tossed the Soul to the side and it was sucked into the Gate.

"Come and burn," I said softly, then I clicked my coms, "Pull."

The Demons charged our little group, and two hundred and thirty two Mages Pulled into the sky. The world seemed to vibrate with a huge *THRUMMM!*

Lyrica snatched that power, and created the giant maelstrom of power in the sky above us. I closed my eyes and just used my inner sight to track the power. I could sense the flows all around us and the mighty vortex above us. I raised my arms to the sky and when they came down, gouts of fire slammed into the Earth.

I began the steps of a new dance. This dance was a dance of the mind, a dance of power. This was a dance of destruction. The Dance of Death. I could see all of the power around me, and I brought down Hell on Earth. All around us the fires slammed into the ground.

MOTHER! FATHER! The names of those who had died for me slammed outward from my mind. They were pushed by rage and hate each accompanied by a gout of fire from the sky.

SEARSON! JAYDEN! The names of a hundred and two children and teachers from Morndel slammed outward. They had died for me just as much as my mother and father. Or died because of me.

WILSON! JANICEK! My friends and fellow warriors. Every name of those who have died under my command is etched into my mind. Each gout of destruction to slam into the ground was accompanied by a name.

The earth shook as I added name after name to the list of the Fallen. My friends, my brothers and sisters, all of the fallen Soulguards I have known were names on that list.

NORA! JENNA! The names roared out across the field. I didn't even realize that they were slamming into those around me from my mind. The list was in my head, and I was Lashing each time with those names. Both Kresh and Human alike felt those names slamming through their minds like hammer blows. The list continued through every single one of the Fallen.

FORTRAINE! A Gout of fire hit thirty feet in front of the interlocked shields held in a circle around the Jaeghernauts with a mighty BOOM!

RICTOR!!! And the world began to shake in one continuous blast at the very last name on my list. As the name of my friend slammed outward with all of the loss and pain I was feeling, I began ripping Power down without the tempo of the list. I ripped multiple gouts of destruction down from the heavens all around us.

BUUURRRRNNN!!!!! The word ripped out from my mind, and rolled across the massed horde of screaming Kresh. It was Lashed out with all of the rage and hate I felt.

I was lost in the destruction. Lost in a world of hate and rage. My tears fell as fiery drops of Soulfire. So many people had died for me and that list had grown this day, I knew. There would be a whole new list of names for me to remember.

"Enough, Son."

I heard Kharl's voice from my right, and I felt the squeeze of the hand on my right shoulder.

I opened my eyes to a sight right out of Hell. The ring of Mages were standing in a circle around me and outside that circle, the earth was melted. Some spots flowed like water. What few Demons were left scrambled for the Gate or just stood dazed out in the midst of that apocalypse.

I looked out at the stragglers and a vision of my friend's Soul being snuffed like a candle in the wind flashed through my mind.

"It will never be enough," I said bitterly.

I stood there motionless as I watched the remainder flee through the Gate. Then the Gate simply winked out of existence. There wasn't even a trace of the huge portal that had been there.

Then I heard a new sound. It began some distance away but it grew louder. A mighty cheer rolled through the ranks of warriors surrounding the smoking field. We had won but I couldn't bring myself to cheer. I saw a dying Trainee I had brought into this place, I saw my best friend incinerated by an explosion. These are what I will remember from the Second Battle of Kansas. These things will haunt me for a great deal of time.

Both of them died as heroes. And they will be remembered as such. Even after letting the Soul free from my grasp, I could feel the new well of hatred and rage inside me.

Yes they will be remembered, and yes, they will be avenged.

Chapter 48

My body felt like it had been seriously abused. So much power had ripped through me in a short amount of time. I felt drained, even though I was filled by a fifteen inch Soulstream. It was not just a physical weariness, it was emotional weariness. I was just tired and sore all over.

I made myself move toward the melted earth to the west of us, toward the spot where I could see her Soul. It shone like a beacon in the darkness and I walked toward it. I crafted a bridge across the melted and blasted earth as I walked toward her. The Jaeghernauts followed behind me in rows of four with Kharl walking directly behind me.

I met her at the edge of the blasted landscape, and she was in my arms and holding me. Her head rested against my chest and I held her tight. Our Soulstreams merged and some of the physical weariness fell away but the emotional weariness would take time.

Not only had I lost my best friend, I had become something else out there on that battlefield. I'd known for years about the Demon DNA, but I now had a second Soulstream that led to that spot that had always been empty. It was an ugly Soulstream and it fluctuated with the opening and closing of the portals out on the field. It seemed to vanish as the last of the portals shut down but I could still feel the reservoir of that ugly power down inside me.

I don't know where that ugliness will take me in the future. It is the price I paid for the victory we achieved. The price I will always have to pay for the things I can do that no one else can. The things needed to fight this war against the Kresh.

As we walked toward the crowds of Soulguards and National Guardsmen the cheers continued, louder and louder. Let them have their moment of victory. We are far from finished, but the Kresh now know that the first battle of Kansas was not just a fluke. They were destroyed because we destroyed them. They'll think twice before coming back to Kansas.

The crowds parted as we walked through toward the headquarters. We must have been a real sight. A lot of my insane charge toward the shielded Demonmages I had been unshielded and I was covered in both Demon blood and a lot of my own. Once it was on me it was there. The shields would burn the blood away but my shields were outside of that. There is a certain distance from the body that is imbued with my Soul, or I would always come back from a fight naked. That would be a sight as well I guess.

Here I was covered in blood, and beside me walked Lyrica with some of that blood smeared on her from our embrace. It wasn't bothering her very much as she held tight against my side. She was just worried about me. She had seen what I had done, seen what had sparked my unstoppable rage. She could see into my Soul, see what I had done to myself.

The crowd parted as my group made our way through toward our HQ. I just wanted somewhere I could sit and be still for a few minutes. We reached the HQ and I walked inside. The Jaeghernauts remained outside in formation at the door facing the cheering crowd.

As the door closed behind me I turned my back to the wall and slid to the floor. Everything began to register on my mind, and the new well of rage was right under the surface. There were things I needed to know. Where was my mom? How many trainees had died out in that mess for me? How many Guards? How many of my friends?

My mental state was a far cry less important than these things. It was more pressing on me right this moment than the others, but I didn't have time to do anything about it right then. Lyrica sank to the floor right beside me, and her arms wrapped around me. We didn't say anything, we didn't need to. Our Souls merged, and she could feel everything I did. Just as I could feel everything she did. We just sat there for a while.

***

"It was easy to say Code Alpha," Marcus said, "but to actually see it is something else, Colin."

I sat in the office of General Polomo. Marcus Stratton and Polomo sat in the other chairs in his office.

"You can say that again, Marco," Polomo said.

I looked at Polomo and Stratton.

"You didn't think we hadn't heard of your little nicknames for us, had you?" Marco asked.

"It just seemed a little disrespectful to call you Marco and Polo," I said with a short chuckle.

"First time I've heard a laugh from you since the battle, Colin," Polo said. "I know some serious shit happened out there, but you know we stand right behind you don't you? If you need someone to talk to, either of us will be there."

"I thank you both," I said, "and perhaps, I can talk about it later. Right now there is too much to get done and not a great deal of time to do it in."

Polo nodded, "That's a damn fact. We're still sifting through the ashes, so to speak."

"I do have one question, Colin," Marco said. "Were you aware that the names you were calling off were heard in the minds of everyone within five miles of here?"

I shook my head. I had known they were slamming outward telepathically, but I wasn't aware of how much power I was throwing behind those names. It seems that the link I made to their Source boosted my telepathy much more than it had been before.

"I learned I could use this telepathy on other humans some time back, but I never realized it was so strong. It didn't hurt anyone, did it?" I was worried about the effects of my telepathy on others since the forced Mark of my Romanians.

"No, it didn't hurt anyone," Marco said, "but who were they?"

"All of the people who have died for me in my thirty three years, or because of me. That list grew quite a bit Monday."

He nodded, "I thought as much. You know we are here because this is what soldiers do, don't you? This isn't your fault, they invaded our world and we'll fight them tooth and nail. This isn't because they want you alone. If you only listen to one thing I'm saying, listen to this."

"If not for you we would have lost the battle today. There would be a radioactive wasteland where we now sit and none of us would have survived. There isn't another person who could have done what you did out there. The fact is, we all expected to have to call down the bombs long before this even started."

"After the horde spewed out of that gate, we almost knew it would take nukes to stop them. We've never faced anything like those bastards. What they sent to the cities were just the 'attack dogs' you were describing to us. We thought we had a handle on the situation until Monday."

"But your Soulguards are amazing," Polo interjected, "just straight up amazing. It's hard to believe that a normal human can become what you have made of them."

"None of which was anywhere near what you did, personally," Marco said. "It was unbelievable, and if I hadn't seen it with my own eyes, I wouldn't believe it at all."

"There's film of it from fairly close up. Mostly from behind you. That camera man who was out there shot your run from the moment you left that shield to the Code Alpha. They tried to get him to leave the shield and go to safety, but he and the reporter refused to budge, and the engineers said the safest place they could think of was that shield they were inside of so the whole group stayed till the battle was over."

That sounded like Alstead, all right. She would walk through Hell if she could get the story she sought. I wasn't too happy with the fact that they had been focused on me. They had to have seen things I would prefer not to have ever been seen by another human being. Things I don't even like to think of myself.

"But back to the work at hand," Polo said. "The forts are not usable anymore. We need facilities farther out. No one realized how fast our lines would be pushed back. And we need more planes."

"I can get those," Marco said, "so if we can get enough Mages to work the guns we can get as many planes as we want."

I nodded, "And we need to work as fast as we can. I don't know if they'll come back here, but we need to be prepared for it. My fear is that they will just start opening Gates all over the world. So far, they focused on the US because, if I'm guessing right, I am here. If they decide to just pour their numbers through in other countries, we're looking at a long bitter fight."

"Casualties will be catastrophic," Polo agreed. "We don't have any ideas where these other Gates are?"

"There was the one in Romania, but we buried it under about a hundred thousand tons of mountain. We don't know where the others are. I've spoken with my Shak'Tar, and they don't know where the others are either. They all came here through the Romanian Gate."

"The future looks bleak," Marco said, "but we'll face it as it comes. It's what we do, we Humans, we survive."

Chapter 49

I was looking for my mom. She hadn't been with Kharl when I went to the barracks. He was pretty shaken. She was blaming herself for the loss of eighty-seven Trainees. She had been very distant for the last two days, and I wanted to talk with her.

I left the barracks and opened my inner eye, my Sight. I found her Soul and headed toward the remains of the battlefield. I know how she feels, but her actions saved more lives than I could count.

I passed several Soulguards as I headed for her.

"That's him," I heard whispered.

"You see what he did?"

"Ripped that things Soul apart."

"Saved our asses, he did."

They were unaware of the sensitivity of a Mages hearing. I hated that what some remember is what I did to the Farrara'Ti's Soul. I hated to even think I could torture another living being as I had done the Kresh. It's one thing to kill them. It's another thing altogether to torture one as I had done. The Soul is a living thing until it is absorbed back into the Source and it had been aware of all that I had done to it.

I got far enough that I didn't hear the whispers. They were always present now, every time I was near anyone. Both Soulguard and National Guard, all of them had seen what I had done and they felt the hammer blows of my telepathy as I recited the list of my dead. They all know I am not just human now. Some don't understand what it is that they know exactly. But some understand much more than I would like anyone to know about me.

I found her out at a spot that I had visited several times already. The spot where Rictor had died. It still doesn't completely compute in my mind, I can't quite believe that my friend is gone. I've come out here and sat, just as she was sitting and tried to figure out what the Hell is going on in my head.

I walked up beside her and sat down.

"Why did he do it?" she whispered.

"It's what we do, Mom," I answered. "We do whatever it takes to save our brothers and sisters. We do whatever it takes to save our race. You think it would be easier if he hadn't saved you? Not to those of us who love you. I would be mourning the loss of my mother instead of my friend."

"But I brought them out into this," she said softly. "It was my place to die for them. Not them for me. They were children."

"They were Soulguard," I said, "And they were soldiers, and they saved more lives than they even knew when they joined the fight. The next line of defense was the National Guardsmen. How many of them would have died without the Trainees actions?"

"Hundreds, maybe thousands," I said, "but your actions are the same as I would have done in your place. And I would feel the same as you feel. But the action was still the right one. Your forces held the lines. Without them we would have failed. They learn their dedication from you, Mom. They need you back and teaching them just as before. We need you back and teaching them. Don't give up on me, now."

She took a deep breath, "I won't give up, Son. It just makes me feel so damn old. I've lost friends before but this is so different than anything the Soulguard has faced in my lifetime. No one except maybe Dietrich has seen anything like this."

"I know," I said, "And I fear it's going to get worse before it gets better."

"Me too," she said and stood up, "Thanks, Son."

She placed her hand on my shoulder and squeezed. Then she turned and walked back toward the base. I don't know if anything I said helped her. It helped me to take those same words, and apply them to myself. She blamed herself for the loss of eighty-seven trainees. I feel the loss of those Trainees just as well. And the thirteen hundred and twenty three other lives lost in the Second Battle of Kansas.

Out of the six thousand three hundred and thirty Soulguards who participated in the battle, we lost fourteen hundred and ten men and women. They were still running the figures from the Gate. There had been drones high in the air, observing the Gate. The consensus was somewhere around six hundred thousand Kresh came through the gate. It's unknown how many escaped back through the Gate. The maelstrom in the sky had blocked the drones from seeing anything after the Code Alpha.

The casualties had still been too high. We needed more defenses, and we needed more planes. We needed Howitzers, and we needed so many weapons that they couldn't see the lines for the guns. And we needed Mages. We needed so many Mages. That, I could provide. The tests were going quite well with the new Mages, and I intended to start making more immediately.

"Perhaps you're the lucky one, Buddy," I muttered, "You get to stop now. I'm just beginning. I'll see you soon enough, Ric-maybe not today, but soon enough."

The rage was still dangerously close to the surface. I'd spent some time trying to erect the walls back around the rage in my mind, but it wouldn't stay caged. It was right below the surface all the time now and ready to erupt at a moment's notice.

***

I looked out at the crowd of people looking at me. The number of Soulguards had grown to well over ten thousand for the last rites of the fellow warriors who fell at Second Kansas.

My Company was right out in the front of the crowd. I could see Andrea Prada, standing straight. She had been wounded a few times in the fight, but Mages heal faster even than Guards and she was back on her feet. I saw Lyrica, with Trent and Mattie, ever at her side. I hated that I couldn't spend as much time the two of them as I wanted. There never seemed to be enough time.

Not only were there thousands of people watching, but there were several news crews, including Jennifer Alstead.

"Today we mourn the loss of many of our brothers and sisters. Each and every one of them died while performing the duty of protecting the Human race. This is what we do. This is what we are."

"I am saddened by the loss of so many of our friends and family--family. This is what the Guard is to me. You are the only family I have ever known. Kyra Nightwing and Kharl Jaegher raised me from the day I was born, my mother and father in every way but blood-- Soulguard--family. I look out at you, and I see my brothers and I see my sisters--my family."

"Today we mourn the loss of one thousand four hundred and ten of our brothers and our sisters. It leaves a great hole in my heart when I think about them. But they gave us victory. They bought that victory with blood and they will never be forgotten!"

With that word, the huge structure behind me was unveiled. It was the beginning of a monument that would hold the names of all of our dead. It was the first huge block of a marble wall and on the front of it were the gold plaques of fourteen hundred and ten names.

"Behind us is a great victory, but before us looms a desperate future. More will come and we will stand and fight, just as the Human race has always done. I was asked once if this was Armageddon, the End of Days. I was asked if these Kresh were the armies of Hell come to devour the world."

My rage was touching the surface, and I was seeing through heat waves as my eyes burned with Soulfire.

"I say no they aren't from Hell. They haven't seen Hell. I am going to show it to them! They call me Rash'Tor'Ri, Life Ender. That's not really accurate, alone, I am just a Mage. But as long as you are with me, *we* are Rash'Tor'Ri! And together, you and I, we are going to show each and every one of those bastards who set foot on our world what Hell truly is!"

I'm not sure if I was projecting the emotions I was feeling but the Soulguards facing me stood and raised fists in the air. The ground seemed to shake with the roar that erupted from the throats of ten thousand Soulguards. I joined them with my own yell of fury.

The rage was barely under the surface after my touching of the Kresh Source, but I managed to sit down and observe the rest of the Memorial service.

The Guard had never been much on medals and awards. We were born in secrecy and our triumphs were largely unsung. But all of that changed when they invaded our world in numbers that couldn't be hidden. The Council had begun the crafting of medals for those who go above and beyond the call of duty, much like the Congressional Medal of Honor. It would be awarded to those who had done just that. Trainees had no business in the battlefield, but those very Trainees were the reason the lines held. They had truly gone beyond the call of duty and each of them was awarded the Medal of Valor.

Eighty seven Trainees received this medal posthumously, including Cordell Fortraine, Julius Samson, and Malcolm Kenner. These three were gang members in New York a few months before Second Kansas, and they showed me what the human race is capable of. Thugs and criminals became heroes when our world needed them.

They had tried to award me with the same medal. I refused. I just did my duty, nothing more. It was argued that First Kansas was definitely beyond the call of duty. My response was simple.

"If we start awarding past actions, the whole Soulguard will need the damn things. Every damn one of them has done no less at some point in their past."

I got my way on the subject.

But we did receive dress uniforms with campaign ribbons. The Military has inspired us to show what we are proudly. Before, we used secrecy. Now, we wear our Soulguard uniforms proudly and wear our Campaign Patches with pride as well.

My uniform held ,both, First Kansas and Second Kansas, The Battles of New York and Chicago. I had a suspicion there would be more of those campaigns in the future, many more.

Chapter 50

I saw Pelin moving down the hallway with another Shak'Tar I didn't recognize. I was watching with my Sight. I sat in my office looking at the massive list of the fallen. I need to remember them. I need to remember them all.

"Come in, Pelin," I said as she neared the door.

Unlike most, the Shak'Tar aren't made nervous by my extraordinary skills, both from my Soullord heritage and my Kresh blood. She entered the office with a man who I didn't remember, but the moment he saw me I knew him.

He carried the Mark I had put on Gorvelis and the others, but it was just a bit different. He was one that the Mark had spread to. His name was Fero Jintera, and he was from another world than Earth or Kresh. He was from a world called Cerres, a world under the yoke of the Kresh. I knew all of this the second I saw him, and I could tell by his aura and by the feelings I was feeling from the man that he was in utter awe of the only human to ever Mark another being.

"Master," he said as he knelt, "I have news for you from Gorvelis."

I shouldn't have been able to understand him. His language was totally alien to me but my link seemed to translate as he spoke.

I nodded, "There's no need to kneel to me, Fero."

He looked confused and he stayed on his knee, "You are the Master."

I sighed, "Ok, what's Touran been up to?"

"He approached us on Cerres and the Mark spread across us. Immediately we began to pull people out of the villages and hiding them."

"Just remember," I said, "You only have to remember, Fero."

He was silent for a second and nodded. I concentrated and watched/lived a memory.

***

I rode the memories of Fero as he watched the approach of Gorvelis and a large group of the Clan. In moments the Mark slammed through Fero and the others around him. He was on his knees holding his head as the Mark ripped apart the Mark of his former Master. This new Mark was utterly amazing. Never had he felt anything of the sort from any of the Kresh.

His mouth fell open as he realized that the Mark was from a Human! And what a Human it was. In the moment of the Mark, Fero knew this man. He knew him to his core and as he learned his new Master, tears streamed down his face. For so long he had hated his Masters, but this one didn't instill hatred. It was truly amazing.

He turned to his left to see Sureta Golin down on her knees as well. Her face was pale and her eyes wide in amazement.

"He is Human?!" she exclaimed.

"Very much so," answered Gorvelis.

I followed memories through some time and watched as the Night Clan, which is what Shak'Tar translates as, began hiding people from the Kresh. This went on for months as Gorvelis and his men worked their way through Cerres spreading my Mark.

It all culminated in one final memory. Gorvelis stood in front of nearly five hundred Shak'Tar. He was facing a giant of a Kresh. It had to be a Farrara'Ti. They were surrounded by thousands and thousands of Kresh.

"I could rip you apart and eat you," rumbled the voice of the Farrara'Ti, "But I will not. I will destroy this new Master's Mark and take you as my own, slave."

Touran Gorvelis smiled.

"You are welcome to try," he said, "but you will fail. Better to kill us all than face my Master. Better to run to the farthest corner of Cerres than make war on the Clans of Rash'Tor'Ri!"

"Rash'Tor'Ri! He is a story to scare whelps! I fear no Rash'Tor'Ri!"

"Then you are welcome to try to take his Mark from me!"

Everyone felt the Lash of the Farrara'Ti. Gorvelis staggered and there was blood running from his eyes, mouth, and nose.

"Now!" he roared.

Something that no Kresh had ever done started then. Five hundred Shak'Tar Lashed together. They Lashed with one thing, my Mark.

Each of those Lashes were pushed, not outward but directly through Gorvelis. He rose to his feet and raised his arms as he slammed it all into the Farrara'Ti.

The giant Kresh staggered and fell to the ground, screaming. Each of the Shak'Tar could feel the changes take shape in the mind of Pos'Far'Nadir, the Farrara'Ti who had controlled Cerres for the last century.

Gorvelis walked forward toward the Kresh who was on all fours in front of him. It's head was hanging down and it raised as Gorvelis approached. Their eyes were on the same level and Gorvelis stared into the confused eyes of the giant.

"Your mistake was to think you faced only one," he said and placed his hand on the enormous shoulder of the Kresh before him, "Welcome, brother. Welcome."

He turned to the other Humans, his Clan, and motioned for Fero to step forward.

"It is time to send word to the Master, Fero," he said, "You will go to him and tell him something for me. Tell him that the Revolution has begun!"

There was a great roar around them as both the Shak'Tar and all of the Clans of Kresh raised their fists in the air and let rip a shout that would be heard throughout the fifteen worlds. I could see the seeds of the destruction of the Kresh Empire in that shout, and it took all that I had not to shout with them. These were my soldiers in a war that covers multiple worlds. They are mine and they are doing the things I can't do yet. But, one day I will join them and we will bring that Empire to its knees. We'll burn it down, Humanity will be free!

"Stand, Fero," I said, "I expected great things from Gorvelis and the rest of you but this is amazing. You have my gratitude, and when I can rid this world of the influence of the Kresh, I will be going through the Gate to join you all."

"Understood, Master," he said with a fervor that scares the hell out of me, "We will continue and anticipate the time when you can come."

I turned to Pelin who had shared in the memory as well, "See that he is fed and treated well. I have to think for a while on what response to send to Touran. He seems to have things well in hand. I believe I'll leave things in his capable hands."

"Yes, Master."

"You don't have to call me that."

"I know, Master."

I sighed and she chuckled.

"Do you mind if I share with our brother what happened here?"

"Not at all, I was going to send a report back to Gorvelis anyway."

She turned to Fero and I saw the flood of images that crossed to the man. I had thought she was just talking about telling the story but I should have known better. They are telepathic after all.

They replay of the battle was very coherent and I could tell it came from the memories of many people, including myself. I had to remind myself that this was all they had known and it wasn't unusual for them to garner information in this manner.

But watching what I did from the vantage of the other people in the field was quite disconcerting. I can see why the others feel the fear after seeing what I am capable of.

After she finished, Fero turned to me with awe, "Please, Master, do me the honor of placing your Mark on me in person. Never would any of us ask one of the Kresh to do this, but you are not them. Your Mark is a joy to carry."

I didn't see the harm in it so I concentrated on the Mark inside him and I focused my will on it. I slammed my will into that Mark and it blazed inside Fero.

"Thank you, Master," he was once again on his knees.

"Stand, Fero," I said. "You don't have to kneel to me. You don't have to call me Master. My name is Colin Rourke."

He nodded and stood. Pelin led him out of the room, and she looked back at me standing there with the discomfort I feel when dealing with the near slavery of the Shak'Tar. She chuckled again and shook her head.

Chapter 51

"Ma'am," I stood and strode across the room to the woman who was shown into my office, "Welcome."

She was a heavy set black woman and she was followed by a man in his twenties and a teenage girl. I could see the family resemblance and I knew that they were her other children.

"Mr. Rourke," the older woman said, "I come out hea cause you asked me to. I already knew one day I would heah dat useless boy done died in da street."

I could see the conflicting emotions in her two children. Both seemed to have felt the way their mother did but I could see a glimmer of hope in the young woman.

"Ma'am," I said through my own well of emotion about the loss of Cordell Fortraine. He had been my responsibility and he'd died because I had brought him to this place.

"Please allow me to show you something," I said, "I have certain abilities that are beyond the normal. Let me show you how your son died. You can judge from there however you want to."

"How you gon show me?"

I smiled gently, "It won't harm you in any way, Ma'am."

I projected a memory from the gathered memories of the group that had held their ground protecting the civilians.

Her eyes widened as she saw Jennifer Alstead fall and a young black man step across her and protect her as she was dragged into the circle.

This was the last act of Cordell as he was ripped by a soldier that got through his defenses. He could have lived if he'd not stepped out alone, but it had happened so fast.

There were tears in all three of their eyes as she looked up at me, "Dat's my boy?"

She asked me in a tone of utter astonishment. She had known of his gang ties, his criminal acts, but this was something out of a dream.

"Yes Ma'am," I said, "Cordell Fortraine died a hero. He died in a battlefield I brought him to. He died a Soulguard."

I handed her a black box gilded in silver. She opened it to find a simple silver medal.

"Ma'am," I said, "this is the Soulguard Medal of Valor. We're relatively new at awarding medals for our troops, but your son earned it. He left that past that you knew of and forged himself into the man you saw. I was and am very proud of his actions and gladly present this medal to you."

She clutched the box to her chest and muttered, "My boy was a hero."

There was a great surge of pride in her wayward son rolling through her aura, as she clutched the box.

"Thank you Mr. Rourke," she said to me and she turned and followed by her other son and daughter, walked away.

The daughter turned and looked back, "Thank you Mr. Rourke. I've waited a long time for him to change. I just wish I could have seen him before he was gone."

She turned away and followed her mother and brother.

That had been hard, but I felt so much better after seeing a mother regain the pride in a child that she had lost her pride in a long time ago.

I had spent days searching for the next of kin for the fallen, and I had found most of them. I was looking at the form in front of me--Rictor Hughes. There was only one person listed on his form. He, like me, had no family except the Guard. He had listed me as his next of kin, and I sat there with tears in my eyes as I looked at the page. He was my best friend, he'd been a sort of mentor when I got to Knoxville, and we'd been working together ever since. I have friends I've known longer than I knew Ric, but none who were as close. He knew more about my heritage than any other person. He'd pushed me to find out what was wrong with me. He'd followed me into Hell so many times I had lost count.

I put the form down and stood up. I needed to find Rostov. He'd said something about the finest Vodka in the whole world and I could really use a drink.

***

Alexei Rostov was sitting in the barracks when Lyrica Jayne found him. He saw her coming and smiled. He liked the young woman and he knew she was good for Colin. He'd learned a few things about the both of them since his arrival in Kansas--he the eternal warrior, she the healer. Right out of a grand story they were, he thought.

"Hey Alexei," she said, "Have you seen Colin around?"

"Yes, he came by a few hours ago to talk me out of a bottle of the finest Vodka that Russia has ever produced. It seems a bit of a waste, since he can't really get drunk from it."

Her eyes seemed to lose focus for a moment. It was truly eerie when either of them did that. He knew they were looking at the energy flows of the world when it happened but it was weird anyway.

Her eyes crossed the north where the battlefield had been and her eyes narrowed.

"Oh no," she said in a voice that made his heart jerk, It was filled with a sadness he hadn't seen in her before.

She turned and shot back out the door. He jumped up and followed. Her two shadows were just steps behind her as she shot to the north. He followed in their wake.

They ran through the destroyed landscape toward a spot that Rostov knew from the battle. He was a little worried too, now. This is where Hughes had fallen. He knew how much it had hurt Colin to lose his right hand. The Soullord's Pitbull, they had called him. Rostov had no doubt that Rictor Hughes would have done anything the Soullord asked. He would have followed him into the Demon world if Colin had asked him.

He reached the spot to find Lyrica sitting on the ground, holding his head in her lap. She brushed his hair from his forehead.

"He tied himself from the Source," she muttered.

"Damnit Colin," muttered Trent Deacons. Mattie Riordan was silent but she stood Guard at Lyrica's back.

"What the Hell was he thinking?" Rostov exclaimed, "Doesn't he know how dangerous this is? Doesn't he understand how much we need him?"

Lyrica looked up with a fire that looked a great deal like his in her eyes, "Do you know how hard that is? To be the one who has to save the world? Do you? He just lost the one person who probably understood how hard that is, the one of the few who would treat him as a person instead of this friggin' messiah. Do you know how hard that would be?"

Rostov actually took a step back as her words hit him.

"We spend so much time looking at him as this Messiah, we forget he is just a man," he said as he nodded to Lyrica, "my apologies."

"It's not really your fault, Alexei," she said. "I just hate to watch him torture himself. He blames himself every time."

"Da, I heard the list, as well," he said.

"Don't worry, Alexei," She said and gently stroked the hair of the man who's head rested in her lap, "I'll keep him safe."

"I have no doubt of that," Rostov said and walked back into the darkness to give her as much privacy as she needed.

He waited three hours out in the darkness until she picked up the Soullord and carried him back to his quarters. He followed at a distance to make sure she got him in alright. Like there was anything that could stop her if they tried, he thought.

***

The golden Valkyrie bent over me, and kissed my lips. I could see her face.

"Mine forever," her words flowed through me.

I opened my eyes to see that beautiful face a few inches from my own. She was sleeping there beside me. All of my worries of Gods and Goddesses had been just that, worries. My Goddess was right here beside me and I could remember clearly now how she had driven off the darkness that had wanted to consume me.

I reached down and opened the portal I had put in my Stream so I could get drunk and forget for a while.

As the portal opened, and the awful pain in my head slipped away, her emerald eyes opened.

I kissed her and pulled her close. Her lips were soft, her skin like silk, and her Soul...her Soul blazed like the Sun. Our Soulstreams merged and we were lost in each other for quite some time.

She is the other half of my Soul. She's the best part and I now understand that I cannot survive without her. She is my life, she is my love. With her at my side, I know we can accomplish anything we set out to do and the future of our world looks just a little less bleak.

Epilogue

A man crouched on a rise looking at the huge facility down on the plain. There was a shimmering portal at one end of the great platform.

The man rubbed at the scars along his right arm. They were the scars from a severe burn. He knew he could reach the portal, perhaps even without the Kresh even seeing him.

There was a disturbance behind him, and he looked down into a ravine to see a group of twenty or so people running up the sloped ground. Behind them a group of ten Kresh loped. They ran around the people in the back and knocked them rolling through the dirt. Then they would let them up to run again.

Rage surged through the man on the hill. He looked over his shoulder at the shimmering portal one last time and snarled in frustration.

Then he turned and leapt seventy five feet to land near the pursued group of humans. Then with a roar of fury he charged into the group of Kresh and tore them apart.

299